Hawk had been beautiful.

The way he walked, the way he and the mare moved together…it was like poetry in motion.

Now Sheryl looked at his face, lit by the glow of the dashboard. It was a hard face—unforgiving, but also honest. One more step toward him and she knew she'd be in too deep. This man oozed animal magnetism. What drew her to him? Chemical attraction? Biological need?

Whatever it was, she didn't need it, a voice warned inside her head.

But like it or not, she wasn't ready to turn her back on Hawk Donovan and his mysteries. Yet as she looked at his profile and tried to make sense out of everything she'd seen of this man, she got the distinct feeling that she didn't want to know all his secrets….

Dear Reader,

It's fall and the kids are going back to school, which means more time for you to read. And you'll need all of it, because you won't want to miss a single one of this month's Silhouette Intimate Moments, starting with *In Broad Daylight*. This latest CAVANAUGH JUSTICE title from award winner Marie Ferrarella matches a badge-on-his-sleeve detective with a heart-on-her-sleeve teacher as they search for a missing student, along with something even rarer: love.

Don't Close Your Eyes as you read Sara Orwig's newest. This latest in her STALLION PASS: TEXAS KNIGHT miniseries features the kind of page-turning suspense no reader will want to resist as Colin Garrick returns to town with danger on his tail—and romance in his future. FAMILY SECRETS: THE NEXT GENERATION continues with *A Touch of the Beast*, by Linda Winstead Jones. Hawk Donovan and Sheryl Eldanis need to solve the mystery of the past or they'll have no shot at all at a future…together. Award-winning Justine Davis's hero has the heroine *In His Sights* in her newest REDSTONE, INCORPORATED title. Suspicion brings this couple together, but it's honesty and passion that will keep them there. A cursed pirate and a modern-day researcher are the unlikely—but perfect—lovers in Nina Bruhns's *Ghost of a Chance*, a book as wonderful as it is unexpected. Finally, welcome new author Lauren Giordano, whose debut novel, *For Her Protection*, tells an opposites-attract story with humor, suspense and plenty of irresistible emotion.

Enjoy them all—then come back next month for more of the best and most exciting romance reading around, only in Silhouette Intimate Moments.

Yours,

Leslie J. Wainger
Executive Editor

Please address questions and book requests to:
Silhouette Reader Service
U.S.: 3010 Walden Ave., P.O. Box 1325, Buffalo, NY 14269
Canadian: P.O. Box 609, Fort Erie, Ont. L2A 5X3

A Touch of
the Beast
LINDA
WINSTEAD
JONES

Silhouette®

INTIMATE MOMENTS™

Published by Silhouette Books

America's Publisher of Contemporary Romance

Special thanks and acknowledgment are given to Linda Winstead Jones for her contribution to the FAMILY SECRETS: THE NEXT GENERATION series.

For Kathleen Stone. It's readers like you who make telling stories such a joy.

 SILHOUETTE BOOKS

ISBN 0-373-27387-8

A TOUCH OF THE BEAST

Visit Silhouette Books at www.eHarlequin.com

Printed in U.S.A.

Books by Linda Winstead Jones

Silhouette Intimate Moments

Bridger's Last Stand #924
Every Little Thing #1007
Madigan's Wife #1068
Hot on His Trail #1097
Capturing Cleo #1137
Secret-Agent Sheik #1142
In Bed with Boone #1156
Wilder Days #1203
Clint's Wild Ride #1217
On Dean's Watch #1234
A Touch of the Beast #1317

Silhouette Books

Love Is Murder
"Calling after Midnight"

The Sinclair Connection

Family Secrets
Fever #8

LINDA WINSTEAD JONES

would rather write than do anything else. Since she cannot cook, gave up ironing many years ago, and finds cleaning the house a complete waste of time, she has plenty of time to devote to her obsession for writing. Occasionally she's tried to expand her horizons by taking classes. In the past she's taken instruction on yoga, French (a dismal failure), Chinese cooking, cake decorating (food-related classes are always a good choice, even for someone who can't cook), belly dancing (trust me, this was a long time ago) and, of course, creative writing.

She lives in Huntsville, Alabama, with her husband of more years than she's willing to admit and the youngest of their three sons.

She can be reached via www.eHarlequin.com or her own Web site www.lindawinsteadjones.com.

FAMILY SECRETS: THE NEXT GENERATION

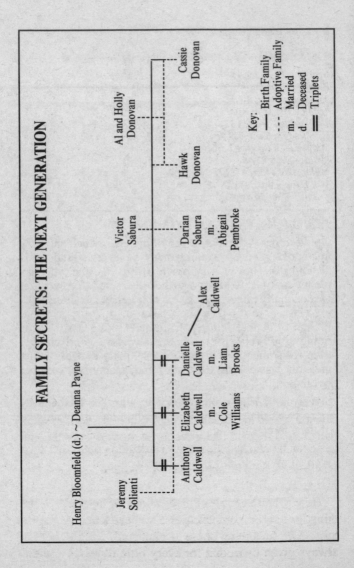

Henry Bloomfield (d.) ~ Deanna Payne

Jeremy Solienti

Anthony Caldwell

Elizabeth Caldwell
m. Cole Williams

Danielle Caldwell
m. Liam Brooks

Alex Caldwell

Victor Sabura

Darian Sabura
m. Abigail Pembroke

Al and Holly Donovan

Hawk Donovan

Cassie Donovan

Key:
— Birth Family
--- Adoptive Family
m. Married
d. Deceased
≡ Triplets

Chapter 1

Hawk studied the boxes and bottles of remedies that were neatly arranged on the shelf. Greenlaurel's sole pharmacy, Chapman Drugs, usually had everything a man might possibly need. But since the doctors were stumped about the cause of Cassie's sudden onset of seizures, Hawk had no idea what to buy to make his sister feel better.

What he really wanted to do was hunt down one Dr. Shane Farhold and break the man's scrawny neck. Farhold had always seemed like a decent enough guy, not the kind of man who would knock up a woman and then disappear. Hawk knew he'd be angry even if Cassie hadn't been having strange spells.

He grabbed a couple of medications off the shelf. Something for nausea, something else for headaches. At the last minute he snagged a bottle of pink stuff. His mother had always given them that for every little illness. He didn't really think it would do any good, but he had to try something. On the way out of town he'd stop at the grocery store for ginger ale and soda crackers. They were as likely as anything else to work.

Deep down he knew the medicines that might help Cassie with her normal pregnancy ailments would do nothing at all for the mild but disturbing seizures no one could explain. And he didn't dare ask anyone about a treatment for the odd flashes of precognition that followed the episodes.

"You won't find what you're looking for here," a smoky voice whispered.

Hawk turned sharply to find an older woman, one he did not recognize, standing just a few feet away. He hadn't even known she was present until she'd spoken. In ordinary circumstances he knew very well what was going on around him; his worry for Cassie had clouded his senses.

The woman who looked up at him with fearless green eyes was not a resident of Greenlaurel, Texas, or the surrounding county. Hawk had grown up on a ranch outside this small town, and with the exception of his four years in the military, he'd spent his entire life here. Besides, except for Harmony Eastwood, a middle-aged, self-professed, die-hard hippie who had been emulating Stevie Nicks for more than twenty years, the ladies of Greenlaurel didn't dress this way. The woman's silver-streaked dark hair fell well past her shoulders, and the long, loose-fitting black dress she wore could have come straight out of the seventies.

"How do you know what I'm looking for?" Hawk asked sharply.

The woman leaned in slightly closer. "Your sister is ill, and you want only to take care of her. What she needs, for herself and for the baby, you won't find in any pharmacy."

Great. Apparently word was already out that Cassie was pregnant and sick. Not that Hawk cared, or ever had, what people thought about him or his family. But Cassie deserved better.

"Whatever you're selling, I'm not buying." He headed for the cash register at the front of the store.

"I'm not selling anything, Hawk."

He wasn't surprised that she knew his name, either. In a small town, information was easy enough to come by. Hawk glanced through the glass front door of the pharmacy and smiled at Baby. The big yellow dog—a mixed breed with a healthy dose of golden retriever—sat right where Hawk had told her to stay, watching for him through the glass and waiting patiently.

Hawk placed his purchases on the counter, and Ike Chapman began to ring them up. Slowly. "I heard that Cassie wasn't feeling well," Ike said with a nod of his balding head. "I hope she gets to feeling better real soon."

"Thanks," Hawk said succinctly.

The strange old woman circled around him, as if she were headed for the front door. Ike watched her as closely as Hawk did. After all, she was a stranger, and strangers in Greenlaurel were always suspect. The woman moved gracefully, but before she passed by, she swept in with a swish of her skirts to grab Hawk's hand. She pressed a piece of paper into his palm and folded his fingers over the note. "What you need can be found here. Look to the past for your answers, Hawk."

Hawk gently but firmly took his hand from the woman and reached into his back pocket to grab his wallet so he could pay Ike for the medicine. The bell on the front door rang gently as the woman in black opened the door.

He was about to toss her note into a trash can behind

the counter when she said in a very soft voice, "By the stars above, you look so very much like your mother."

Hawk's head snapped around just in time to see the door slowly close. He bolted, leaving his purchases sitting on the counter as he ran after the woman. A newly arriving customer, agonizingly slow and nearly ancient Addie Peterson, opened the door before he reached it. Standing front and center and planted there like a tree, she said hello, smiled and began to tell Hawk about her newest ailment. He nodded curtly, obviously impatient, and waited for her to move out of the doorway. When she took a step forward, he slipped around her and burst through the pharmacy doors.

Hawk searched up and down the street for any sign of the woman who'd given him the message, but she was already gone. Where could she have disappeared to so quickly?

Baby stood. Her ears perked up and her tail wagged furiously. Hawk dropped to his haunches and looked the dog squarely in the eye. He reached out to stroke firmly but gently behind Baby's left ear. "Where did she go, girl? Show me."

Baby ran down the sidewalk, turning sharply into the alley between the pharmacy and the coffee shop next door. Hawk followed. Through the narrow alley they ran, then down a grassy hill and into the parking lot of the restaurant that had closed down last year. In the middle of the small parking lot Baby came to a dead stop. Confused, she walked in a tight circle and then turned her gaze toward the street.

Hawk cursed under his breath, and Baby looked up sharply.

"Not your fault, Baby." Hawk reached down and rubbed her head. "You did good." But the strange woman was nowhere in sight. She'd obviously left a car waiting in the parking lot, and she must've run from the drugstore in order to escape. Even with Mrs. Peterson slowing him down he should have been able to catch the woman who'd pressed the note into his hand.

When she'd said that Hawk looked like his mother, she must have been talking about his birth mother. The woman he'd called Mother all his life had been five foot one in her best heels. She'd had a round and cheerful face with dimples that appeared when she smiled, blue eyes and blond hair. No one had ever mentioned a resemblance before, because there wasn't one.

Hawk's eyes and hair were dark, and he'd always been tall for his age. In his youth he'd been lean, but in the past few years he'd added some muscle to his frame. His disposition was nothing like his mother's, either. She'd been sunny. She'd been able to laugh easily. She'd loved people and they loved her.

Nope, Hawk Donovan had nothing in common with his mother.

From here the odd woman could have gone anywhere. He could try to follow her, but by the time he got to his truck on Main Street and picked a direction, she'd be long gone, and he didn't have time to waste. Not today. Crap! How could an older woman move so quickly? He should have caught her long before she'd reached the parking lot and driven away. Obviously, she'd known he would follow…and she had no intention of getting caught.

Hawk stood tall and opened his fisted hand, unfolding the scrap of paper the woman had placed there. It said 204 Pine Street, Wyatt, North Carolina. There was nothing else written there, no clue as to what he might find at this address. He turned and headed back to the pharmacy to collect his purchases, retracing his steps up the hill and through the alley to the sidewalk on Main Street. A few shoppers walked along that sidewalk, purchases in hand, but for the most part it was a quiet September morning in Greenlaurel.

What if the old woman was right, and there was nothing here in Greenlaurel that would help Cassie? The knowledge that there might be no way for him to help her was scary. They'd lost their parents nearly three years back; Dad in a car accident, Mom from a heart attack not four months later. Hawk's twin sister was all the family he had left. Her and the baby she carried. He would do anything to help them.

There was certainly no guarantee that he could find what he needed, what Cassie and the baby needed, at the address on the sheet of paper he still held in his hand, but he was desperate.

Desperate enough to travel to North Carolina on such thin evidence?

Back in the pharmacy, Ike handed over the small bag of items, then took Hawk's money and made change with maddening deliberation, counting out each coin as if he'd just learned to count. He'd been making change just this way for more than forty years.

Addie Peterson, who was apparently put out because Hawk had brushed past her in midailment, lifted her nose and continued to study the selections on a shelf not far from the front counter.

"That woman who was in here a few minutes ago," Hawk said as he returned his wallet to its place in the back pocket of his jeans. "Do you know her?"

"Never saw her before," Ike said. His old eyes twinkled. "Strange-looking lady, I must say. I would guess she was just passing through. What was that she said to you as she left? Something about your mother?" Ike Chapman was certainly old enough to remember when the Donovans had brought their newly adopted twins home, some twenty-eight years ago, and he'd known the Donovans well.

But Ike's old ears weren't as good as Hawk's. In truth, Hawk didn't know anyone who could hear as well as he did. "I don't think she was talking to me," he said. A blatant lie, since the woman's words had sent him racing out of the store. "You wouldn't know where she might be staying?"

The old man shrugged his thin shoulders. "If she's staying in town I reckon she's at the Sunshine Motel, though she might be out at the RV park near the old campgrounds."

Hawk thanked Ike and stepped onto the sidewalk, where once again Baby waited. She wasn't as calm as she had been before; she'd picked up on Hawk's own frustration.

He was going to search for the old woman at the motel and the RV park, and he'd drive his truck down the road, just in case he got lucky and spotted her along the way. But he had a feeling he wasn't going to find her. Not here in Greenlaurel, anyway.

Maybe he'd find her in Wyatt, North Carolina.

Sheryl Eldanis locked up the veterinary clinic and headed toward home, walking as always. Laverne, that obstinate gray cat, walked beside her but a little ahead. Laverne wasn't the type to follow. Ever.

Sheryl and Laverne had a lot in common these days. Neither of them wanted to be told what to do.

She couldn't help but be pleased with the way her life was going now. Things had been working out well in the few months she'd been here. Wyatt was a smaller town than the one she'd grown up in, and she hadn't been sure exactly how she'd take to living in such a place. But it suited her. She knew all her neighbors and they knew her. Town socials were frequent and low-key and surprisingly fun.

Now if she could just convince the local population that she wasn't interested in dating, dancing or marriage, she'd have it made.

Her last romantic relationship had been bad enough to make her swear off men forever. She didn't need a man, not for financial support or emotional support or sex. She was a veterinarian with her own business, and finances, while occasionally tight, were under control. For emotional support she had Laverne. And Bruce and Howie and Bogie and Princess and Smoky. As for sex…she could learn to live without it, if the occasional thrill meant letting a man disrupt her well-ordered life.

Yeah, Michael had taught her well. Romance just wasn't worth all the trouble that came with it.

"Hi, Sheryl."

The next-door neighbor—a tall, slender and attractive woman who always seemed to be smiling—rose from her place in the front yard where she'd been planting mums in an obscenely neat flower bed, dusting dirt from her knees and then pulling off her gardening gloves.

"Hi, Debbie." Sheryl took a detour and headed down the walkway that led from the sidewalk to the neighbors' front door. "Pretty day."

Debbie's smile widened. "I love autumn. September is my favorite time of year."

"I like spring myself," Sheryl said. "Autumn runs a close second, though." She was happy to see the heat of summer wane. And traffic through town decreased substantially when the summer beach traffic let up.

Debbie studied the clear blue sky for a moment before asking, "What are you doing this weekend?"

"Sleeping, mostly," Sheryl answered.

Debbie laughed. The woman had so much energy. She had a husband who worked on the road most of the time, three kids and a part-time job. And yet she never seemed to be overwhelmed. Did she ever sleep? Maybe that was the secret. No sleep.

"The autumn festival is next weekend, don't forget," Debbie said.

"I won't forget." How could she? Someone reminded her on a daily basis. She looked forward to her weekends, since she worked a half day on Saturday and was off on Sunday. Unless there was an emergency, of course. All her clients knew how to reach her on the weekends and in the middle of the night.

"My brother-in-law is coming to town for the festival," Debbie said much too casually. "Maybe you can show him around while he's here."

"No, thanks," Sheryl responded, not at all surprised or dismayed. Debbie was always trying to fix her up, and she was forever raving about the joys of marriage and motherhood. Sheryl had learned to take the friendly interference in stride, just as Debbie was learning to accept the fact that her new friend wasn't at all interested in the things that made her own life complete. She wasn't quite there yet, though.

When she'd moved to Wyatt, Sheryl had never expected her new best friend to be eleven years older than she, a married woman with three kids and an unnatural fixation for The Home and Garden Channel.

The Home and Garden Channel gave Sheryl a headache.

After talking to Debbie for a few minutes more, Sheryl headed for her own house, ready to kick off her shoes and plop down in a comfortable chair. She'd have to feed and water the animals first, but once that was done they'd let her have a breather. A short one.

Her own yard was not as well kept as Debbie's, and was not nearly as large. Sheryl had bought the smallest house on the block, but it was more than sufficient for her needs. The clapboard ranch was square and ordinary, but there was something warm about it. The previous owners had painted the house a pale yellow, and she liked it. She had never thought of herself as a yellow-house person, but this one… She loved it. Inside there was a large kitchen, a spacious living room, a dining room, two large bedrooms and a big bathroom that needed updating but was functional and roomier than most modern ones. The attic was unfinished and strictly for storage, but the extra space was nice. After years of living in apartments, she found the yellow house was a real luxury.

Laverne waited on the deep front porch, her gray tail swishing with impatience. Sheryl collected her mail from the metal box beside the door, but waited until she'd unlocked and opened the door before leafing through the envelopes. Bills, ads, a letter from her dad.

There had been a time when something as simple as leafing through the mail had made her heart beat too fast. After she'd broken up with Michael there had been too many angry letters waiting for her in the mailbox, too many unwanted messages on her answering machine. She hadn't heard from her ex-fiancé in four months, but still every now and then she expected him to rise up out of the bushes.

Yeah, romance was nice enough, but it just wasn't worth the hassle.

As she walked through the front door, a chill ran down her spine. She felt as if someone was watching her. Sheryl turned around slowly, and her eyes swept the empty sidewalk. Debbie was busy working in her flower bed again, and no one else was in sight.

She brushed off the odd feeling, attributing it to unpleasant memories of her ex, and closed the door behind her.

"It's such a long shot," Cassie said as Hawk threw sloppily folded clothes into his suitcase. "And North Carolina is so far away. I can't believe you'd listen to a crazy woman who accosts you in the pharmacy."

"What makes you think she's crazy?" Hawk glanced up as he closed the suitcase. His sister was pacing near the door, her hands clasped tightly. She wasn't usually so tense, but with everything that had happened lately, she had just cause.

"Everything you told me about her," Cassie snapped. "The way she dressed, the way she sneaked up on you, the completely insufficient note. An address, that's it. How do you know that address even exists? She might've made it up or it might be the address of a dry cleaner or a bakery or some poor person's house. What she said about you looking like our mother, that's definitely crazy. What do you think you'll find at that address, anyway? Another weird woman offering riddles about the past?"

Compared to Hawk, his sister was tiny. But the vast difference in their body mass had never stopped Cassie from standing up to him and speaking her mind.

"I don't know what I'll find."

Cassie ran a nervous hand through her hair, brushing the black strands away from her face. "I know you, Hawk. You think you're going to drive up to a house with a white picket fence, knock on the door, and our bio-logical mother and father will come to the door with open arms, wondering where we've been all these years."

He'd quit expecting anything like that years ago, though there had been a time when he'd been absolutely obsessed with finding his birth parents. "You'll be okay while I'm gone."

"I know I'll be okay," she said, a little bit calmer than she'd been a few minutes ago. "It's just...I can't talk to anyone else about what's going on. They'll think I'm nuts! And I am worried about you, you know. I don't want you to go all that way and be disappointed when you don't find what you expect to find."

"I don't expect to find anything."

"Yes, you do," Cassie said softly. "Hire someone to check out the address for you. You can find a private de-tective in North Carolina and have him check it out. That way you can stay home and no one gets hurt."

"And what exactly would I tell this private detective?"

Cassie just pursed her lips. She knew too well that they couldn't bring anyone else into this mix.

"I'm not a kid anymore," Hawk said. "I don't expect to find anything but answers about your condition."

"My condition," Cassie scoffed. "I hate having a 'con-dition'!"

"Call me anytime you need to talk. I'll have my cell phone on twenty-four/seven."

His sister almost pouted. "It's not the same."

Cassie Donovan wasn't one to pout, not for any reason. But the episodes were tough on her. She'd always had dreams that seemed more real than dreams, but something unexpected was happening with these seizures.

She was seeing a few minutes into the future immediately after each convulsion. It was hard to swallow, impossible to explain. But over the years they'd learned to accept that some things were just that way.

Impossible.

Cassie sighed, apparently resigned to the fact that he was going to North Carolina. "If you insist on making this trip, you could fly instead of driving," she said as she followed him down the long hallway. "It would be much quicker. Fly over, visit this address, fly home."

"I don't know how long I'll need to be there, and besides, flying would only save a day or two." He glanced down at the dog who walked beside him. "Baby hates to fly, and I can't leave her here. Last time I went on a two-day trip, she didn't eat the whole time I was gone."

"You love that dog more than you love me," Cassie said, sounding very much the way she had at the age of twelve.

Hawk hid a smile. "You know that's not true."

"What if I tell you that *I* won't eat until you get home?"

He laughed. "The way you've been eating lately, I know that's a hollow threat."

Cassie hit him lightly on the arm as she danced around him. "That's not very nice."

"But it is true."

Again she seemed to pout.

Hawk dropped the suitcase and took his sister's face in his hands. His tough, tanned hands only emphasized her paleness. There were dark circles under her eyes, and while she'd been eating plenty lately she wasn't gaining weight. The thinness of her face told him that she'd lost a few pounds. She might not like it, but he had to do something.

He couldn't possibly sit around here and twiddle his thumbs and just wait for something to happen. If he could find an explanation for what was happening to Cassie, maybe even a cure, then he could rest easy. Maybe.

Protests about unrealistic expectations aside, he had to admit that the woman's final comment had been haunting him for the past two days. *You look so very much like your mother.*

"What if our biological mother gave us up because she knew we were different?"

"We were infants," Cassie argued. "How could she possibly have known?"

Hawk brushed one thumb over his sister's ashen cheek. "That's what I'm going to find out."

Chapter 2

"Hey, there's someone here to see you."

Sheryl looked up from her chore as Cory stuck his head into the room. She never knew what color her young part-time helper's hair would be. This week it was black. And spiked. Odd appearance aside, the teenager was wonderful with animals. Sheryl's patients didn't seem to mind what his hairstyle was like. They also didn't mind that his pants usually hung so loose on his narrow hips they looked like they were about to fall to the floor.

"A drop-in?" she asked.

"Not exactly. He's an inspector or something. He has a clipboard and a business card. I told him he could wait in your office."

Sheryl's heart sank. Just what she needed! There was bound to be something in this old building that wasn't up to code. "I'll be right there."

"He's kinda nice lookin', for an old guy," Cory added with a grin. "Maybe you shouldn't leave him waiting too long." He wagged his eyebrows suggestively.

"Not you, too!"

"Not me, too, what?" Cory asked, almost pulling off the innocent expression. "I'm just trying to, you know, fix you up. You're hot, for an older woman. If you weren't too old for me, I'd definitely ask you out."

She'd never imagined that she'd be "too old" at twenty-six. "Cory, do you like your job?"

"Sure!"

"Then I suggest you shut up."

Cory locked his lips with nimble fingers and watched her work. Silently.

Sheryl finished with the small dog on the table, then handed it over to Cory for grooming.

Her offices were located in an old building. True, the place needed some work, but the rooms were spacious and the hallway was wide, and some of the interior walls were red brick, giving the place a solid and homey feel. In addition to the equipment necessary for her practice, she'd livened the place up with plants and hung framed pictures—photographs and drawings of animals—down the long hallway. The clinic wasn't home yet, but it was certainly beginning to feel that way.

The man who waited in her office was indeed "kinda nice lookin'." But he didn't look at all like a building inspector. Did men who worked for the state of North Carolina dress in black, wear their hair in a short ponytail and sport a gold earring in one ear? She didn't think so.

"Dr. Eldanis." The man, who hadn't been waiting in a chair but was perusing her bookshelves, offered his hand for a quick shake. "Tony Carpenter, North Carolina Department of Structural Safety. I need to ask a few questions and take a look around the building, and then I'll be out of your hair."

"Sure," she said, seeing this intrusion as an annoyance that came with owning an old building.

"You've been here how long?" he asked.

"Three months."

He nodded curtly. "And the building was empty for several years before you bought it, correct?"

Sheryl cocked her head and studied the man's face for a moment through narrowed eyes. "Yes. The building was empty for quite some time. Don't you have this information in your files?"

He gave her a practiced and disarming smile. "The database is woefully out of date, I'm afraid. I always find it best to cover everything pertinent when I conduct an inspection."

Sheryl no longer trusted disarming smiles. In fact, they put her on edge.

Over the next several minutes, Mr. Carpenter asked a few questions about the condition of the building. He made a couple of quickly scribbled notations on the paper on his clipboard, and while he certainly wasn't nervous, he was definitely wound a bit too tight.

There was something about the way he glanced around her office that made Sheryl suspect that he was a little bit too interested.

"Did the previous residents leave any materials behind?" he asked, finally laying his eyes on her again. "I understand that several years ago there was a fertility clinic at this location."

"Yes." Sheryl crossed her arms across her chest. "That was quite a long time ago, Mr. Carpenter."

There was that smile again. "Call me Tony."

Oh, I don't think so. "A few years after the clinic closed, a doctor's office opened here. After that the building stood empty for more than five years before I bought it."

"I see," he said, making a notation. "And you didn't come across anything out of the ordinary when you moved in? Sometimes businesses will leave files and materials behind in their haste to leave."

Sheryl backed slightly away from the so-called inspector. Why wasn't he asking questions about the plumbing and the electrical? Why didn't he want to know if the roof leaked when it rained, or where she stored her fire extinguishers? And why was this inspector working on a Saturday morning? It just didn't add up.

The fertility clinic he seemed to be so interested in had been closed for close to thirty years.

"Can I see your ID, please?" she asked him.

"I showed your assistant...."

"I'd like to see it myself."

The man with the ponytail reached into his pocket and withdrew a business card. Sure enough, it read Tony Carpenter, North Carolina Department of Structural Safety. Looked to Sheryl as if the card had been printed up on a computer. A very good computer but still... She could print up a card declaring herself a queen, but that wouldn't make it so.

"Wait right here," she said with a smile of her own. "I just remembered I have a phone call I need to make. I'll be right back, Tony." She left the room as casually as possible, then once the door was closed behind her she hurried down the hallway to the lobby. She snagged the phone on the front desk. Every instinct told her that the man in her office was not who he said he was. If she was wrong, she'd be embarrassed. But if she was right...

Wyatt had a small police force. They weren't exactly NYPD but they did their best, considering that most of the officers were younger than Sheryl and the chief was a good ol' boy who had grown up here and was trusted not because he was good at his job but because everyone knew him from way back.

Sheryl asked for a policeman to be dispatched to the clinic and then hurried back to her office. She might need to stall the so-called inspector for a few minutes, since law enforcement response was erratic at best. She burst into the office, ready to answer any question the ponytailed man might have.

Her office was empty.

It was a two-day trip by pickup truck from Greenlaurel, Texas, to Wyatt, North Carolina. Two full days, with a few hours' sleep at a hotel in Tennessee along the way.

Hawk was tired, he was cranky, and with every mile that had passed he'd wondered if this impulsive trip was a mistake. Cassie needed him, the horses he'd left behind needed him.

But the odd woman's words kept echoing in his head. She said the answers to his questions could be found in the past. What if Cassie's new health problem was genetic? What if the address in Wyatt somehow led to their birth mother? It was a long shot, but he had to do something.

Cassie would be in good hands during his absence, and so would the horses he trained and cared for. The Donovan Ranch was a good-size organization, not a two-man operation. There were people to care for Cassie, if she needed help, and there were employees to care for the horses. If there was even a small chance that he might be able to help his sister by coming here, he had to try.

Wyatt was a small community, smaller even than Green-laurel. It boasted a town square, complete with courthouse, sheriff's auxiliary office and local police department. The square was completed with shops necessary for a small town to survive. Maybe they picked up some of the tourist traffic that ventured off the interstate. There were a couple of antique shops, a candy shop, two small restaurants, a bookstore and other assorted businesses. All around town, signs advertising Wyatt's autumn festival were posted. This weekend. With any luck, he'd be long gone by then.

Two turns off the main square, he found Pine Street. There it was, 204. The freshly painted sign out front read Eldanis Veterinary Clinic. Hawk parked his truck at the curb and reached over to run his fingers through Baby's fur. She whined, as if she knew what awaited her here.

"We're just visiting," Hawk said as he left the truck. Baby came with him, though not as enthusiastically as usual. "No shots, I promise."

Baby perked up considerably, and they walked into the clinic side by side. Down the hallway that led to individual rooms, a thin teenage boy with spiked hair was pushing a broom. Curious, the kid glanced toward the lobby, checking out both Hawk and Baby as he continued with his chore.

A woman stood at the counter with her head down, a phone in one hand, a pen in the other, as she made note of an appointment. She said something pleasant to the person on the other end of the phone and smiled as she lifted her head to see who had arrived.

Sleek, dark-blond hair had been pulled back into a long ponytail, and intense blue eyes sparkled when they landed on him. Pretty girl. Very pretty. Hawk had to remind himself that he wasn't here to admire the scenery; he didn't have the time. Still, he had to admit that she had a nice wide mouth and a genuine smile…and man, were those eyes blue.

The smile was wider and more real for Baby than it was for him, even at the end of the day. According to the hours on the sign at the entrance, the place would be closing in five minutes.

"Can I help you?" the woman asked as she walked around the counter. She wore a long white smock that disguised her figure. Beneath her smock baggy trousers hung loosely around her legs. Her shoes were of the sensible sort.

Could she help him? It would be a whole lot easier to figure that out if he knew what he was looking for. "I guess I need to speak to Eldanis."

"I'm Sheryl Eldanis," she said, her smile fading slightly. "What can I do for you?"

Sheryl Eldanis was definitely the cutest vet he'd ever laid eyes on, shapeless clothes and all. And he'd known his share of vets. "I'm not really sure," Hawk admitted. It didn't really matter what she looked like. He needed answers, and if she was the one who had them, he didn't care how pretty she was.

"I'm looking for information. Have you been in this location very long?" She was much too young to have been here more than a couple of years at most. "What I'm looking for is probably going to go back several years. I'm not even sure what it might be, exactly. Some information from past activities in this building, I imagine."

All pretense of friendliness disappeared. The smile vanished, the blue eyes went hard. Her stance changed, as she became defensive, and the muscles in her body tightened.

"What are you?" she asked sharply. "The second team? I don't go for the fake building inspector, so two days later they send in an aw-shucks cowboy to charm the files out of me?"

"I have no idea what you're talking about."

She lifted a finger and wagged it at him. "You can tell your friend that I called the police after he disappeared. It only took one phone call to find out that there isn't any Tony Carpenter. There isn't even a Department of Structural Safety!" Eldanis stepped behind the counter and lifted the phone, dialing with anger and precision. "Let's cut out the middle man this time around. You can talk directly to the chief of police.

"Sandy?" she said into the phone.

Hawk glanced down at the gray cat that had begun to weave between his legs. In and out, around and around, that long tail twitching and twining. He smiled and reached down to snag the friendly feline with one large hand. He felt her deep purr in his palm as he said hello.

"Hey!" Eldanis called, moving the phone away from her head so she wasn't shouting into the receiver. "Laverne doesn't like—"

She stopped speaking when the cat in question purred and wound its way around Hawk's neck to settle comfortably on his shoulder. The long tail twitched and wound around his head.

"Never mind, Sandy," Eldanis said in a calmer tone of voice. "False alarm. I'll call you later if I need help with anything." After she ended the call, she leaned onto the counter and studied not Hawk's face, but the way her cat had made a home on his shoulder. She didn't relax all at once, but gradually her distrust of him faded. A little. Maybe a trace of the smile crept back, and her expressive eyes definitely changed.

"Laverne seems to like you," she said. "That buys you three minutes to explain yourself. I suggest you make the best of it."

Sheryl stayed close to the phone. In fact, she kept one hand on the receiver, just in case. She was absolutely stunned by Laverne's reaction to the man in the waiting room, and she couldn't ignore what she saw. The stubborn cat never cuddled up to anyone, and yet she had definitely made herself comfortable on the stranger's wide shoulders.

"My name's Hawk Donovan," the man said simply. "If you want to call the police, go right ahead. I don't have anything to hide."

That was a good sign, Sheryl decided. She relaxed a little bit. "What do you want?"

"I'm not sure," Donovan said. "You mentioned files. What kind of files?"

Was it possible that her two visitors were not connected? Possible. Not likely. And she still didn't trust this man—or any other. She especially didn't trust men who looked like this one. He was too pushy. Too *big*. And he had a fascinating face that suggested women had been doing whatever he asked of them all his life.

She didn't allow herself to be pushed around, not anymore, and no one told her what to do. Especially not men. "Don't try to turn this around on me. Why are you here?"

He didn't answer. At least, not immediately. Hawk Donovan, if that was indeed his name, was not at all bad looking. Not at all. He had the required iron jaw, and the hard body and the way of moving that came from being in the kind of physical shape most men simply dreamed of. There was something sleek about Donovan, in the way he walked, in the way he moved his head. He reminded her of a caged an-

imal. Beautiful, fascinating, but also dangerous and un-
predictable.

Big men could be aggressive, so for a moment she ignored the fact that he was over six feet tall and wide in the
shoulders. His hands were big, too, and they were definitely a working man's hands, weathered and scarred.

His dark hair might've been conservatively cut a while
back, but was growing out just a tad on the shaggy side,
untended and thick. Those eyes set above killer cheek-
bones were deep and dark and warm. His face would be
like granite, if not for the unexpected and subtle dimple in
his chin. Well-worn jeans hugged muscled thighs, and the
shirt he wore was a plain and sturdy denim. The boots were
leather, expensive and had seen better days. There was no
cowboy hat in sight, at least not today, but she'd bet her
last dollar that he had one at home.

"My sister is sick," he said in a lowered voice. "The doctors are having a problem coming up with answers for us.
Since we were adopted as infants, we don't have any family medical history available." The dog who'd arrived with
Donovan sat at his side. Laverne continued to rest on his
shoulder, and instead of dismissing the cat, as many men
would have, Donovan seemed to have forgotten she was
there.

"Don't tell me," Sheryl said sternly, not at all convinced
by his supposedly tender words or swayed by the fact that
he was mouthwateringly studly and intriguingly different
in a way she could not explain. "You want the files from
the fertility clinic to assist in your search for answers."

He didn't smile, but it seemed that the muscles in his
face relaxed as if he were thinking about it. "Fertility
clinic?"

Disgusted, Sheryl waved her hand at him. "Don't play

games with me, Donovan. Don't stand there and pretend you don't know exactly what I'm talking about." What could possibly be in those old boxes that was suddenly so desirable? Maybe she should have looked through a couple of them when she'd moved them from the basement of this old building.

Donovan reached into his back pocket and pulled out a thick wallet. "I don't know what's going on here exactly, but it seems to me you'll rest easier once you know that I am who I say I am." He withdrew a driver's license and tossed it to her. It landed on the counter and skidded to a stop directly in front of her.

She glanced at the authentic-looking license. "Fake IDs—"

"Call your police chief," Donovan interrupted briskly. "Have him check me out if it'll make you feel better. Have him call anyone in Greenlaurel, Texas, and ask them about me."

She picked up the phone, ready to call his bluff. "Fine."

Instead of challenging her, Donovan walked to a lobby chair and sat. Laverne remained on his shoulder. His dog, a large, yellow, mixed breed who obviously adored him, curled up at his feet. An absent hand, tanned and long-fingered, reached up to stroke Laverne's thick gray fur, and the usually unsociable cat purred and swished her tail.

Donovan hadn't been exactly warm in dealing with her, but any man who was so obviously adored by animals couldn't be all bad.

"Aren't you going to make your phone call?" the cowboy asked as he waited. At the sound of his deep voice, both Laverne and the yellow dog turned accusing eyes to her. This was her clinic, and that gray cat usually wouldn't let anyone but Sheryl near her. So why did she suddenly feel like the outsider here?

"No." He didn't care about her phone call to the police, which meant that, true or not, his story was going to check out. She still didn't trust him. "Come back tomorrow."

He stood quickly, one big hand on Laverne so the cat wouldn't be frightened by the sudden move. "Tomorrow? What's wrong with right now?"

Carpenter had been smoother than this! The last thing she needed was a bossy man showing up to issue orders.

"It's late, and I'm tired," she said. "I'm sure the hotel has a room available. It's cheap and just a couple blocks away."

"But—"

"Tomorrow," Sheryl said. She stepped out from behind the counter. "And if you don't mind, I'd like my cat back."

He reached up and grabbed Laverne in one large hand, swung the cat down and handed her over. Laverne allowed herself to rest in Sheryl's arms for about three seconds, and then she leaped to the floor. She and the dog were nose to nose for a moment, and then Laverne began to once again wind her supple body around Donovan's legs.

Anthony Caldwell made his way out of town, empty-handed and frustrated. According to the computer file he'd stolen, thirty-odd years ago genetic experiments had taken place in that building where Sheryl Eldanis now operated her veterinary clinic. There should be something that had been left behind. Something concrete. Proof.

Nothing remained in the building itself; he'd confirmed that for himself. After darkness had fallen and Eldanis had gone for the night, he'd searched the place from top to bottom and found nothing out of the ordinary.

That didn't mean what he wanted didn't exist; it just meant it was going to be tougher to find than he'd imagined it would be. Did Eldanis have possession of that "something concrete?" Or was it long gone? Somehow he'd spooked her, and he hadn't had a chance to look around the clinic properly on Saturday morning. He'd watched her for a few days before visiting the clinic, and he'd watched her over the weekend. Not that there was much to see. She led an ordinary, dull life—her and her animals.

A neighbor had seen him last evening, dammit. She hadn't said anything to him, but Anthony knew he'd been seen. And a woman at a store in town, where he'd stopped twice for supplies, had started asking why he was in Wyatt. Time to get out of town, at least for now.

There was a festival this upcoming weekend, and the town would be filled with strangers. He could blend in with a crowd, he knew.

He was leaving Wyatt behind him for the moment, but he'd be back.

Hawk arrived at the vet's office shortly after eight in the morning. Sheryl Eldanis was already in and supposedly hard at work. Her cat met him before he'd taken three steps into the lobby.

There were two customers in the waiting room, even at this early hour. An older lady, who cradled a small dog in her generous lap, and an equally older gentleman with a calico cat curled up on one thigh. Both animals perked up as Hawk walked into the lobby and claimed a seat to wait. Eldanis's cat seemed anxious to reclaim her place on his shoulder, so he moved her there. Baby curled up at his feet.

After a moment the small dog jumped from the lap

where he'd been sitting contentedly before Hawk's arrival. The cat followed suit a few seconds later. They both gravitated to Hawk, and without hesitation he reached down to give them each a gentle stroke on the head. The cat leaped into his lap. The little dog, whose leaping days were over, went up on his hind legs. Hawk reached down and snagged the dog, and made a place for the animal on his lap, there beside the cat. They did not hiss or growl at each other, but settled in much as Laverne had.

Animals had always liked him, and he'd always liked them. They were less complicated than humans, more honest and open and loving. An animal would never betray or lie. They loved completely and without demand.

For a long time Hawk hadn't questioned his affinity with animals. It hadn't seemed at all odd that there were times when he simply knew that one of his pets was ill or afraid. He'd called it instinct and left it at that. As a child, as a young man, he'd understood that the other people he knew didn't have this instinct, but he didn't worry about that too much. Everyone had his own talents.

He had been nineteen when he'd discovered that his talent with animals went beyond the ordinary.

The calico purred, and the little dog rested his head on Hawk's knee and closed his eyes. Hawk laid a hand on the small canine body, and for an instant, just an instant, he felt the sharp pain in the animal's hip.

Arthritis was a bitch, no matter what species it attacked.

Hawk laid his big hand on the dog's head, and everything else faded away. In spite of the pain, the animal was happy. He was horribly spoiled, in fact, and was already thinking of the treat that would be hand-fed to him when he got home. Colors faded as Hawk saw through the dog's old eyes. His vision wasn't as crisp as it had once been, and in true canine fashion there was no color. Ah, but he heard everything, and he lived in a world of smells. He could even smell the woman who gave him shots and fed him treats and clipped his toenails. Sometimes she hurt him, but he liked her all the same because she knew just where to rub his tummy and she kept those treats nearby.

"What are you doing?"

Hawk's head jerked up at the sound of that annoyed voice. For a moment Sheryl Eldanis and everything around her was gray. Gradually, color and depth came back, and he found himself staring into a very pretty—and very annoyed—face. He realized, as he removed his attention from the animals who had gathered on and around him, that he was not alone in this room. The owners of the small dog and calico cat were staring at him with wide, confused eyes.

Go. The command was silent and friendly, and the animals on his lap obeyed. The calico cat jumped to the floor and sauntered to her owner, and the little dog stood shakily. Hawk wrapped one hand around the small furry body and lowered the dog to the floor.

"You wearin' bacon under them pants?" the old man teased as his cat leaped into his arms.

"No," Hawk answered.

"My, the animals surely do like you," the little dog's owner said as she retrieved her pet. "Why, I haven't seen Toby move that fast in five years or more." She cast a sharp glance at the cat owner. "Though I have to say, Harold Johnston, it's quite rude of you to suggest that the young man is hiding bacon beneath his blue jeans."

"I was just having a bit of fun, Mildred," Harold said with a snort. "I shoulda known you wouldn't recognize a joke if it walked up and bit you on the—"

"Mrs. Harris," Sheryl interrupted brightly, "you and Toby are next."

The woman rose, offering the old man, Harold, a lift of her pert nose and her double chin as she carried her little dog to the veterinarian, and the two women began walking down the hallway. Eldanis glided; Mrs. Harris waddled. The pretty vet gave Hawk one last, sharp glance before she disappeared from view.

Sometimes Hawk wished he could read humans as easily as he could read animals. Other days he was very grateful that his talents were restricted to the animal world.

"Hot broad, ain't she?" Harold said once the women were well down the hallway and out of hearing range.

"Dr. Eldanis?"

"Her, too, I reckon," the old man said. "Though she is a mite young for me. Shoot, I've got grandkids her age!"

Which meant Harold was talking about Toby's owner, the older woman who had turned up her nose at his supposed joke.

"You're a young fella," Harold continued, even though Hawk did not participate in the conversation. "How does a man go about asking a lady out these days?"

"I wouldn't know," Hawk answered.

"Handsome young fella like you?" Harold protested. "Surely you can give an old man some pointers. Help me out here. I'm spending a small fortune, bringing Bitsy down here every Tuesday morning just because I know Mildred is going to be here with her cantankerous mutt. Usually we don't talk at all, and if we do it's mostly arguing. Stubborn woman," he added beneath his breath. "It ain't easy to start all over again, you know. I was married for forty-one years before my wife passed. Mildred had been married almost as long when her husband passed away last year. What do you think? Should I ask her out to supper? Maybe I should just invite her to take a walk around town with me, though with my bad knee that might not be such a good idea. Maybe we could go out for an ice cream cone. I just don't know."

Hawk stood, at the same time scooping the gray cat from his shoulder and placing her on the ground. "Tell Dr. Eldanis I'll be back this afternoon," he said as he and Baby headed for the door.

"Okay. But what do you think I should do about Mildred? You never did say."

"Sorry. I don't know," Hawk said as he pushed the clinic door open and stepped onto the sidewalk, his mind filled with questions of his own. Maybe he could find some answers at the courthouse, if they kept decent records. All night his mind had spun and danced. A fertility clinic! Had his birth mother been here, in this very building? His biological father?

Perusing old records was preferable to offering advice to a man old enough to be his grandfather. Even if he were inclined to chat with strangers, he was the last man who should be giving anyone advice on romance.

Chapter 3

At five minutes to four, Laverne began to pace before the door. She even seemed to peer through the glass to the sidewalk, as if she were looking for someone.

Someone. Sheryl shook her head as she rearranged a new display of dog collars near the front desk. Who was she kidding? Laverne was anxiously waiting for Hawk Donovan to show up.

Sheryl was not. It would suit her just fine if the man never showed his face here again. He was trouble through and through; she knew that with every fiber of her being. Still, she couldn't help but wonder what was in those fertility clinic files that would interest both a fake building inspector and someone like Donovan.

When she'd arrived here this morning and discovered that someone had broken in last night, Donovan had been her first suspect. But if Hawk Donovan had broken into the clinic last night looking for the files, why had he shown up here this morning? If he'd searched the clinic last night, he knew the documents he wanted weren't here.

This morning she'd been so tempted to accuse him of breaking into her place, but she hadn't wanted to make a scene in front of two regular clients. Gossip in Wyatt traveled at the speed of light, and she had no desire to be the subject of that gossip. Twice in the past three weeks, Doc Murdock had shown up unexpectedly to see if she needed any help. The veterinarian who'd retired just before Sheryl opened her practice was already bored. His retirement was the reason she'd opened her practice here, instead of in a larger city. She wanted to be her own boss, to have her own clinic, but if Doc Murdock decided to reopen his practice, she was finished. Especially if people thought this clinic wasn't safe.

As far as the break-in went, her money was on the man who'd called himself Carpenter, and that was what she'd told the police chief when he'd shown up to talk to her, around ten o'clock—three hours after her initial phone call.

Tonight she'd go home and take a look for herself. Maybe she should just call Chief Nichols, explain what had been happening and turn the boxes over to him. Once they were out of her hands, someone else could deal with Donovan.

She hadn't even mentioned the files to the chief. Nichols was a nice man, and it wasn't that she didn't trust him. But what if Carpenter showed up with a new name and a new ID? Chief Nichols would hand the boxes of documents over and be glad to be rid of them.

Laverne quit pacing at ten after four, and stood in the middle of the lobby with her eyes riveted to the front door.

Sure enough, not three minutes later the door opened and Hawk Donovan and his dog walked in. Donovan looked to be as surly as ever.

There was something unusual about the man, surliness and good looks aside. The way he moved... He was sleek and strong enough to make any red-blooded woman's mouth water. She had never known it was possible for a man to be graceful, in an entirely masculine way, but Donovan pulled it off. It was downright eerie, and more than a little fascinating.

Laverne, the traitor, meowed and greeted Donovan as if he were her long-lost and much beloved owner. The big man relaxed visibly, and even had a smile for the fat cat. Did he respond that way to any human? She thought not. Laverne didn't take up residence on Donovan's shoulder this afternoon, but settled into his arms with a purr.

Donovan did not have a smile for Sheryl. He fixed dark eyes on her and said, "We need to talk."

"No, we don't." She turned and walked away from him. He was the most infuriating man! Demanding and cantankerous and...and Laverne really did love the big guy. Sheryl stopped before she reached the hallway and turned to find that Donovan hadn't moved. He stood in the waiting room with a contented Laverne in his arms and a happy dog at his feet.

Yeah, a man like this one was nothing but trouble.

"Did you break in here last night, searching for your damned files?" she asked sharply.

He looked properly shocked. Was the reaction genuine or a well-planned act? She didn't know him well enough to judge for herself.

"No, of course not. Someone broke in? Was anything stolen?"

Naturally, he was worried that someone else might have gotten their hands on what he'd come here for. "A lock on the back door was broken, and a few things in my office and in the basement were moved. As far as I can tell, nothing was taken."

If she was reading Donovan correctly, the news of the break-in sincerely disturbed him.

"I did some research at the courthouse today," he said. "In the seventies, there was a fertility clinic in this building. They were shut down for some reason, and a couple of years later a doctor had his offices here. He retired, and the building stood empty for a few years. Three months ago you moved in."

"You're not telling me anything that I don't already know."

He was not deterred by her attitude. "What I'm looking for is paperwork that might've been left behind by the fertility clinic. Maybe by the doctor," he added with a frown. "I can't be sure."

"And you expect whatever it is you're looking for to be here after all this time?" she snapped.

For a long minute he didn't answer. She wished he would give away something with his dark eyes, but they—and he—remained a mystery. If he would smile at her and try to beguile the files out of her, she'd know he was just like Carpenter and she could toss him out with a clean conscience.

But he didn't. Instead he finally said, "I don't know exactly what I'm looking for. Something important is here, in this building. Or was. There could be medical information that was left behind. About my birth mother." He said the words reluctantly, as if they'd been dragged from him one syllable at time. He might be great with animals, but he was not the kind of man who shared personal information easily or often.

Heaven above, she did not want to feel even an ounce of sympathy for him! "Even if I do happen to know where some old documents are, how do I know you're not lying to me?"

"Why should I lie?"

"Why should two men suddenly show up at my clinic looking for a bunch of moldy old files?" And what if she made a mistake and turned them over to the wrong man? What if there truly was something important in that mess of papers?

Donovan almost smiled. His lips twisted a little, and his eyes softened. Oh, eyes like that should be illegal, she thought. The man might be a cowboy, but he had gypsy eyes that were not only dark but mysterious. Soulful. "So," he said, "they're moldy?"

She was saved from explaining herself when Mort Dermot pushed his way through the front door, using his left hand, since his entire right arm was in a cast. Sheryl was happy enough to turn away from the maddening man who had bewitched her cat.

"Hi, Mort," she said. "What happened to your arm?"

"That damn mare," he answered softly. "I can't do a thing with her and neither can anyone else. Do you have the name of that guy in Raleigh who handles horse disposal? I'd put her down myself, but…" He shook his head and stared at the floor. "I just don't have the heart for it. But I can't have her hurting one of my kids, and I can't in good conscience sell her to somebody else who might get hurt. What else can I do?"

Donovan turned all his attention to Mort. "Let me have a look at her," he offered in a low but intense voice.

"Thanks, mister, but—"

"It's what I do," Donovan said. "I work with difficult horses. At least let me spend a few minutes with her."

A disgusted Mort was already shaking his head.

"If I don't have her gentled in three hours, I'll buy her from you," Donovan said. "I'll give you double what you paid for her."

Mort was as surprised as Sheryl. Donovan made the offer without even knowing how much such a purchase would cost him.

"I don't want to take advantage of you, mister. She really is just a bad horse. It happens."

"Please."

At that moment something in Sheryl's heart melted.

Somehow she knew that Hawk Donovan would never say please for her or any other human.

The dun mare was so afraid, the fear radiating from her in waves touched Hawk to the bone.

Dermot had a small horse ranch a few miles away from town. Nothing like the Donovan Ranch, but respectable, just the same. He boarded and occasionally trained horses, but he wasn't an expert by any means. The circular corral where the dun mare had been restrained, after kicking at Dermot and breaking the man's arm, was in good condition.

A lot of horses had been broken here in the past. Hawk could practically smell old fear in the air. Blood and fear and forced domination. He could almost hear the pounding of hooves on the hard ground, could almost smell the blood on the air, even though it had been a long time since anyone had broken a horse here. Most of the horses who entered this corral these days were already tame.

But not the dun mare.

The vet and the man with the broken arm stayed out of the corral. Dermot tried to caution Hawk as he stepped toward the horse, but it only took a few seconds for Hawk to completely dismiss the people who watched as he approached the mare. It was like coming home, stepping into the corral. He belonged here. He was himself here in a way he would never be anywhere else.

"It's going to be okay, girl," he said as he approached. Before he proceeded, he untied the mare. Not only had she been tethered to a post with a short rope, her hind legs had been bound. No wonder she was frightened. Her ears were flattened to her head, her eyes were wild. As he released her bonds, he stroked gently and murmured kind words. Meaningless words. Calming sounds that came from deep in his throat. He let the sound of his voice and the touch of his hands soothe her.

When she was free from her restraints, the mare ran. She raced in circles along the boundaries of the corral, snorting and blowing, while Hawk watched silently. He tried to touch the mare's mind with his while she ran, but she fought against him. Hawk didn't push to connect with the animal, but he didn't back away, either. He remained steady. Calm. Gradually the fear in the dun mare faded.

Now and then Hawk glanced at Baby, who had made herself at home near Sheryl Eldanis. Baby didn't take to many people. She was slow to trust, with good reason. Before Hawk had found her, she'd been treated badly. It had taken years to get her to trust people again. For years she'd flinched when a person came too near. She'd cowered and hidden and waited for blows that would never come again. The mare would be the same way. Trust would not come easily.

When the time was right, Hawk lifted his hand slowly. The mare came to him, no longer running, but loping easily. She walked directly to Hawk, never hesitating, never acknowledging those who watched.

Hawk stroked the mare between the eyes, silently telling the fine animal that he didn't want to hurt her, that he didn't intend to break her. They would work together, a team united. No one would be her master. No one would break her spirit. There was no need for fear.

She wasn't easily convinced. Dermot had tried to break her the old way—with pain and fear. The dun mare's heart was too wild to be broken, but she would make a fine ally.

Time passed, but Hawk was not aware of it. He linked his mind with the mare's in a way that was ancient and primal and inexplicable. The dun mare was no longer afraid of him, but she had not forgotten the way she'd been treated in the past few weeks. He whispered in her ear; she responded with a soft snort. Before Dermot there had been another man who'd tried to incite respect with a whip. The mare bore the marks of that method on her flanks. She would never forget, and any rider who tried to take a whip to her might truly be endangered.

But the mare came to trust Hawk. She knew without doubt that he would never hurt her, that he had no desire to possess her.

When the wildness in her eyes had gone and her ears were perked up, Hawk remembered that he and the mare were not alone. Judging by the way the sun hung low in the sky, he'd been out here well over an hour. He glanced at his watch. Almost two hours. He walked toward Eldanis and Dermot, and the mare followed.

People who had never seen him work were usually stunned the first time. These two were no exception. Eldanis wore an easy smile and an expression of bewilderment, but Dermot was truly shocked.

Hawk leaned against the fence, and the dun mare nuzzled him gently. She wanted to play; she wanted to talk. "I'll need a place to board her until I go home. Is there another stable nearby?"

Dermot wasn't anxious to believe what he'd seen. His logical mind was trying to dismiss what his eyes showed him. "I haven't exactly sold her to you yet. You said three hours, and the way I see it you have an hour left." His chin came up defiantly. "Maybe I should just go ahead and sell her to you, though. She looks fine at the moment, but how do I know she won't start kicking again as soon as anybody else steps into the corral? This is a fluke, that's all. Some kind of trick."

Hawk had no desire to prove anything to this small-minded man who was still breaking horses the same way it had been done a hundred years ago and more.

In Dr. Eldanis's eyes he saw something much more interesting than disbelief. She was impressed and intrigued. She was interested in what she'd seen him do. Like it or not, he needed her on his side, he needed her to trust him. Since he'd never been a smooth talker, he wasn't going to win her over with polished explanations and charisma.

But maybe, just maybe, he could convince her that he was trustworthy simply by doing what he did best.

Hawk took a close look at her. She didn't wear any makeup that he could tell, but then again she didn't need it. She had a fresh, clean look and flawless skin that didn't need to be covered. He wondered how she handled the larger animals she treated, since she was petite. Even her face was delicate. Not for the first time, he had to remind himself that he wasn't here to hook up with a pretty woman, not even for a few hours.

But dammit, he needed her cooperation. He needed her to be on his side.

"I could ride her myself, but that won't prove anything," he told Dermot. Then he looked back at Eldanis. "Dermot has a broken arm. What about you?"

Without hesitation she nodded her head.

This afternoon she'd left Cory in charge of the clinic and ridden to the Dermot ranch with Mort and his eldest son, who'd driven his father to town to have the broken arm set. At that time Donovan had followed in his pickup. Now, just barely past dark, she was headed back to Wyatt with Donovan at the wheel and Baby and Laverne curled up in the small back seat. Both animals were fast asleep.

"I want to know everything," she said, her eyes on Donovan's impassive face. She sounded much too interested, much too excited. But she couldn't help herself. Donovan had put on an amazing display. One she could not explain away. "How do you do that? Can you teach me?"

After he had easily hefted her onto the mare's back, she'd ridden the horse that Mort Dermot had been so sure no one would ever ride without risk of injury. Hawk had stayed close by, ready and able to sweep her off the mare if necessary. But of course, that had not been necessary. Her ride had been uneventful.

Needless to say, Dermot had decided not to sell the mare to Donovan.

"There are a lot of trainers who don't break horses in the old way," Donovan explained. "If you're interested in the various modern methods of horse training, there are classes available across the country. Take your pick."

"What about you?" she asked quickly. "Do you teach classes?"

"No." He sounded a little horrified by the prospect.

She had a feeling Hawk Donovan hadn't learned his skill in any class given by any other trainer. What he had was a gift.

After Donovan had finished his display, Mort had been full of questions. Questions Donovan had either half answered, ignored or bluffed his way through. He did give Mort a list of instructions on how to deal with the mare in the coming days. She was not to be whipped or sacked, she was not to be bound. Mort had agreed to everything, and more questions had been fired at Donovan. They would have been there all night if Donovan hadn't insisted that he needed to get back to town.

His affinity for four-legged creatures definitely didn't extend to the people around him. Donovan had been gruff and impatient with Mort and with her. But when he'd been in the corral with the mare he had become beautiful. Sheryl couldn't explain it and she didn't even want to try. The way he moved, the way he looked at the mare, the way they'd moved together… It had been like watching poetry. She couldn't explain it, except to come to the conclusion that Hawk Donovan was obviously more comfortable with animals than he was with people.

She could empathize.

Donovan's face was lit by the green glow of the dashboard, since the sun had set more than an hour ago. It was a hard face, unforgiving and without gentleness or humor. But it was also an honest face, unlike that man Carpenter. Was Hawk Donovan truly searching for information about his mother?

One more step, and she would be in too deep. The best thing she could do for herself—for her sanity and her peace of mind and the conservation of her well-ordered life—

would be to send Donovan packing. She could even offer to ship him the files, if he'd just get out of her life and stay out.

She'd learned to live without a man, without even the hope of one day having a romantic relationship, even though friends and family tried to tell her that she was too young to give up on the concept of love. One bad experience shouldn't stop her from living, they said.

One bad experience. More than a year of living hell was more like it. Michael had only hit her one time. One time had been more than enough. She'd left him that night, walked out with her pride and her cheek stinging. Her cheek had healed; her pride was still a little bruised.

As if that hadn't been enough, Michael, a man she had once loved, had turned into a stalker. He'd fooled her completely, swept her off her feet with his charm and his undivided attention and his apparent love. And then when he had her where he wanted her—*boom*—he'd shown his true face. Could she pick 'em or what?

Since walking out on Michael, Sheryl hadn't looked at any man or admired one in any way. Pretty faces were a dime a dozen. Hard bodies were easy to come by.

Until Hawk Donovan had walked into her clinic, she hadn't given much thought to what she'd given up in the name of security. It wasn't her fault; the man oozed animal magnetism in a way she had never before encountered. What drew her to Donovan? Chemical attraction? Biological need and bad timing? Whatever this was she really didn't need it.

But like it or not, she wasn't ready to turn her back on Donovan and his mysteries.

"I'll make you a deal," Sheryl said as the lights of Wyatt, such as they were, loomed closer. "You teach me how to do that, and I'll let you search through the files."

His head snapped around, but the truck didn't swerve. He, and the vehicle, remained steady. "You do have them?"

She nodded gently. "They're in my attic at home. I moved them there when I set up the clinic. I have to warn you, they're really a mess. I thought about tossing the old boxes out instead of moving them, but at least some of them are the doctor's files and may be important to local residents who saw him way back when. So I moved the boxes to the house and planned to go through them when I had a chance. Haven't thought about them much since, until a few days ago when a man impersonating a building inspector showed up at the clinic and ended up asking about the fertility clinic records."

"Do you think that's the same man who broke in last night?" he asked.

"I do." She was suddenly sure Donovan would never do such a thing. He might bully his way past her and demand to see what he was looking for, but he would never sneak in and nose around. It wasn't his style.

He braked, for no apparent reason, and slowed the truck to a crawl. They were still miles from town, and there wasn't another vehicle in sight. Before she could ask why he was stopping, a deer bounded across the road, caught in the beam of the truck's headlights. If Hawk hadn't stopped, he surely would have hit the doe.

As he put the truck in motion again, she asked, "How did you—"

"I'm starving," he interrupted. "Do you eat?"

It was such an inelegant and obviously unplanned invitation, she had to smile. "Just about every day."

"The hotel where I'm staying has a restaurant and the food is pretty good. Wanna grab a bite?"

She hadn't had a date since moving to Wyatt. Not that

she hadn't been asked, but with her new business and fixing up the house she'd bought and taking care of her animals she simply hadn't had time for a social life. To be honest, she hadn't had a date since ending her relationship with Michael. Love hadn't been enough to get past his demands. He'd been looking for a wife who would be there every night when he came home. A woman who would put his desires and career and worth above her own. The first and only time she'd challenged him outright, he'd responded with a fist.

He hadn't let her go easily. For months she'd turned around and found him watching. He had never touched her again, but the way he'd followed her, the way he'd hung on…it wasn't natural. It was no wonder that she was still skittish where men were concerned. Dating was just too risky.

Not that dinner with Donovan would be a date, mind you, but they would be eating together, and people were bound to notice and talk. Still, it had been two years since she'd sent Michael packing. Maybe it was time.

"Sure," she said, her heart fluttering briefly.

Donovan obviously didn't want to talk about the deer, and maybe that was for the best. As she watched his profile and tried to make sense of everything she'd seen of this man, she got the distinct feeling that she didn't want to know all his secrets.

Chapter 4

Hawk almost groaned aloud when he reached the top of the pull-down stairs, flipped the switch that turned on the uncovered bulb that hung in the center of the room and peered into the attic. There were dozens of cardboard boxes stored here and there, most of them unmarked, all of them showing signs of years of wear and neglect. He glanced over his shoulder and down to where Sheryl stood at the foot of the rattletrap steps.

"You moved all these boxes up here by yourself?"

She shrugged and smiled.

In spite of the fact that she didn't look strong enough to handle the task on her own, he wasn't really surprised. Moving all these boxes from the clinic to this attic had been a tough job, but Sheryl Eldanis had energy. Not a too-much-caffeine kind of energy, but a real, pure strength and quiet enthusiasm. He didn't imagine she'd ever considered a chore and wondered whether she could handle it. Besides, when he'd lifted her onto the mare he'd discovered that, petite or not, she had muscles. Even though his reason for being here was an important one, the man in him couldn't help but wonder what she'd look like in something other than those baggy clothes. Or even better, in nothing at all.

He stepped into the center of the attic and turned around slowly. It was an ordinary enough attic, with bare wood floors and exposed beams and two windows that looked down on the front yard. The ceiling was high enough for him to stand here in the middle of the space, but if he moved more than a step or two to the side he'd have to duck.

And like most other attics, it was full of junk. Along with a broken lamp, a rusty birdcage and a rocking chair that had to be older than the house, there were newer boxes mixed in with the older ones he was interested in, most of them labeled with black marker. Kitchen. Bedroom. Linens. Winter clothes. Sheryl's own things stored with the rest. Unlike her boxes, the ones he needed to search weren't marked at all. Where to start?

Sheryl didn't join him, but she climbed up the stairs to peer through the square opening in the attic floor. "If you need help, I can come back after I get the animals fed."

"No," he said, his eyes on one particularly nasty-looking stack of mildewy boxes. "I can't even tell you what I'm looking for. I guess I'd better just dig in and see what I can find." He grabbed a box at random and set it on the floor, then knelt down to open it. It smelled of musty old paper, and while there were a few file folders in the box, most of the paperwork was loose and completely unorganized.

"Okay." Sheryl backed away slowly. "Holler if you need

anything." And then she was off to feed her animals. From what little he'd seen as he'd walked in through the kitchen and to the stairway, she had a few. Cats, dogs, a colorful parrot that had called him "meathead" as he'd walked past the living room downstairs.

Hawk had learned to tune down his abilities when he needed to, and he did that now. He adjusted the part of his brain that could see and feel and hear things others couldn't even imagine and concentrated on the papers before him.

Somewhere in here was information that could help Cassie. The woman in the pharmacy hadn't sent him on a wild-goose chase. What they needed had to be in one of these boxes; he couldn't entertain any other possibility.

A fertility clinic. Even though he had never expected to find such a place in his background, he shouldn't be surprised. All his life he'd wondered about his parents. Who were they? Why had they given their twins away? When he'd discovered his gift with animals he'd wondered if they'd known. Was that the reason they'd given him up? Now there were Cassie's flashes of precognition to take into account. But how could their parents have known when they looked at their infant twins that they'd be different?

He hadn't given his biological parents much thought in the past few years. In adolescence he had almost become obsessed with them, but eventually he'd decided to put them, and their reasons for giving him up, out of his mind. If his parents hadn't wanted him, then why the hell should he care who they were and what they were like? It was easier to put them out of his mind than it was to wonder all the damn time. Cassie's seizures had fired up his curiosity all over again.

Hawk took his time with the task before him, carefully

studying each sheet of paper. Most of what he scanned didn't make any sense to him. Chemistry had never been his best subject in school, and this... A lot of what he discovered were formulas and medical data. Much of what he found in the manila folders was private information, women's medical files. He felt strange, perusing such personal information. But he couldn't set aside the papers without checking each one. Notes were scribbled in the margins here and there. Names that meant nothing to him appeared more than once. He tried to drink it all in, just in case a name or a date came to mean something to him later.

Hawk tossed one useless folder aside and grabbed another. Maybe Cassie was right and he should've hired this chore out. He didn't know what he was looking for, and besides, he didn't spend his time at home sitting in a cramped room going through papers. He practically lived outdoors. He needed fresh air in his lungs, sunshine and moonlight on his face.

But this was not a job he was willing to hand over to anyone else, no matter what the cost might be. His secrets, and Cassie's secrets, wouldn't be safe with anyone else.

Not even an unusually pretty vet.

"You stink."

Sheryl added water to Bruce's dish. "Can't you say 'Polly want a cracker' like a normal bird?"

"Bite me."

Normally finding a home for a beautiful talking bird wasn't a problem, but Bruce had been trained in a home where his primary teacher had been a teenage boy who thought it was funny to train the colorful parrot to insult everyone who passed by. "You stink" and "bite me" were actually not too bad, considering Bruce's repertoire.

Sheryl's mind was elsewhere as she fed the other animals. Two dogs, three cats and a bird. Some of them she'd brought to Wyatt with her; others she'd collected since her arrival in town. They'd all taken to the new house well, settling in as if they'd always lived here. She had a variety of animal beds here and there, and there was a small doggie door in the kitchen that allowed the animals to go into the fenced backyard at any time.

The pets she had accumulated over the years were her family. They loved without question or demand, and it was nice to have them waiting for her when she came in the door after a long day. They needed her; she needed them. And yes, they were her family. Like most families they were a bit dysfunctional. Bruce was temperamental and was given to bad language. Bogie was the shy ugly duckling, and Howie could be aggressive on occasion, like all Chihuahuas. There were times when Smoky and Princess tormented the dogs, as cats often do, but the situation never got out of control.

Laverne was independent and thought herself better than all the pets who had come after her, which was why she usually went to work with Sheryl. It was just safer that way.

The other animals in Sheryl's house were suspicious of Baby at first, but once they'd all sniffed one another properly, they got along just fine. Besides, the big yellow dog had the Laverne seal of approval, and the others all knew that didn't come easily.

Considering the way animals took to Donovan, Sheryl was a little surprised that they didn't all climb the rickety stairs to stand watch while he pored through the files. But they didn't. The animals left him alone.

So did she, even though she was dying to go up there

and jump into that nasty chore with him. There was something desperate and touching about his need to find this information about his mother, and she wanted to do what she could. Sympathy: it was her downfall. It was the reason she had three temperamental cats, two ugly dogs and a personality-challenged bird no one else wanted. The last thing she needed to do was add a surly man to her menagerie.

Dinner at the hotel restaurant had been pleasant enough, even though she'd done most of the talking. Donovan had paid attention, especially when she'd spoken about her practice. His love for animals was genuine and deep. If they had nothing else in common, they had that. But there was a definite wall, a barricade so tangible she could almost count the bricks. She just didn't have the time, or the heart, to try to break through that wall.

Besides, Donovan would be gone as soon as he found whatever he was looking for in her attic. He might thank her, and he might even mean it, but once he had what he'd come here for, he'd go home to Texas and she'd never see him again. So it would be foolish to get interested.

She'd been foolish before, and it was no fun.

When he'd been up there for more than three hours, she couldn't stand it anymore. She made a large glass of iced tea and carried it up the stairs. All the kiddies—her animals—were sleeping. Even Baby. She needed to get to sleep herself. Tomorrow would be an early day, as every day had been since opening her practice. Besides, her animals wouldn't let her sleep late, even on Sundays. The cats might let her lie in bed past six on occasion, but the dogs were relentlessly cheerful in the morning, and they wanted everyone to rise with the sun.

Donovan was startled to see her when she popped into the attic. The strain of sorting through the mess was showing on him already. His eyes looked tired, and he'd run his fingers through his dark hair more than once, probably in sheer frustration. The heavy stubble on his cheeks indicated that it had been a long day.

He looked much too tempting, sitting there. Sheryl wanted to do more than bring him tea. She wanted to run her fingers through his hair, lay her hands on those broad shoulders, tell him everything was going to be all right, even though she had no idea if anything would ever be right again.

At some time during the evening he'd set a couple of boxes to one side. He'd probably been through those already. A few pages that had caught his interest had been set aside. It was a dismally short stack.

When she offered him the tea, he stood and stretched out a few muscles before taking the cold glass. Hmm. Donovan looked as if he'd just climbed out of bed in the morning and was working the kinks out of that incredibly fit body. Even when he stretched and turned, there was a sleekness about him, a masculine grace.

If he moved this way when he was working out the kinks in his muscles, then what might he be like when he—

Oh, dear. Her mind simply could not go there.

"I guess you want me to get out of here," he said, casting one glance into the box he was currently sorting through. "I know it's getting late."

Yeah, she was such a sucker. Hawk Donovan was not the kind of man anyone took pity on. Ever. Was that almost-desperate expression a put-on? Did he know that no red-blooded female could say no to a face like that?

"You can stay awhile longer if you want," she said softly. "I'm going on to bed. Lock up when you leave."

He nodded, obviously grateful that she wasn't going to

kick him out, and then he took a long swig of the tea. He drained the glass quickly, then returned to his knees to continue sorting through the box in the center of the attic floor.

Sheryl watched Donovan as she carefully moved down the steps. He was already intent on the contents of that box again, as if she'd never been here, as if he had never been interrupted.

She hadn't even offered to ship the documents to Texas and let him go through them there, at his leisure, away from her house and out of her hair. That would have made perfect sense. The files would be out of her possession and no longer her concern, and Hawk Donovan would be out of her life for good. The man was definitely trouble—even if he was on the up-and-up. Especially if he was on the up-and-up! Her life was settled now; it made sense. The last thing she needed was trouble.

Hawk woke up to a familiar sound and sensation. Baby was licking his face and saying good morning with a growl and a whine. But this morning Baby was not alone. Laverne was curled up on his stomach, and two other cats—one black and the other calico—had burrowed into the crook of his elbow. A Chihuahua who thought he was a rottweiler stood on Hawk's chest, staring at his face and waiting for a response, and another dog—a black-and-white mixed breed with the homeliest face Hawk had ever seen—panted close by.

Hawk lifted his head from the attic floor, and the animals all perked up considerably. Even Laverne, who refused to be disturbed from her perch on his stomach, seemed to smile.

It was nothing compared to the smile he got from the woman standing above him.

"Coffee," she said.

She was dressed for the day in sensible trousers and a cotton blouse that should have been plain but somehow looked sexy. Like the smile, and the way she pulled her hair away from her face, and the way her fingers wrapped around the white mug she carried.

Hawk closed his eyes and took a deep breath, breathing in the scent of coffee and old paper and animals. And her. She'd had a shower, and she smelled faintly of shampoo and soap. The soap was scented with a trace of lavender.

"I didn't intend to stay the night," he said, ignoring the way Sheryl smelled. He moved Howie from his chest and Laverne from his gut and sat, then stood slowly. When he reached out for the coffee cup Sheryl offered, her smile faded. Just a little. "I decided to rest my eyes for a few minutes and—"

"I know that feeling," she interrupted. "It usually hits me when I'm trying to watch TV, even though I'm too tired, and I decide to close my eyes during the commercial. The next thing I know it's three in the morning and I wake up to find that I've missed the end of my movie and some cheesy infomercial is on." Her voice was too bright, too quick, as if she were trying to hide the fact that she was uncomfortable. Of course she was uncomfortable. He'd been here all night, sleeping above her head.

"Yeah." He took a long sip of coffee and glanced down at the box he'd been going through when he'd decided to take a break. This chore was taking much too long, but an extended break was not an option. This was too important, and he didn't have a day to waste. Not an hour or even a minute. A good night's sleep was a luxury he could do without for a while. "I know you have to work, but if you don't mind I'm going to—"

"I do mind," she said sharply.

He was disappointed, but not surprised. It was more than he'd expected that she'd allowed him to spend all night up here, though that hadn't been his intention. Or hers. Of course she wasn't going to trust him to stay here in her house while she was at work.

She shook her head as if she could read his mind. "You're exhausted. You spent way too much time going through those files last night, and I can tell just by looking at you that even if you came upon something important this morning you wouldn't see it. Go back to the hotel, get a shower and a few more hours of sleep, and after lunch you can start again." To his surprise, she handed him a single key on a simple key chain.

"Don't look so shocked," she said with a smile. "I don't have anything worth stealing, unless you want to take Bruce with you when you go."

"Bruce?"

"The parrot who called you meathead last night. Trust me, it could have been worse."

Hawk wanted to argue with her, but like it or not she made a lot of sense. He probably needed to go through that last box all over again, just to make sure he hadn't missed anything thanks to sheer exhaustion.

"There's a price, don't forget," Sheryl said, wagging a finger at him but not quite poking him in the chest.

"A price?"

"You can spend all afternoon up here if you want, but when I get off work you're taking me to Dermot's farm and giving me a lesson."

He had promised her that, he supposed. What was he going to do when that time rolled around? What he did couldn't be taught. It couldn't even be explained.

"Don't give me that look," Sheryl said lightly. "You're not weaseling your way out of this one, mister."

No, he probably couldn't weasel his way out of anything where Sheryl was concerned. He could only hope he'd find what he was looking for before she got off work today.

Sheryl was having a surprisingly good day, all things considered, until Doc Murdock came in and asked if she needed any help. The gleam in his eyes when he looked around her place told her more than she needed to know.

He missed working. One of these days he was going to decide to reopen his veterinary practice, at least part-time, and all his old customers—Sheryl's customers—were going to flock to him because they'd known him all their lives and he was their beloved friend. And her business would go under in a matter of months. She just didn't have enough cash to sustain that kind of hit.

She could go to her folks for money if that happened, but she didn't want to do that. This was her business. Her life. She wanted to make it on her own, not go running home to Mom and Dad when the going got rough. She could pack up and start over in a bigger town where it wouldn't be a problem if there were more than two practicing veterinarians. But giving up and starting over would feel an awful lot like failure. Besides, starting over meant start-up costs again, and she didn't have the cash handy.

She was already envisioning the worst. First thing, she'd have to sell her house. It was old and needed work…. But she loved her house!

While Doc Murdock followed her around the office, admiring the way she had the clinic set up, Sheryl's mind wandered to another place. Her attic. Was Donovan there yet, going through those old boxes? Of course he was. He probably hadn't waited until after lunch, but had grabbed a shower and an hour or so of sleep at the Wyatt Hotel and then headed back to her place.

Sheryl turned on a surprised Doc Murdock and smiled. "Do you really want to help out around here?" she asked.

His eyes went wide. "I'd love to."

"I have an errand to run this afternoon. Want to watch things for a while? Cory will be here as soon as school is out."

"Sure." He tried to sound nonchalant, but the light in his eyes and the wrinkling of the crow's-feet at the corners of those eyes, told another story altogether. He'd just been retired a few months so his license was still good. Maybe helping her on occasion would keep him from entertaining thoughts of getting back into the business.

Besides, Donovan and her lessons were waiting.

Sheryl walked home, leaving a very happy Doc Murdock in charge of the clinic. It was one of the things she loved about Wyatt; she could walk anywhere. Her clinic was two blocks from downtown. Her house was another three blocks from the clinic. There was a small section of shops downtown that offered just about everything she needed for her everyday life. A small grocery store, drugstore, dry cleaner, ice cream shop. Yes, she did occasionally miss browsing through a really good department store, but she was less than an hour and a half from a decent mall, and a day trip wasn't out of the question. She had a pickup, for the occasional trip to a neighboring farm or that mall, but on a day-to-day basis she walked just about everywhere, and that truck stayed parked in the separate garage in her spacious backyard.

She and Laverne were home in a matter of minutes.

Donovan's truck, which was much finer than hers, was parked at the curb, and the sight gave her an unexpected thrill. He was here. Her heart skipped a beat—or danced or did something equally bad.

The neighbors were probably talking already. Debbie must be having fits, wondering who belonged to that truck. It had been there last night. All night. It was back again, and Sheryl was home from work earlier than usual. She could practically feel the curious eyes on her as she walked to the front door, but she didn't actually see anyone.

She never came home early, and all her neighbors, especially the nosy ones, knew it.

None of the animals met her at the door. She wasn't surprised, not even when Laverne broke away and ran for the hallway. The gray cat was headed, no doubt, for the attic stairs.

Sheryl didn't fly, but she didn't waste any time, either. She found Donovan sitting on the attic floor with an open box in front of him. The stack of interesting papers had grown some, but not much. Three cats and three dogs had formed a rough circle around him, all of the animals relaxed but alert. Oddly enough, they looked as if they belonged together, Donovan and his dog and her animals.

Was there room for her in that circle?

"Kiss my ass."

Sheryl's head jerked around. Her parrot had found himself a new home on her grandmother's rocking chair. "What's Bruce doing up here?"

The bird was out of his cage, perched well away from the others and yet somehow a part of the crowd.

Donovan lifted his head and looked at Sheryl. "He was making so much racket downstairs, I decided to bring him up here. I hope you don't mind."

"If you can stand him, he's all yours."

"Bite me," Bruce responded.

Donovan turned his gaze to the bird. "That's not nice," he said slowly and distinctly. "Apologize."

Sheryl started to laugh. Bruce apologize? She'd been trying for months to get the parrot to say something, *anything,* that wasn't an insult.

"Sorry," Bruce squawked. The big bird ruffled his feathers as if the curt apology had been physically painful.

"How did you…" Sheryl didn't even bother to finish asking the question.

And Donovan didn't offer any explanations. He glanced at his watch. "You're earlier than I expected."

"You don't have to sound so disappointed."

That dark head snapped up. He needed a shave. The stubble on his cheeks was thick and dark, and while it should've made him look unkempt and less than gorgeous, it didn't. The roughness suited him.

"I didn't mean…" he began.

"I was just kidding," Sheryl said with a smile. Donovan was so relentlessly serious, so intense. "Had any luck today?"

"No. I hope you don't mind, but I borrowed your computer." Donovan returned his gaze to the papers in his lap. "There are a couple of names that keep popping up. Agnes Payne and Oliver Grimble. Do either of those names mean anything to you?"

Sheryl shook her head. "Sorry. Did you find anything interesting online?"

She knew by the expression on his face that he had not. "No. You'd think there would be something. A genealogy site, or a tidbit in a newspaper. It's almost disturbing that there wasn't anything at all."

"You know what they say. The Internet is a million miles wide and a quarter of an inch deep. Just because you didn't come up with anything, that doesn't mean the information isn't out there somewhere."

"Somewhere," he repeated softly.

"You need to get out of my attic," Sheryl said with a grin. "I'm ready for my lesson."

He hesitated, but not for long. "Fine. Let's get this over with."

"Faith Winston." Faith juggled the phone and the baby, while two-year-old Daniel and almost-four Abby entertained themselves with coloring books and a big box of colors.

"Dr. Winston, this is Agent Tom Phillips with the NSA." The voice was crisp and businesslike and unfamiliar. "We've just intercepted an Internet search for Agnes Payne and Oliver Grimble. You're at the top of my list of those to alert in such a circumstance."

Faith, who had been spending the day at home immersed in the simple chore of taking care of her children, held her baby a little bit closer. If she never heard those names again, she'd be perfectly happy. Still, considering the developments of the past few months she shouldn't be surprised that someone was digging into the past.

"Where did the search originate?"

"In Wyatt, North Carolina, on the computer of a Dr. Sheryl Eldanis."

Chapter 5

Before they began, Hawk spent a few minutes talking to the mare. Walking with her in a circle around the corral, stroking her neck, whispering, connecting in that way he would never be able to explain, let alone teach. When he was certain she was calm and wouldn't mind being ridden, he saddled her. He didn't stop talking but kept his voice low. Even Sheryl, who sat atop the fence while she watched and waited, wouldn't be able to hear him.

They were alone at the moment. Dermot was still curious about Hawk's methods, but he and his kids were all busy with other chores. Just as well. Hawk always worked best alone. People made him nervous, especially when they watched so intently and asked endless questions. They messed with his concentration, and concentration was often crucial to his job. His calling.

When he helped Sheryl into the dun mare's saddle as

he had last night, Hawk noted once again that her body was tight and solid, an unexpected contrast to her cute face. Cute women should be soft and girlie, not hard. The clothes she wore disguised the fact that she had a killer body. Did she hide her strength on purpose?

Of course she did. Sheryl disguised her strength the same way Hawk hid what he could do. Most people underestimated cute women.

He would do well to remember that underestimating anyone was a bad idea.

She expected a lesson, and he was going to give her one. "Just like people, horses respond much better if you ask them to help you instead of ordering them to obey. Particularly if that order is delivered with a whip in one hand."

"But horses aren't smart enough to understand what you're asking of them," Sheryl said, looking down at him from her perch on the mare's saddle. "Are they?"

"As with people, some horses are smarter than others," he explained.

"And Matilda?"

The horse began to walk, each step smooth and without the panic she'd felt just yesterday. "Matilda?"

"That's her name." Sheryl didn't look at him now, but kept her eyes on the animal who bore her. Even though she trusted Hawk enough to sit in that saddle, she hadn't forgotten that this was the animal who'd broken Mort's arm. "I called Mort this morning to see how he and the mare were doing, and he called her Matilda. So, is Matilda one of the smart ones?"

"Yes, she is."

"You're just saying that because she obviously likes you." It took Hawk a moment to realize that Sheryl was teasing him. It was the smile that tipped him off. No one teased him. Ever. Except Cassie, of course, who occasionally tormented him in a sisterly way. He didn't know how to respond to such lighthearted jesting, so he didn't respond at all.

Comfortable with the horse, moving along smoothly, Sheryl turned her gaze to him again. "All animals seem to like you. Even that crotchety parrot of mine. I didn't think Bruce was capable of warming up to anyone, much less learning to apologize. Think you can teach him to lay off the bad language so I can find him a good home?"

"Maybe," he said grudgingly.

He had come here on a mission, and he should be anxious to get back to the files. But in spite of the fact that he shouldn't be here, Hawk liked this moment. He liked the sound of Sheryl's voice and the way the light breeze ruffled the soft strands of her hair. He liked the fact that she was so obviously comfortable in his presence. The three of them—he, the mare, Sheryl—had formed an odd kind of triangle. Other people never came between him and an animal, but this… It was curious.

It was nice.

"I've never seen anyone who drew animals to them the way you do," Sheryl said. "What's your secret?" She grinned. "The way my dogs took to you, I'm beginning to think 'bacon under the pants' isn't such an outrageous suggestion."

He didn't respond.

"So, is that your secret?" she continued. "Pork?"

He explained his ability away the way he always had. "I grew up around animals. They know I like them—that's why they're comfortable with me. It's that simple."

She rode awhile longer, moving in a circle around the corral while he stood in the center and watched. "So," she finally said, "are you one of those people who likes animals better than people?"

"Yes," he answered without hesitation.

Instead of being insulted, she smiled again. "Me, too. What does that say about us, Donovan?" It wasn't a question that required an answer, rather a statement on the fact that they were both somehow different.

She had no idea how different he was, and if he had his way she never would. The moment was comfortable. One day he'd remember his trip to Wyatt with the kind of fondness he never, ever experienced. The last thing he wanted was for Sheryl to look at him as if he was a freak.

He liked the way she was looking at him now, as if he was a man. Nothing more, nothing less. If he had the time… If he ever intended to hook up with a woman for more than one night… If he wasn't so damned different…

But he didn't have the time; he'd never have a permanent woman in his life; and he was different. So standing here and wondering what if was a waste of time.

After a half hour or so of riding a cooperative Matilda, Sheryl dismounted. The sun hung low in the sky, and the lesson was over for today. It hadn't been much of a lesson. He knew it and so did Sheryl. Would she push for more? Or did she realize that he couldn't teach anyone to do what he did?

They handed Matilda over to Mort, who had arrived to watch the last few minutes. He was still amazed at the progress Hawk had made with the mare, and as he led her away he was shaking his head and talking to Matilda. It was a good sign that he was calling the mare by name and speaking to her. He intended to keep her for a very long time.

As they walked toward the truck, Sheryl began to sing,

almost absently and in a very soft voice, "Waltzing Matilda." She had a sweet voice to match her cute face, and as she sang Hawk realized that in spite of her tough exterior, deep down she was a happy person. She wasn't naive, and she had her own reasons for not giving her trust easily. But there was more to her than distrust and suspicion. He didn't know anyone who was truly happy. Not like this. At the moment Sheryl Eldanis appeared to be completely care-free.

She stopped when they reached the truck, and turned to face him. The song ended abruptly. "Is that what you did with me?" she asked.

"What do you mean?"

"Asking instead of ordering. You did strike me as a bit of a bully at first, but for the most part…" She smiled, and her blue eyes sparkled with life. "Do you get results with women the same way you do with horses?" Before he could answer she continued. "Of course you do. You did everything but rub me between the eyes! Guess what? It works. You really do catch more flies with honey than with vinegar. I never would've allowed a man who tried to push me around to spend the night in my attic."

Instead of getting into the truck or allowing him to open the door for her, she leaned against the passenger door and looked up at him.

"I didn't treat you like a horse," Hawk said softly.

Her smile didn't fade. "I'm not saying you did it on purpose."

Sheryl really was a happy person, she was content with her practice and her animals and her life. But all Hawk had to do was look at her to know something was missing. The same something that was missing from his life.

Wyatt's young veterinarian was more than cute in this

light and with that smile on her face. She was tempting and sexy as all get-out. Hawk usually controlled his impulses, but with Sheryl it was getting harder every day. She was hot, and he was tired of ignoring the fact that she turned him on with a smile or a word. He was tired of ignoring the unexpected pull between them.

A cool autumn breeze washed over them both. Kissing her seemed like the thing to do, so he leaned in and down and laid his mouth over hers. She was surprised at first, but she didn't seem to mind that he kissed her.

For a moment she was still. She didn't answer the kiss, but she didn't turn away, either. Soon she responded. Gently, at first, and then, a moment later, more strongly. Her mouth molded to his, her lips and her tongue moved subtly; just enough to push him a little bit closer to the edge. The kiss was as gentle and moving as the breeze and the way Sheryl smiled.

There wasn't much gentle in Hawk's life, so he enjoyed the kiss longer than he should have. He didn't grab her; he didn't press his body to hers even though that was exactly what he wanted to do. But their mouths continued their tender but deep exploration. He tasted her; he claimed her; and for a moment he forgot why he couldn't have her.

Her lips parted, and she moaned low in her throat when his tongue danced with hers. He did not reach for her, but she laid her hands on him—one on his forearm, the other on his shoulder. Her body began to list toward his, as if he were a magnet and she a piece of steel. The hand at his shoulder drifted up, and a gentle thumb raked over his jawline, rasping over the two-day beard.

If Sheryl pressed her body to his and parted her lips a millimeter more, he'd end up making love to her. Here. Now. He wanted to be inside her; he wanted to make her scream and lurch beneath him. The way the kiss went on and on, the way it deepened and changed, told Hawk that Sheryl wanted that as much as he did.

But it was just a kiss, and no matter what his body tried to tell him, Sheryl was not his for the taking. Knowing she wasn't his didn't make him want her any less.

By the time he moved away they were both breathless.

He couldn't stay in Wyatt, and Sheryl wasn't the kind of woman who'd offer herself for a one-night stand. She'd expect more. She'd expect him to give something of himself besides his body, and he couldn't do that. One night, maybe two, was all Hawk had to give. Not just to Sheryl, but to any woman.

When he found what he was looking for in those files, he'd be leaving town—in the middle of the night, if necessary. Cassie needed him, and he didn't have time to waste pursuing pretty vets. Thinking of anything beyond this one kiss was ridiculous.

But his mind went there, anyway.

"I'll buy you dinner," he said quickly, as he turned away to walk to the driver's side of the pickup.

"Not tonight." Sheryl opened the passenger door and stepped up. Her voice trembled, just a little.

Crap. He never should've kissed her. She was scared, wary, and now she was going to kick him out of her house and he'd be back to square one. Maybe she'd let him buy the contents of those boxes in her attic. If he offered her enough money...

"I'm cooking tonight," she said as she buckled her seat belt. She cleared her throat and took a deep breath, and the tremble in her voice disappeared. "Lasagna, salad, garlic bread and banana pudding."

"Sounds good," Hawk said as he started the engine,

hiding his rush of relief. She wasn't kicking him out. At least, not yet. She just didn't want to eat out tonight.

"You can sort through the boxes while I cook," she continued, "take a break and eat, and then get back to work. You'll be more alert while you're searching through those files if you take a breather now and then."

It took him a moment to realize that she was offering to cook for *him*. "That would be nice," he said.

They didn't talk as the truck took them back toward Wyatt. Though they didn't mention the kiss, it was there, between them, unfinished. Shimmering in the air as if it had taken on a life of its own.

Hawk wasn't one for romance. He'd been engaged once, but he'd been much too young, and the engagement had been a mistake. Sara had married another man while Hawk had been in the military, and after he'd come home he'd just never found the heart to even think about romantic relationships. He didn't hate Sara for leaving him; he didn't even blame her.

How could he consider making a woman his wife, or even an important part of his life, when he knew he'd never share with her the connection he felt with a stray dog he'd found on the side of the road? Animals were open to him. He understood them; they understood him. There were no secrets, no games, no puzzling questions when he linked with an animal in mind and spirit. People, on the other hand, were mysteries. Complicated, impossible-to-read mysteries.

Especially women.

Sheryl hadn't cooked for a man in two years, and she wanted everything to be perfect. The food, the setting, the conversation.

Of course, Donovan wasn't much of a conversationalist, unless that was a talent he'd been hiding from her.

She didn't set the rarely used dining room table, but laid out plates and fresh-cut flowers at the round oak table in the kitchen. Dinner would be cozy, friendly but not necessarily romantic. Warm and sociable but not fancy.

She didn't want Donovan to think she was being forward. Cooking for him was just an amiable gesture. That was all. He was a nice guy, and he was having a bit of trouble, and she was doing what she could to help. She would have wanted to help even if he didn't have those dark, gypsy eyes. Even if he wasn't an extremely fine specimen of manhood. Even if he didn't make her knees weak when he kissed her.

Yeah, right.

In the back of her mind, she figured part of her attraction to Hawk stemmed from the fact that he was safe. Since he wasn't going to stay in Wyatt, he couldn't become a permanent problem. He wouldn't be here long enough to make demands she couldn't agree to, or to get annoyingly proprietary, or to overwhelm her with expectations she could never live up to. More important, he wouldn't be here long enough for her to fall in love with him. But if there was an attraction on both sides and if they wanted to act on that attraction, what would be the harm?

She left the garlic powder off the bread, just in case.

There hadn't been a man of any kind in her life since Michael. It had been safer that way. Easier. There was less turmoil in her life simply because there was no man in it. Donovan made her realize what she'd been missing. Her heart had been safe, man free, but her days had also become routine and even boring. She was twenty-six years old, much too young to be satisfied with boring.

When dinner was almost ready, Sheryl moved to the foot of the ladder and shouted, "Five minutes!" Then she washed her hands and her face in the bathroom. After studying her face in the mirror for a moment she let her hair down and combed her fingers through the silky strands. She wasn't going to win any beauty contests, but she did have nice hair and she might as well show it off. That done, she returned to the kitchen to take the bread out of the oven. If there was a knot of excitement in her stomach, it was because she hadn't dated in years and now there was a man headed to her kitchen for supper. A man who'd kissed her.

A man who was going to leave as soon as he had what he'd come here for.

She felt as much as heard Donovan enter the kitchen. "Any luck?" she asked as she put the hot garlicless bread on a serving plate.

"Not really. I did add a couple of papers to the interesting stack, but for the most part it's like reading another language and trying to find something that makes sense."

He sounded tired. No…more weary than tired, she decided. This task he had set for himself was an important one.

When she turned around she half expected to see all the animals, his and hers, lined up around Donovan like a devoted entourage. Surprisingly, he was alone.

"Where is everyone?" she asked.

He looked almost sheepish. "They're guarding the boxes in the attic."

She smiled. "You put the animals on guard duty?"

"They volunteered."

Which meant they were probably all asleep, and that meant they'd be awake and kicking before dawn. "Let's eat," she said as she placed the bread on the table. "And when we're finished I'll help you."

"You can't—"

"Don't argue with me, Donovan," she said as she took her seat. "I might not know what you're looking for, but I can help you get organized. Another pair of eyes might see something you missed."

He didn't sit until she was settled in her chair. "You don't have to do that. I'm sure you have more important things to do."

"Yeah," she said. "But not tonight."

Sheryl was obviously surprised to find that he'd been telling the truth. Three cats, three dogs and one surly parrot were guarding the files. He couldn't explain to her that they knew something here was important to him, and keeping the boxes safe was their way of doing him a favor.

He didn't think she'd be able to help, but Sheryl took the stack of papers he'd set aside as potentially important and sorted them with paper clips. By names, by dates, she tried to make sense of the mess. When the time came to make something of what he'd found, it might be helpful.

If nothing else, she looked good sitting on the attic floor with her legs tucked beneath her, and her occasional attempts at conversation kept him alert. She'd swapped her usual professional and baggy clothing for something more casual. A pair of flannel pants and a snug-fitting T-shirt that showed off the nice muscles in her arms and her back. More than that, it molded to her breasts. Sheryl had small, firm breasts that would be just the right size to fill his hand. And either it was cold up here or she was turned on by sorting through old files.

Her nipples pressed against the cotton that hugged her

torso. Dammit, he could not think about nipples at this stage of the game.

Sheryl Eldanis was sexier than he'd imagined she could be. Prettier than he'd thought her to be when he'd first seen her.

But more than that, she was a distraction. It was impossible to keep his mind on the task at hand when she was so close. She was more than nice to look at, and she smelled good, and if it didn't make him look like a complete fool he would be content to just sit here and watch her. He had no time for distractions, though, and neither did Cassie.

Every minute wasted might be important to his sister.

When Sheryl yawned for the third time, Hawk pushed aside the box he'd been searching in and turned his full attention to her. "You don't have to stay up with me. Go on to bed. I won't sleep here all night again, but I can't quit just yet."

"I want to help," she said sincerely.

"You're tired and you have work tomorrow morning."

"I don't mind."

No, she didn't mind. And that was the problem. Sheryl looked so good sitting there. So bright and pretty. So full of hope. And beyond the body that seemed to call out to him, there was something fetching in her blue eyes, something that invited him to be a part of her life. To share that happiness with her. To kiss her again.

He didn't have time for any of that, no matter how good the unspoken invitation felt.

"You've obviously got some wrong ideas about me," he said hoarsely. "I didn't come here looking for a friend. I appreciate all your help, I really do, and I've tried to be civil about this, but..."

"But I'm getting in your way," she finished for him, her happiness and that unspoken invitation quickly and completely gone.

"Yeah."

Sheryl stood and brushed off her flannel pants, sending particles of dust flying. "Sorry to be so much trouble," she said sharply.

The animals all reacted as they picked up on her anger. Baby's tail twitched, the Chihuahua growled deep in his throat, the ugly mutt shivered. The cats were less obvious, but all feline eyes turned to Sheryl. Bruce chirped happily, "Holy crap!"

Sheryl ignored them all. Her eyes were on him. "If I'm just getting in your way, then why did you kiss me?"

If he told her he'd kissed her because he hadn't been able to stop himself, that wouldn't help matters at all. If he told her she'd drawn him to her like honey draws bees, she might take it the wrong way. So he told her what he had to, in order to get her out of the attic so he could concentrate on the job at hand. "It was just a kiss. Didn't mean anything."

Before she turned away from him she looked stunned, as if he'd slapped her. "Now I remember why I gave up on men two years ago," she muttered as she hurried down the steps. It was a comment not meant for his ears, he knew, but he couldn't help hearing. He heard one more angry word as she moved away from the attic. "*Civil.*"

Hawk sent the animals after her, and they went. Reluctantly. All but Bruce, who remained perched on the old rocking chair. When everyone else was gone, the bird squawked, "What a loser!"

Smart bird.

* * *

Just a kiss. Didn't mean anything. Sheryl was tempted, so tempted, to climb up the attic stairs and tell Hawk Donovan to get out of her house and stay out.

But she didn't. She'd made more of the kiss than she should have, and that was her own fault. Donovan had been honest, in that annoyingly direct way of his, in telling her that she meant nothing to him.

A lesser man probably would have slept with her just to make sure he continued to have access to those files that were obviously so important to him. A lesser man would've taken advantage of her temporary insanity.

In a perverse way, she wished Donovan were a lesser man.

She got ready for bed. The process always took a while, since it included playing ball with Bogie and scratching Howie's stomach. The animals all needed a moment of individual attention, something to assure them that they were important to her, that they were loved, that this house wouldn't be the same without them.

Was that why she wanted Donovan, when she'd been perfectly happy without a man for two years? Did she need a man to make her feel important and loved and necessary?

She would not be one of those women who relied on a man for their feeling of self-worth. Maybe she wanted Donovan in a purely sexual way, but she certainly didn't need him. She didn't *need* anyone.

It wasn't him, she told herself. Two years was too long for a healthy woman to go without sex. If Donovan hadn't come along, she probably would've gotten the hots for Chief Nichols, or the cute guy at the antique store, or Mark Singer, who had all those dogs. She tried to imagine any one of them kissing her, and no matter how she tried she felt nothing even resembling desire.

Men were simply not worth this kind of trouble. What she really needed was a vibrator and a lifetime supply of batteries.

The animals wouldn't rest well if she closed her bedroom door, so she left it open just enough to allow them to move in and out.

Donovan didn't make a sound. He was completely quiet in the attic as he pored over his papers. Sheryl didn't worry much about him bothering her during the night. He wasn't interested in her, only in the moldy papers in her attic.

The way he'd kissed her had convinced Sheryl that he *was* interested in her, but apparently her imagination had been working overtime.

As she threw herself into bed and pulled the covers to her chin, she whispered, "Get a life, Sheryl."

Bogie and Howie hunkered down in the doggie bed by her dresser, and the cats found their own places here and there. They loved to sleep in the bed with her, and sometimes she let them. But not tonight. Baby left the room, headed no doubt for Donovan's side.

Soft light from the hallway illuminated the room. She hadn't had a lot of money for decorating when she'd bought this house, but she had splurged on the bedroom. It didn't make sense to spend a lot of money on a comforter the dogs and cats would lie on, or to buy furniture the cats would use as scratching posts, but a woman needed a pretty place to come to at the end of the day, a serene place to dream. So she'd bought a solid oak bedroom suite, a silky blue comforter, pretty pictures for the wall and nice lamps for the tables. She even had a couple of silk flower arrangements, and fine lace curtains for the windows. Candles that had never been lit had been placed here and there, on the table by the bed and on the long dresser.

One by one, the animals fell asleep. They made their own noises in the night. Purrs, the sounds of evenly expelled breaths, the occasional whimper from a dream. The noises didn't disturb Sheryl; they actually soothed her. This was her home. The animals were her family.

She didn't need anything else.

Chapter 6

Spending the better part of two days going through boxes of papers that meant nothing to him only frustrated Hawk. Nothing he'd found would help Cassie, nothing pointed toward even the tiniest bit of information about their birth mother. He was wasting his time here.

The situation with Sheryl only added to his frustration. In another time and another place, maybe things would be different. He liked her; she liked him. But he'd never see Sheryl in another time or another place. This was it. He was here to find what he could and then hurry home, and she had a life here. A good life.

If he thought they could have a little fun and then say goodbye without regrets, he'd be tempted to take what he could get. They were both single, healthy and interested. But Sheryl wasn't the kind of woman who'd have a casual fling. And casual was all he had to give.

Besides, if she knew the depths of what he could do…she wouldn't want to have anything to do with him. It was best this way. He could be a jerk, and she'd be glad to be rid of him when the time came.

He'd fallen asleep on the attic floor again, and awakened to Baby's own special alarm—a friendly tongue on the cheek and a nudge of her paw—just before Sheryl had stuck her head in the attic and told him to get out. There was no coffee this morning and no smile. Just as well, but…dammit, he missed them. He missed the coffee and the smile, and the hint of something more he couldn't explain away.

Hawk left the house a few minutes after Sheryl, headed for the hotel. He carried a few of the files with him. Maybe after a nap he could lay the papers out on the table by the bed in his hotel room and see something he'd missed the first time.

"Good morning!" The bright voice caught him by surprise, and he turned to face the smiling woman who cut across the lawn, heading unerringly in his direction.

Hawk's first thought was of escape. But he recognized right away that it was too late.

"Hi!" In one sweep she took in the rough beard, the wrinkled clothes, the hair that hadn't seen a comb other than his fingers for days. "I'm Debbie Willis. I live next door. Are you…a friend of Sheryl's?"

There was so much emphasis on that word. *Friend.* "Yeah."

"Are you Michael, by any chance?" Something in her eyes flickered.

"No." Who the hell was Michael? "Hawk Donovan."

The woman, a slim brunette who stood just a few inches shorter than Hawk, breathed a sigh of obvious relief.

"Thank goodness. When I saw your truck out here all night again, I just assumed...well, I have a tendency to assume the worst, you know? And Sheryl is such a sweet girl, she deserves so much better than that."

Hawk was tempted to toss the woman a quick goodbye and get to his truck. But he didn't. Sheryl deserved so much better than *what?* Or was it *who?* "Who's Michael?"

The brunette pursed her lips for a moment, then said, "Okay, obviously I've said more than I should, but I don't guess I can leave you hanging. Basically, Michael was an old boyfriend, and things didn't end well. That's really all I can say." She pursed her lips again, but that didn't last long. "Sorry. I just... The guy was a real jerk, a stalker, to be honest, and the whole experience really spooked Sheryl, as you can imagine. That's why I was so glad to see your truck, and you hanging around. Sheryl has been very reluctant where men are concerned. No, *reluctant* is not the word. A stone wall is more like it. So I was thrilled that she'd met someone who, you know, changed her mind about completely writing off the opposite sex. But then I started worrying—what if Michael came back? What if he's... Well, you know."

Hawk didn't know, but he could imagine.

"I'm so glad you're not Michael!" Debbie said, smiling widely. "Well, relieved, I guess. I'm very much relieved. Oh, you two have to go to the dance Friday night!" She reached out and patted his arm as if they were old friends.

"Dance?" He didn't mean to sound horrified, but...

"It's the kickoff of the festival. Food. Music. Dancing." Debbie used her hands as she spoke, gesturing this way and that with great animation. "The food's great. The music is so-so. The dancing is amateurish. But we have fun, I promise, and it would be a great time for you to meet everyone."

"I, uh, don't know if I'll be here that long."

"Don't be silly. It's tomorrow night!"

"Yeah, but…"

Debbie waggled her eyebrows. "Oh, I bet Sheryl can convince you to stick around at least one more day. And it would be so good for her to get out and about. She keeps too much to home, just her and her animals. I mean, animals are great and all, but even a veterinarian needs to be around people now and then." She laughed at her joke— which was not so much of a joke as she seemed to think it was.

"We'll see." Hawk backed away, glad to finally make his escape. He was very aware that Sheryl's curious next-door neighbor watched until he was out of sight.

Sheryl answered the phone with a gruffer than usual "Eldanis Veterinary Clinic."

There was a moment of silence on the other end, and she almost hung up. It had been a long day, and the last thing she wanted to do was deal with telemarketers. But a soft voice soon said, "Dr. Sheryl Eldanis?"

"Yes."

"You're a…veterinarian?"

Sheryl sighed and closed her eyes. After the disaster with Donovan, she was dangerously close to hurting someone. Anyone. "Yes, I am."

The caller quickly got over her surprise. "Good afternoon. I'm Dr. Faith Winston. It's come to my attention that you own a building that was once occupied by a fertility clinic run by Dr. Agnes Payne and Dr. Oliver Grimble. Is that correct?"

A shiver ran down Sheryl's spine. Another one? After all this time, there were *three* people looking for those files.

Carpenter, Donovan and now this Winston woman. Why? "There was a fertility clinic located here," Sheryl said cautiously. "But that was years ago."

"I see," Dr. Winston said thoughtfully. "I know it's a long shot, but is it possible that in their haste to depart they left something of importance behind? Equipment, paperwork…anything?"

Sheryl was tempted to hang up on the woman. In fact, she automatically moved the phone slightly away. But she gathered her composure and returned the receiver to her ear. *Panic* was not the answer. "No. As far as I know they didn't leave anything behind. Sorry."

Sheryl expected the so-called doctor to hang up on her, but instead the caller remained polite. "It's been a long time," the woman said, friendliness and composure remaining steady in her voice. "But I did have to ask. If you by chance run across anything interesting that might possibly be related to the old fertility clinic, please give me a call." She proceeded to give Sheryl her home, office and cell phone numbers.

"Doctor," Sheryl said, before the woman could say goodbye, "what exactly are you looking for? It's been such a long time, I can't see that files so old would be worth anything."

"They don't have any real value," Dr. Winston answered. "Though there might be some obscure tidbits of information there that would be of interest to someone working in the same field."

"Do you?"

"No."

"Then why do you want them?"

The pause that followed was just long enough for Sheryl to know the answer would be a lie. "My interest is purely academic."

"Well, if I run across anything, I'll give you a call."

"Thank you so much."

Sheryl stood at the counter with her hand on the receiver, minutes after she'd ended the call. What the hell did she have in her attic?

Faith looked Luke squarely in the eye. "Dr. Eldanis says she knows nothing. I suppose it's possible that she's telling the truth, but I really can't be sure. If she hasn't found anything of interest, then why did she enter those names into a search engine?"

"Call Jake," Luke said. He sat beside her and juggled his two youngest children quite adeptly.

"Jake is on vacation," Faith argued. "He hasn't taken any time for himself in so long, I refuse to interrupt his time off simply because a woman decided to investigate the former owners of her building."

"You don't know that's all it is."

"She's a veterinarian, Luke. I hardly think she's following in Agnes's and Oliver's footsteps. But with everything else that's going on…I just can't be sure. I should have done those DNA tests myself. What on earth is taking so long?"

Her husband smiled at her. "We have a new baby. We have three children under the age of four. Didn't we have this talk about delegating responsibilities months ago?"

"We did," she said sheepishly. Her husband knew delegating was a real challenge for her.

Faith Martin Winston wasn't about to give up her career as an epidemiologist. But she wasn't going to give motherhood anything less than her best, either. It was hard work, balancing a career and family. Fortunately, Luke was the best of fathers. He changed diapers. He played educational games. He watched *Barney.*

If only she could teach him to breast-feed.

Luke leaned forward and kissed her lightly.

Faith tried to completely dismiss the conversation with Eldanis from her mind, but that was easier said than done. Why should the woman lie? And in all probability she had lied. Maybe she was covering up her nosiness because she was embarrassed to be caught snooping, but then again, it was always possible that Sheryl Eldanis was not who she claimed to be.

"She sounded so nice over the phone," Faith mused.

Luke balanced Daniel on one knee and held his baby daughter, Emily, in the crook of one arm. Abby, his daughter from a previous marriage, their daughter now, was totally captivated by a purple dinosaur on the television. Faith loved these family moments, hectic as they might be.

"Call Jake," Luke said once again.

It would make perfect sense to call her brother, but he so desperately needed this vacation. "I do hate to call him on his cell phone and interrupt his time off just because someone is nosing around a bunch of old information. Agnes and Oliver are dead. They're not a threat."

"You're not going to call him," Luke said. "He will be so pi—" He glanced down at Daniel, who always listened intently and had begun to repeat everything he heard. "He will be very angry with you," he said.

Faith smiled at her husband. "I'll call him next week, when he gets home."

Daniel squirmed down off his father's lap and joined his eldest sister in a dance before the television.

Her children had extraordinary talents, but Faith did her best to make sure they led normal lives. They colored and watched television and had birthday parties. And they sang and danced quite enthusiastically and, well, badly.

"You're not getting enough protein," Faith said, standing and kissing Luke quickly. "I'm making a pot roast for supper, and it needs tending."

His eyebrows rose slightly. "You're not getting enough sleep," he countered.

"It's not my fault Emily has decided to be a night person."

Luke stood, the baby snug in his arms, and followed her to the kitchen. "You're not even a little bit worried about this? The NSA wouldn't have called if they didn't think this information was important."

"Important, perhaps. But not urgent."

"And yet you called this Dr. Eldanis."

Faith turned and leaned against the counter in her state-of-the-art kitchen. "I just wanted to know why," she said softly.

She wished she had gotten a simple explanation. The Eldanis woman had run across some old papers and gotten curious. Someone had mentioned the doctors' names and she'd decided to do a little digging into the past. Instead of explaining the Internet search away, the veterinarian had denied all knowledge of the scientists who had once occupied her building.

"Why would Dr. Eldanis lie unless she has something to hide?"

"Call Jake and let him handle it," Luke insisted. "You don't need anything else to worry about."

"I'm not worried," she insisted. "And I will call Jake. When he gets home."

"Stubborn woman." Luke headed for the family room with the kids, leaving Faith to her kitchen.

It looked almost like a lab, but with spices instead of vials of vaccines and a blender instead of a microscope.

She hadn't become a good cook overnight, but with Nelda's help she was getting there.

Finding her family so late in life was one of the reasons she treasured her sister and her brothers so. Maybe she was, occasionally, a little bit bossy, but there were times when she knew what was best for them. And Jake needed some time away from his responsibilities.

Next week would be soon enough to call Jake. Neither Wyatt, North Carolina, nor Dr. Sheryl Eldanis was going anywhere.

Waiting for DNA results that might very well link Faith and her siblings to the Caldwell triplets had Faith on edge. Now this. She had never been very good at waiting.

Luke had taught Faith patience. Waiting patiently didn't come easily to her and neither did delegating work to others.

But she was learning. Whatever was going on with Dr. Eldanis, it could wait.

Rain moved in, ending any thoughts Hawk might've had about another lesson with Sheryl. Just as well. He had a feeling he didn't have much time left here, and he needed to spend it as productively as possible. Dinner tonight had consisted of a hastily constructed sandwich, but at least Sheryl hadn't kicked him out on his ear.

She could have. Maybe she should have.

Hawk cursed himself as a fool a hundred times as he went through the boxes in Sheryl's attic. When he touched animals, he knew their pain, their fears, their needs. But with Sheryl he had missed all the signs that anyone with half a brain should've deciphered! She was skittish; she'd taken the time to build her strength so that she was strong enough to fight back; she didn't trust easily.

But there was enough heart left in her to allow him access to these boxes. To smile. To kiss like she meant it. And what had he done? Told her the kiss meant nothing. That *she* meant nothing.

He was an idiot.

"Loser," Bruce squawked harshly.

"Yeah," Hawk replied in a soft voice.

Most people thought he was a hard-ass. He was quiet; he kept to himself; he didn't socialize. He preferred working with his horses to carrying on conversations with people. That, combined with his size, gave him the appearance of being unbearably gruff.

But he wasn't *completely* hard. He'd do anything for his sister. He would never purposely hurt anyone, any more than he'd purposely hurt an animal. And in the back of his mind he often wondered what it would be like to have the things other men took for granted. A woman. Someone to lean on at the end of a hard day. Maybe even children.

He'd hurt Sheryl. It had seemed like the right thing to do at the time, but now… Bruce was right. He was a meathead. A loser.

Pushing the box aside, Hawk left the attic. He wasn't seeing the print on the pages clearly anymore, so taking a break made sense. He was beginning to think he was manic about those files for no reason at all. There wasn't anything here that would help Cassie. If there ever had been anything meaningful, it had been moved years ago. After all, who would leave important information to mold for nearly thirty years?

Sheryl sat at the kitchen table going through a stack of mail. As she had last night, she'd changed into a pair of flannel pants and a T-shirt that was a size too small. The pants were loose; the shirt was not. It molded to her body like a second skin. She seemed completely unaware of how she looked. She didn't know she was beautiful. She didn't know she was sexy as hell in that snug shirt and baggy pants.

She didn't even glance his way when he entered the room, even though she knew he was there. He could tell by the sudden shift of her body, the tension that radiated off her like a Texas summer heat.

"Mind if I make a pot of coffee?" he asked.

"Help yourself." She didn't look up from her chore.

Hawk knew how the kitchen was arranged by now, and he quickly got the coffeemaker started. The aroma of the strong brew filled the air. Yeah, it would help him make it through the night. A few more hours, anyway.

But caffeine wasn't going to solve this problem.

Hawk took a couple of steps toward the table where Sheryl sat, crossed his arms over his chest and planted his feet. "I'm sorry," he said gruffly.

"For what?" Sheryl moved a bill to one stack, an advertisement to another. Still, she didn't glance his way.

"You know damn well for what."

Finally she looked at him. There was a flinty gleam in her blue eyes, but a vulnerable gentleness touched her lips. Dammit, he didn't know what to make of her! Not now, not ever.

"That's the rudest apology I ever heard."

Hawk knew plenty of men who could seduce the toughest shrew with a couple of words and a false smile. Not him. Yesterday Sheryl had accused him of treating her like a horse. He wished he could do just that. He wished he could touch her mind with his, stroke her between the eyes and make everything all right.

"I understand there's a dance tomorrow night." The word *dance* almost stuck in his throat.

"Yeah," Sheryl said softly. "So?"

"Go with me."

Gradually the hardness in her eyes faded. A little. "Donovan, your invitations are as smooth as your apologies."

"If you're looking for smooth, you might as well say no."

She returned to her bills, opening an envelope and studying the statement inside. Hawk turned away from her, willing the coffeepot to finish its job more quickly. While he stood at the counter, waiting for the coffee to be done, a soft voice finally answered.

"Dancing sounds like fun. I wasn't here for the spring festival, but I did make it to the Fourth of July picnic. They do things up right around here. Be warned, Donovan," Sheryl added almost ominously. "I'm not much of a dancer."

"Neither am I."

"We'll just have to stumble through the dance together."

Something hard and tight settled in his gut, and he wasn't sure why. Because she'd said yes to his invitation? Did the very idea of dancing with her cause a physical reaction?

Then again, maybe it was the visual image those words put in his mind that made his stomach react. Stumbling through *together*.

When the coffee was done, he poured a large cup and headed for the attic. Before he'd gone far, Sheryl asked, "Need some help?"

Hawk almost said no, and then he realized that she'd just taken a step much like the one he'd made when he'd asked her to the dance. Neither of them was very good at putting themselves on the line.

"Sure," he said. "I could use another pair of eyes."

* * *

Sheryl surveyed the mess laid out on her attic floor and shook her head. Opened boxes filled with discarded files had been shoved to one side. Stacks of old papers were arranged here and there, amongst her own boxes and the junk she'd stored up here. It was cramped and crowded and musty.

This simply wasn't going to work.

"I have an idea," she said, stepping over a stack of papers Donovan had set aside.

"Any and all ideas are welcome," he answered. She could hear the frustration in his voice, see it in the set of his mouth and the tiredness of his eyes. He'd showered and shaved at the hotel this morning, but the five-o'clock shadow on his jaw was heavy, and a bit of dust had settled in his hair.

"I'm afraid you've outgrown the attic. Why don't we move the files you think might lead somewhere, and the boxes you haven't been through yet, to the spare bedroom? The computer is right there, in case you find any new names to plug into a search engine. I can move some of my books off the bookshelf and make space for you to arrange your files." Donovan looked so tired, she had the urge to reach out and soothe him with her hands in his hair and on his tense shoulders. He needed help. Help and a good night's sleep.

"There's a small bed in the room," she continued. "If you're going to spend the night here, you might as well sleep in a bed rather than on a hard wood floor."

"I hate to impose."

Sheryl laughed as she scooped up a stack of files. "Too late. You have turned my life upside down, Donovan. You've hypnotized my pets, ruined any reputation I might have by leaving your truck out front all night, and—" She stopped abruptly. Best not to tell him that he'd turned her insides upside down, too.

"And what?"

"You and your damn files," she said as she headed down the pull-down stairway. "I got another phone call today."

"From who?" he asked, suddenly intensely interested in what she had to say. He grabbed a box, tucked it under one arm and followed her down the steps.

"A Dr. Faith Winston. Apparently she's developed an academic interest in your files."

"What did you tell her?" Sheryl tossed her stack of files onto the bed, while Donovan placed the box he carried on the floor near the door.

"I told her I didn't have any files."

Donovan smiled widely. Oh, he should smile more often! The grin did things to his face—it made him look not so tough, not so forbidding. The man usually had the look of a brooding gypsy, but that smile made him look infinitely kissable.

"Thanks."

"I didn't do it for you," Sheryl said. She breezed past him, heading for the attic and another load of files. "I'm sick and tired of strangers poking around my clinic. I mean, face it. If there was any important information left behind, don't you think someone would've removed it from the basement before now?"

"I know it's a long shot, but I have to try." Donovan was no longer smiling.

Sheryl was halfway up the stairs. Donovan stood in the hallway directly below, no doubt watching her rear end as she climbed. Great. She should've made him go up first, so she could watch his rear end instead. Maybe then she wouldn't feel so suddenly and inexplicably uncomfortable.

She should've done a lot of things differently, especially in the past few days.

She wished she could dismiss Donovan as easily as she had Carpenter and Winston. But she hadn't. And she couldn't. He might not be warm and fuzzy, but he was honest. He hadn't pretended to be someone he wasn't.

Bruce came out of the attic, wings flapping as he descended. Sheryl was startled, since her mind had been elsewhere, and she lost her balance as the parrot brushed past her. She didn't have far to fall, but she was prepared to land hard at the foot of the stairs, maybe tangled in the wooden ladder slats.

She didn't. Donovan caught her with those long, strong arms that were always so steady. He didn't even wobble as she landed against him, her back thudding against his chest, her legs flailing. With his arms wrapped securely around her, he was solid as a rock, but warm and alive.

"Are you okay?" Donovan's arms didn't move, but remained wrapped around her.

"Yeah, I was just...startled." She was on her feet now, but her heart still pounded too hard. Her breath had a hard time fighting its way out of her lungs. She placed one hand over the forearm that held her steady. What should she say now? Thanks for catching me. Hold me awhile longer. Where have you been all my life?

Instead she said, "I have got to find a home for that bird!"

"He's very smart," Donovan answered. "Clean up his language a little and anyone would be happy to have him."

"Spoken like someone who hasn't known Bruce long." Sheryl swallowed hard. She really should move away from

Donovan…but she didn't. He really should let her go. But he didn't. He was so warm and so steady, and her body responded almost violently to being tucked in his arms. Butterflies fluttered in her stomach, and low in her gut she felt a warmth she had forgotten. A weight and a pulsation and a demand.

She tried to ignore that response. "He's really…I really…" Like it or not she couldn't even think about Bruce, not with Donovan holding on to her this way.

So she just stood there, leaning into him. Listening to the demands of her body. Drinking in the way his body moved when he breathed, the way her breaths came in time with his. She clenched; her mouth went dry.

What was happening to her? This thing she felt, it was some kind of chemistry. Animal magnetism. Whatever it was that drew a woman to a man to the point where she could no longer think straight, Hawk Donovan possessed it. And she had been caught up in that power as surely as if he'd snared her in a net. She liked leaning into him, she liked the way his arms felt around her.

She had a choice, and it had to be made now, with his arms around her and his breath on her neck. She could break away, tell Donovan she was fine and climb into the attic as if nothing had happened. They hadn't yet crossed that line that could not be uncrossed. She could move up the stairs, not look back, and while they might both be a little uncomfortable for a few minutes, eventually they would forget what this holding felt like. They'd forget how close they'd come to becoming more than friends.

Then again, she could stay here. Right here, with Donovan's chest at her spine and his arms wrapped around her. She could relax. She could close her eyes and drink in the delicious sensation of being held. She could stop fighting that flutter in her gut and instead listen to it. Revel in it.

She could forget that she'd written off romance and men as not worth the trouble and just let herself feel. No thinking allowed.

She didn't think, just for a moment. She didn't worry.

It was nice.

She relaxed.

Chapter 7

Moving very slowly, Hawk lowered his head and pressed his mouth to Sheryl's skin. With her hair pulled up and back, her neck was fully exposed. It was a decidedly feminine neck, long, pale and soft. And he'd been aching to taste it for days now. *Days*.

He tasted her pulse, sucked against the curve where neck became shoulder, flicked the tip of his tongue across her tender skin. And she melted in his arms. He felt her desire for him in the way she breathed, in the way she fell into him and trembled down deep.

He had never been so intensely attracted to a woman before. Never. He had never come so close to losing control, to forgetting who and what he was. But somehow Sheryl pushed all his buttons. She worked her way under his skin and stayed there. It would be so easy to forget why he was here and what he had to do.

Sheryl turned slowly in his arms to face him, wrapping her arms around his neck and looking him squarely in the eye. Her body was pressed against his; her warm breath touched his throat. Her eyes were boldly fixed to his. Sheryl wasn't the kind of woman who would look away from a man.

"Kiss me," she whispered. "And then tell me again that it doesn't mean anything."

She didn't wait for an answer but tilted her head up slightly as he lowered his. He covered her mouth with his. To his bones, he was controlled by a need that consumed him. His need for Sheryl swept away all reason, all conscience. This wasn't a sweet kiss…not today. It was primal. Deep. And with every second that passed, Hawk moved closer to losing control.

He liked Sheryl; he wanted her. But as their tongues danced, in the back of his mind he kept hearing that damned logical neighbor who'd waylaid him this morning. *She deserves better.*

He raised up slowly, dragging his mouth from Sheryl's. It was harder than he'd imagined it would be to break away. Her eyes drifted open and her lips curved into a soft smile. Already her mouth looked well kissed, damp and swollen and ready for more.

"Nothing?" she whispered.

She was standing so close, so tight against his body, she knew the kiss had definitely meant *something*.

"I didn't come here looking for this," he said. *Looking for you* would sound so personal. So…true.

"I know." She reached up and brushed back a lock of hair that had fallen across his forehead. The touch was tender. Loving, even.

"I can't stay."

"I know that, too." She didn't pull away, and her smile didn't disappear.

"I'm not—"

"Who are you trying to talk down from the ledge, Donovan? Me or you? Do you have a girlfriend back home?"

"No."

"Do you want me?"

"Yes."

"Then stop thinking so much and jump, Donovan. Jump."

She was too close to the truth. They were both teetering on a narrow ledge.

"We don't know what's below," she whispered. "If we fall or if we jump, where will we land? Are you afraid to find out?" She didn't wait for an answer. "I am, a little."

Sheryl's talk of ledges and falling and wondering where they'd land shouldn't make any sense. But it did, in a strange kind of way. Hawk usually knew exactly where each and every step would take him. Every move was calculated; there were no surprises in his well-ordered life.

The best thing he could do for both of them would be to back down. To walk away. To put an end to this, here and now.

Instead, he jumped.

Sheryl pressed her body against Donovan's and closed her eyes as he kissed her again. Logic, which normally ruled her days, told her she was simply hungry for a man. Any man. It had been too long since anyone had touched her, and yes, her body was hungry. She needed this touch; she wanted to feel like a woman again.

But deep down she knew there was something more here than simple desire. She didn't long for any man to hold her, just Donovan. There was no one else who could infuriate, inflame and incite her. No one else who could make her laugh and sing. No one else who could touch not only her body but her heart.

And like it or not, he did touch her heart.

Maybe all she and Donovan had was physical attraction, and she wanted her heart to be involved because that made what she felt at this moment acceptable. How could love play a part in this when she'd just met him a few days ago? She wasn't the type of woman to give her heart so quickly, and she doubted Hawk Donovan had ever given any woman his heart.

Then again, maybe she was making this too complicated, and physical attraction was all they needed.

Donovan cupped her breast and flicked his thumb over the nipple. She felt that touch to her bones, and she quivered. Man, did she quiver. His tongue slipped into her mouth while he caressed her nipple through the cotton tee that was molded to her body. His tongue slipped in, slipped out, slipped in...and her knees turned to butter. Her stomach dropped, and again she clenched.

She felt as if she was truly falling, so she held on to Donovan. She didn't want to land too hard, and she didn't want to land alone. She touched him with curious hands, fluttered her fingers over his jaw and his neck, the broad chest, the rock-hard arms. Did he feel her trembling? Did he know she was so close to falling apart that she could barely breathe?

He slipped his hand beneath her shirt and pressed his palm to her bare skin. That simple touch was enough to make her moan low in her throat. Flesh to flesh, man to woman. The grace and sleekness she had noticed in him from the beginning was evident in the way he touched her, as if every move was made without conscious thought but came to him naturally. As if he had been born to touch her. His fingers stroked her skin, and that caress was intense. Undeniably right. Just as the kiss that went on and on was right. If she had her way, she'd never take her mouth from his.

But she did, briefly. "Do you have a…"

He growled, and the growl sounded affirmative. She didn't ask for details as he claimed her mouth again as if he couldn't bear to stop kissing her. A moment later, he pulled a wallet out of his back pocket, opened it with one hand, delved inside and then tossed the wallet to the floor. He never actually stopped kissing her. At times the kiss was deep and all consuming, and then it turned into a series of brief, hungry, quick kisses.

While his mouth was still on hers, Donovan tightened the arm that was wrapped around her and then swept her up and off her feet. She found herself sitting on one of the steps that led to the attic. Half sitting, half standing, precariously perched before Donovan, she wrapped her legs around his, deepened the kiss and drew him to her.

Her body thrummed. It hummed. It sang and danced and reached for Donovan. Any doubts she might've had earlier were gone. This moment was beautiful and right and powerful, and nothing could ruin it. Nothing.

Donovan stopped kissing her just long enough to draw her T-shirt over her head and toss it aside, and she was glad to be rid of the constricting garment. In a fraction of a second she felt liberated, exposed and greedy for more. It had grown overly warm in this hallway, but the night air on her flesh was cool. Arousing. Donovan laid his mouth over hers while he raked his hands up her side, and then they were on her bare breasts, caressing taut nipples while his tongue barely slipped into her mouth.

Sensations she had forgotten rushed through her body, more fierce and demanding than she had known was possible. There was a fire in her body, a fever that burned away everything but her need for Donovan.

Sheryl leaned back slightly, the stairs at her back, and unbuttoned Donovan's shirt while he kissed her neck again, his mouth raking over skin that was surprisingly sensitive. No one had ever kissed her neck before, not like this, as if he was making love to her throat. She liked it. She loved it. That kiss made her smile and shiver and throb all at once.

She pushed the shirt off his shoulders and it fell to the floor. Oh, she had known all along that Donovan had a great body, and still she was impressed. His chest was sculpted with hard muscles and dusted with just a little bit of fine dark hair. He had a tight six-pack, taut warm muscles across his abdomen that cried out to be touched. She ran her hands over those muscles for a moment, then brushed her fingers over small, tight nipples.

Her skin was on fire. She couldn't get close enough to the man who held and caressed and aroused her. With her body so close to his she couldn't help but feel his erection pressing against her, and that only aroused her more. He wanted her; he needed her. She moved against him, just a little, and he responded with a rumble low in his throat.

Donovan slipped his hands into her waistband and pushed her flannel trousers and underwear down. She stepped out of the garments and kicked them aside, and suddenly she was standing in his arms naked. Naked and trembling and vulnerable. Vulnerable but not afraid. Donovan skimmed his hand along her body, as if he was learning the curves. She closed her eyes, and for a moment it was as if she was learning those curves, too. She had forgotten; she had hidden this part of herself away.

Donovan's touch was gentle, as if she were fragile. Even when he caressed her intimately, arousing her to the point where she could no longer think of anything else, there was tenderness. He stroked, and she soared. He caressed, and she throbbed.

It wasn't fair that she was naked and he wasn't. She wanted to see all of him, and she wanted to touch him the way he touched her. Boldly and yet with gentleness. She unfastened his blue jeans and lowered the zipper, then pushed her hands beneath the waistband to cup his hips. She kept pushing, lowering the garments out of the way. Like his chest, his hips and thighs were muscled and hard. He kicked his boots off and finished undressing in a matter of seconds, and then they were together again, naked and sweating and once again standing on that dangerous ledge.

She didn't know what was at the bottom, but she didn't care anymore. Falling was glorious. She could fall forever.

Donovan unwrapped the condom he'd snagged from his wallet and sheathed himself.

"Here?" Sheryl reached out and touched his face. Her fingers trembled, her entire body shook.

"Yeah." He positioned her against the ladder and lifted her legs in a strong, smooth motion so they were wrapped around him.

"What about the kids?" she asked with a smile, glancing down the hallway to see if Laverne or Baby or any of the others were watching.

"All asleep," he whispered.

"How could you possibly know…?"

"All asleep," he said again, and she believed him.

She could take his hand and lead him to her bedroom, or to the narrow bed in the spare bedroom if the kiddies had already claimed her bed for the night. But that would mean stopping, that would mean letting him go, and she wasn't ready for that.

Sheryl wrapped her legs more snugly around Donovan's hips, and he guided himself into her. As slowly and gently as he had aroused her, he entered her. She closed her eyes and held on as her body adjusted to his size, as she opened for him. Her body shook; the only way to control the shaking was to hold on to Donovan. He grounded her; he promised her so much.

And then he moved deeper, harder, and she held on tighter and gasped at the pleasure.

There was nothing in the world but this. His body and hers; the desire that had spiraled out of control so quickly and completely.

She lifted herself up so she was just barely balanced against a wooden step, and speared her fingers through his hair, pressing her mouth to his while he made love to her. Their tongues danced while their bodies mated, and she gasped as Donovan plunged deeper. Strands of pleasure drifted through her body; sparks of intense desire leaped through her as if a fire ran through her blood.

With the tottery stairs beneath her and Donovan inside her, she felt oddly steady here. Steady and safe. And hungry. She needed this; she needed him. Donovan moved into her so fast and deep and completely the stairway shook. The very house shook. She felt him to her fingertips, to her toes, to the top of her head.

She came with a cry Donovan caught with his mouth. Her body shuddered, as completion made her convulse and moan and hold Donovan even tighter than before. She shattered, lurched and cried, while her body clenched and unclenched. He came with her, finally falling off that ledge and hitting the ground with a bang.

Everything seemed to slow down, and reality started to come back to Sheryl in unwelcome waves. She didn't want reality, not tonight. She wanted this night to go on and on. She wanted this feeling of belonging to and with someone to continue. She wanted to believe, at least for a while, that Donovan was hers and always would be.

He could be hers, for a few hours or a few days. Neither of them were looking for forever, but maybe they could make a memory that would last that long.

For the past couple of nights, Hawk had leafed through old medical files searching for a clue to finding his birth mother until he'd fallen asleep exhausted. Tonight, at least for a few hours, he had forgotten those files and the frustration of not finding what he'd come here for.

He lay in Sheryl's bed under a thick coverlet the color of the evening sky. They were still naked and resting on their sides, her back fitting against his chest as if they were two pieces of a puzzle.

Sex in the past had been unemotional, a physical release and not much else. He had never held a woman long into the night. He'd never slept in a bed that felt more like home than his own. He'd certainly never curled up with a woman who felt like a part of him.

He would worry about the unexpected sentiments he was experiencing if he didn't know this was temporary. His stay here would be a short one, and that was for the best. If he and Sheryl had anything beyond this bed he'd have to tell her everything. It was hard enough hiding his abilities from strangers, but to hide them from a woman who was a part of his life would be impossible. If he told her who he was and what he could do, she'd run from him. She'd run from this.

Abnormal was an ugly word. *Freak* was worse.

Fortunately for both of them, they didn't have to think about the future. There wasn't one, not for them. There was only here and now.

Hawk pressed his hand to Sheryl's belly, his palm resting on the silky skin beneath her navel. Yes, she had muscles in her arms and her legs, and her back was sculpted to perfection. But she was also a woman, fragile and soft. Her skin was so silky and fine he couldn't keep his hands off her.

She turned in his arms. "You're awake," she whispered as her arms draped around him in the dark, beneath the covers, in this world that was theirs alone and wouldn't last.

"Can't sleep."

She smiled and hummed and rubbed the tip of her nose against his chest. "Why's that?"

He took her hand in his and guided it to his erection. She hummed again as she wrapped her fingers around him.

"I have a cure for that," she said.

"I believe you do."

She stroked him gently while she tipped her head back to kiss his throat with lips so soft they felt like satin against his rough skin. "It's not a quick cure, I'm afraid," Sheryl said as she trailed her lips down to his chest and slipped her hand between his thighs to stroke the skin there. "Administered properly, the treatment can take half the night to complete."

He smiled and raked his fingers through her hair. "It just so happens I have half the night."

She lifted up slowly and looked at him. There was just enough light to see her well, with the streetlamp shining through the bedroom window and the night-light on the far wall beyond the sleeping animals adding a glow to the room. In her work clothes, with her hair in a ponytail, Sheryl Eldanis was pretty as a picture.

Rising above him naked, with her mussed hair falling around her shoulders and that gentle smile twisting her lips and her sleepy eyes hooded, she was breathtakingly beautiful.

Half a night wouldn't be nearly long enough.

Benedict left the meeting charged. Apparently someone had been snooping around Wyatt, North Carolina, asking questions about Agnes and Oliver, digging up old information best left buried.

The bit of intelligence he'd just heard forced him to think back. Deanna had destroyed the file that contained the information he'd worked so hard to gather. When she'd told him what she'd done, and that she was planning to leave him and take the children with her, he'd been so infuriated that he'd killed her in a rage. He'd killed her with his bare hands. That bitch! She'd cost him everything he'd worked so hard for. The knowledge, the science…the children.

He didn't have to worry that Agnes might've left something of importance in the clinic once it was closed. She'd been been much too smart for that. Still he wondered. What if something had been inadvertently left behind? What if someone else stumbled across the information he'd struggled for years to gather and understand?

Letting it slip through his fingers would be a mistake.

Before he reached his hotel room, Benedict flipped open his cell phone and dialed the number from memory. Janet answered with a sleepy, "Hello."

"Hello, darling. What are you doing?"

"Sleeping," she said, succinctly but with a hint of a slur. "It's…it's three-thirty in the morning, Ben."

"I'm going on a little trip, and I might have need of your services at a moment's notice." He had to be very careful about what he said over a cell phone. No alarming words could be used. "Bring the RV."

"When?" Janet's voice was now much more alert.

"Now."

He heard her moving about as if she were stretching those lovely long limbs of hers. He could almost see her sitting up, running her fingers through her hair, licking her lips. Oddly enough, he had missed her.

"Where are we going?" she asked, fully alert.

"Wyatt, North Carolina."

Sheryl woke to a normal morning. The sun was barely over the horizon, and already Laverne and the other cats were meowing at her to get up. Howie paced by the bed, and Bogie jumped up and settled on the comforter between her and Donovan.

Donovan had the worst of it. Baby was bigger than her dogs, and she was presently licking her master's stubbled cheek with slobbering enthusiasm.

What had seemed so right last night seemed a little embarrassing by the light of day. It was unlike her to lose control. She suspected it was unlike Donovan, too.

"Good morning," he rumbled.

Sheryl wasn't sure if he was talking to her or to Baby, but she answered anyway. "Good morning."

He rolled toward her, looking deliciously rumpled and not quite awake. "Get enough sleep?"

"Nope," she said with a smile. "You?"

"It'll do."

He was softer in the morning, not yet so very much on guard. A few bricks were missing from that wall he'd built around himself. If they had the time she could take that wall down. One brick at a time. But of course they didn't have the time, so there was no point in wishing otherwise.

She couldn't think about tomorrow, his protective walls or hers, what her mother would think, whether her sister and brothers would get along with him.... None of that mattered. Donovan was hers only for a short time, but he was truly hers. No one else came into the mix.

She liked him this way. A little softer, a little rougher, a little more *hers*. But she suspected it wouldn't last.

She reached out and laid her hand on his shoulder. Not caressing, not pulling toward or pushing away. Just touching. "What are your plans for today?"

"I'll finish moving the files from the attic into the spare room, if you don't mind."

"Of course I don't mind."

"And I might make a trip to the drugstore." He touched her, too, brushing the backs of his fingers across her shoulder.

"Good idea." He'd just had the two condoms in his wallet, and since she'd given up sex when she'd given up Michael, she had absolutely nothing in her house that even remotely resembled birth control.

He moved in with a perfectly wicked grin on his beautiful face. "Do you take a break for lunch?"

"Don't kiss me!" She laughed out loud and tossed her head back. "You have Baby slobber all over your face."

"Okay." He didn't sound at all offended. And then he took a nipple in his mouth and drew it deep, and her body responded as if he were touching her for the first time. She closed her eyes and let the sensations wash through her body from head to toe. Oh, how did he know just where to touch her, just how soft, just how hard? Somehow he knew. What a wonderful way to wake up.

But they weren't alone. Baby jumped on the bed to join the others, and Howie, who was too short to make the jump, started to howl because he was the only one in the room not on the bed. Sheryl laughed, and so did Donovan, who managed to shoo all the animals out of the room with a single word and a wave of his hand.

Sheryl sat up. Alone or not, they were out of condoms and she could not stay in this bed with Donovan and not touch him. "About that lunch break," she said as she left the bed, glancing over her shoulder. "Twelve o'clock sharp. Be there."

Chapter 8

It made a difference, working in the spare room rather than the attic. The air was fresher here, a bit cooler, the space was more open. Hawk didn't feel as if the walls were closing in on him down here. Arranging the files he'd set aside as potentially important actually made him feel as if he might be making progress.

Last night he'd set his job aside to hold Sheryl for a while. He'd forgotten why he was here and had sex. Lots of sex. Good sex. Mind-blowing, where-have-you-been-all-my-life sex. And then he'd slept. He hadn't slept that deeply in so long he couldn't even remember when it might've been.

But today he was focused once again, back to work without the distraction of wondering how Sheryl's bare skin would feel against his.

He called Cassie on the cell phone. She said she was

doing fine, but he could tell by the tone of her voice that she wasn't telling everything. Maybe she'd had another seizure and didn't want him to worry. When he'd tried to press her about the issue, she turned the tables on him, telling him that he sounded different and asking him what he'd been up to.

His denial wasn't accepted any more readily than hers had been. Cassie knew him too well, but she also knew not to push for answers. She'd learned a long time ago that pushing her brother never got her anywhere.

Shortly after eleven o'clock, Hawk headed for town with Baby trailing along behind him. They walked, rather than taking the truck, since the shops he planned to visit were so close and the day was beautiful, with clear blue skies, an autumn breeze and a warm sun.

In the main square Hawk did his shopping. Condoms, a black marker, clear tape and a small sheet of poster board were purchased from a sour old woman at the drugstore. He bought flowers from a small corner stall, and sandwiches and cold drinks from a narrow café located between the barber shop and a dress store.

A block before he reached the veterinary clinic, Hawk stopped. He placed his bags on the ground and searched for the poster board and marker amongst the rest of the purchases. He fashioned a quick sign in a bold, sweeping hand: Back in Thirty Minutes.

When he resumed his walk, he glanced down at Baby, who had, as usual, behaved well all morning. She'd waited outside each shop without a peep, knowing that she wasn't welcome everywhere. Too bad. He'd rather spend his time with Baby than any of the people he'd dealt with today.

"You want to go back to the house?" He could see Baby's thoughts, and at the moment they included the desire for a nap on Sheryl's breezy front porch. Baby didn't care for vet clinics, not even to visit. "Go on, then," he said, giving his permission. "I'll be there later."

Baby took off at a run. Hawk watched as the dog ran toward Sheryl's, her feet flying down the center of the sidewalk, her attention focused on her goal. She wouldn't roam anywhere else, wouldn't be distracted by a squirrel or a stray mutt.

Hawk entered the clinic without his usual sidekick. For the past couple of years, Baby had been with him almost constantly. It felt odd to be standing here without her.

A client who did his best to control an uncontrollable black lab at the end of a leash tried to write out a check while Sheryl stood behind the counter and wrote up a receipt. She lifted her head and smiled at Hawk, not at all surprised to see him here twenty minutes early.

She looked different today, happier than she'd been when he'd first walked into this clinic. Her cheeks were flushed and her eyes sparkled. How could any man look at her and not feel as if he'd just been punched in the gut?

When the customer and the black lab left, Sheryl came around the counter. Her eyes changed. They were slightly hooded now, and the blue seemed deeper than before. Even though Hawk knew this was temporary, deep down he didn't want her to ever look at another man this way.

"Anyone else here?" he asked.

"Nope. I don't have another appointment until one-thirty, and Cory won't be in until after three."

"Good." He handed her the flowers first, and she took them with a widening of her easy smile and a quick kiss as thanks.

He handed over the sandwiches and drinks, which were bulky. She took their lunch and placed it on the counter.

"What's in that sack?" she asked, pointing to the plastic bag that had Wyatt Pharmacy written on the side.

Hawk opened the top of the bag and let her look inside. She spotted the box of condoms first, and her eyes widened. It was a big box, that was true, but as far as Hawk was concerned, better safe than sorry.

Sheryl drew out the sign and smiled as she read it, then reached for the pen and turned to the counter. She scribbled something on the poster and then turned around to present it to him. She'd marked through some of his work and added a few words of her own.

Instead of Back in Thirty Minutes, it now read Back in One Hour.

He put the sign in the curtained window and flipped the lock on the door, holding in his mind the vision of the sparkle in Sheryl's eyes and the unwavering strength of her smile. They would terrify him, if he thought this affair would last more than a few days.

"I've never had sex in my office before." Sheryl wrapped her arms around Donovan's neck as he pulled her closer to him.

"Good," he answered.

She sat on her desk, half-dressed and already dancing on the edge. Literally and figuratively. Donovan was still fully dressed, but that wouldn't last long. Not if she had her way.

If she thought about it—and she had thought about it all morning—she knew this had happened too fast. But she also knew they didn't have time to waste, and she didn't want to let Donovan slip through her fingers. He was special, in a way she could not explain. Handsome, yes, but not the only handsome man she'd ever seen. Intriguing, yes, but she didn't look for mystery in a man. She looked for answers. She looked for absolutes. She had sworn that she'd never allow another man to touch her until she knew him to the core. Surprises were the last thing she needed or wanted, and Hawk Donovan was one surprise after another.

Maybe she should stop thinking and accept that this was physical perfection. Nothing else mattered. Not today.

He lowered his mouth to her neck and sucked there, and she tilted her head to one side to offer him full, unobstructed access. The touch of his lips sent lightning through her body. Just that touch, his mouth on her throat, made her clench and shiver. She closed her eyes and just allowed herself to feel. She felt good, through and through. She felt alive. When Donovan cupped her breast, she shuddered and pressed that breast more firmly into his palm.

She untucked his shirt and skated one hand against his hard belly. She wanted to touch him; she wanted the sensation of his skin against her palm.

Donovan spread her thighs and skimmed his fingers over the soft skin there. His hands were large and weathered, rough and callused, and yet he could be so tender. It seemed that he knew just where to touch her, just how hard, just how soft. A thumb stroked up her inner thigh and back down again, teasing her, coming close to where she was wet for him and then slowly moving away.

And then he didn't move away. His fingers fluttered over her intimately, and she responded. She wanted him already. She wanted him *now*. How was that possible, after last night? She'd gone two years without a man in her bed, and now she couldn't stand to be without Donovan for twelve hours?

The caress grew gradually firmer, more certain, more demanding. No, twelve hours was much too long.

She reached down and stroked his denim-covered erection. Long, thick and hard, he filled her hand. Maybe she did want him to distraction, but he wanted her just as badly. When she reached for his belt buckle, he stopped her with a stilling hand on her wrist.

"Not yet."

"Yes," she insisted.

He smiled at her, and she was reminded that he didn't smile nearly often enough. The smile transformed his face. There was still mystery in his gypsy eyes, but there was also joy. Life. A thousand unspoken promises.

"We have an hour, Sheryl. Trust me."

"I don't—"

"Trust me," he whispered, and then he kissed her and pressed forward, so that she was forced gently but unerringly backward. He removed her blouse, knocking a short stack of papers to the floor in the process. She didn't care. It was nice to know that he could tremble, too, that he could lose control. He kissed her mouth, her throat, her breasts, and while he kissed her his hands caressed her inner thighs and again brushed against her intimately.

She closed her eyes and let herself drown in sensation. Maybe there was a desk beneath her. Then again, maybe she was flying. Maybe her body had changed in a way so dramatic it was no longer earthbound. She didn't think about anything but the way Donovan made her feel... and then she began to think about the way he would make her feel when he pushed inside her. Just thinking of what was to come made her tremble.

Donovan spread her legs wide, lifted her hips slightly, and listed in to flutter his tongue. And she *knew* she was flying. He loved her that way, with his lips and his hands and his tongue, until she shattered, crying out and arching up off the table while the intense orgasm shook her body and then faded away, leaving her trembling and depleted.

Smiling and lethargic, Donovan crept up over her body like a cat. She was practically panting, and he was as serene as she had ever seen him. She was about to come out of her skin, and he looked as if he had all the time in the world. He laid one hand over her breast and very slowly lifted that hand, allowing the fingertips to brush against her skin until they came together at the nipple, where he tweaked gently.

Sheryl quickly unbuttoned his shirt and pushed it away, her hands on his chest and his arms, her breath almost returning. Almost. Her elbow moved and another sheaf of papers fell to the floor. She didn't care.

"What have you done to me?" she whispered as she reached down to unfasten his jeans. Her hands shook.

He didn't answer.

"I've never felt like this before, Donovan."

"Hawk," he said. "My name is Hawk."

"Hawk," she whispered. His given name sounded so intimate. So personal. It was a name she would call in the night, after he was gone. The name of a man she would miss…

But not today. And there was only today. No yesterday, no tomorrow. And she could not afford to think with her heart. Only with her body. She couldn't worry about the empty nights to come. She had to focus on the fact that Hawk was here now…and he wanted her. And even though her body still trembled from the orgasm she'd just had, even though her knees shook so that she knew she wouldn't be able to stand if she had to, she wanted him, too.

She reached for the box of condoms they had wisely opened earlier, and which had not been knocked to the floor. Yet.

"You're wearing too many clothes," she said as she reached into the box and snagged one foil-wrapped condom. "Take them off."

With nightfall and the extra traffic attributed to the start of the festival, Anthony had no trouble sneaking back into town. According to the file he'd stolen, there had once been a major experimental lab where the Eldanis Veterinary Clinic was located. A quick search of the premises had revealed nothing, but he wasn't ready to give up. Not yet.

It didn't make sense that Eldanis herself was involved. She was too young to have any connection with that long-ago past. Her occupation of the building was probably just chance. Bad luck on her part, but one woman's bad luck wasn't his concern.

Dressed in black and standing very still, he waited in shadows across the street from the Eldanis woman's house. There were lots of lights on, but one by one the lamps were being extinguished. Too early for bedtime. Maybe she was going out.

Inside the house one front room remained well lit. The porch light came on and the door opened. Good. She was going out. Not that he expected to find anything in her house, but it wouldn't hurt to have a look around. Eldanis, smiling widely and wearing a pretty blue dress with a long floaty skirt, stepped onto the porch. So did a man, who kept one hand on her in a proprietary way.

A shiver ran down Anthony's spine as he studied the man. His face, well lit by the porch light, was not familiar. And yet…it *was* familiar, in a bone-deep way.

The barking of dogs chased away the eerie feeling. Damn. He hated dogs! Noisy creatures, always popping up where they were least wanted. And it sounded as if Eld-

anis had more than one. More than two. The dogs and the
kids who kept running in and out of the house next door
would keep Anthony from searching her house. Tonight,
anyway. If he felt he needed to come back here, he'd find
a way.

The almost-familiar man turned around and said a word
or two, and the barking stopped. Then he closed the door
and looked down at Eldanis.

Sucker. The man was obviously falling hard and fast.

Anthony didn't move as the couple left the porch and
headed for the sidewalk. When they reached the sidewalk,
the man turned his head in Anthony's direction. Anthony
didn't move, and he was certain he could not be seen in
this position, but it was as if the man stared right at him.
Right freakin' *through* him.

And then the woman took his hand, and they headed for
town. Walking slowly on this fine autumn night, hand in
hand and hopelessly moony.

Just when Anthony felt safe again, the man glanced
back, and the hairs on the back of his neck stood up as if
a jolt of electricity shot through his body.

Sheryl's neighbor had been right on the money when
she'd described the Friday-night dance. Good food. Amateurish music. Lots of laughter. The band was set up in the
town square, and the outdoor party had taken over the entire downtown area. People danced in the streets, filled
their plates from the long buffet line and visited with their
neighbors.

Hawk and Sheryl had been here an hour, and so far they
hadn't danced. That suited Hawk just fine, since he'd never
danced before. When they'd first arrived, they'd claimed
a place at one of the small tables that had been set up on

the south side of the square. They'd eaten, walked around the square and stopped to speak to a dozen or more curious people.

Including Harold Johnston, who had gathered the courage to invite Mildred Harris to be his date for the evening. Also including several of Sheryl's customers and a few of her neighbors. They were all curious about him. Too curious. Curiosity always made him nervous.

The evening was going well, and then Sheryl said those three little words no man wants to hear.

"I wanna dance."

Hawk worked a crick out of his neck. "I thought you said you were a terrible dancer."

"I am," she said brightly, and then she laughed. "That doesn't mean I don't *like* it." Her eyes softened, and she took his hand and threaded her fingers through his. A part of him loved the feel of her fingers twined through his; another part wanted to withdraw from her before it was too late.

Who was he kidding? He was already in much too deep.

"Look around you, Hawk. Fred Astaire is definitely not here. No Gene Kelly, either. Just a whole bunch of people who don't dance well but do it anyway because it's fun."

She was right. He could shuffle with the best of them, if it would make Sheryl happy.

Holding her and moving to the beat of the music made feeling like a bumbling fool worthwhile. It was awkward, for a moment. But only for a moment. Sheryl was delicate and she moved gracefully. Hawk was definitely not delicate, and there were moments when holding Sheryl made him feel as if everything about him was too big, too clumsy. He'd never thought of himself as clumsy before.

After a few minutes he didn't feel as if he was bumbling

anymore. He got the hang of it pretty quickly. He and Sheryl moved together easily, just as they had last night and this afternoon.

"You're beautiful," he said, pulling her closer as a twanging guitar played a slow tune.

"Thank you, but—"

"No buts," he interrupted.

After a moment she gave him a softer, "Thank you."

It was the truth. He'd never seen her in a dress before, with her shapely calves and ankles showing, with the swell of her breasts just barely peaking over the rounded neckline. The dress was modest, by today's standards, but it was feminine and skimmed her curves.

"You're not so bad yourself, you know," she said, laying her head against his chest and moving in until her body was pressed against his from knee to chest. If not for these annoying clothes he'd be inside her; they were that close. If this was dancing, he liked it. He could dance all night, if it meant holding Sheryl this way.

He held her and listened to the music and moved a little. The past couple of days had been amazing, but he couldn't let himself forget why he was here. He couldn't give up on finding something, anything, that would help Cassie. As much as he enjoyed his time with Sheryl, he knew deep down that she was a distraction he couldn't afford to keep.

Too bad. In moments of weakness, he wanted very much to keep her. He wanted to toss her in his truck and take her home and fall into bed with her every night. And on many an afternoon, as well. He wanted to introduce her to Cassie, go riding with her over the hills of his home, find out if she'd be impressed or dismayed by the rodeo buckles he'd won before giving up bullriding.

He even wanted to know if she'd be impressed or dismayed if he told her what he could do, and that could never happen.

The party was still in full swing when they headed for home. Hawk imagined the festivities would continue all night. Tomorrow there would be a parade, a craft fair, a pie contest, a few games and speeches.

"I close up at noon on Saturday," Sheryl said as they walked down a deserted sidewalk. She'd taken to holding his hand, and while he liked it, it also made him a little uncomfortable. Holding hands was too intimate. Too demanding. "Maybe after I close up the clinic we can go to the craft fair and buy a nameplate with Hawk Donovan burned into it, or a homemade Christmas ornament or—"

"I can't," he interrupted.

There had been a healthy dose of humor in her voice, but it disappeared. "Why not?"

"I have to finish going through those files. I have to quit—" He halted, unsure how to finish.

"Wasting your time with me?" Sheryl finished for him. She didn't sound hurt or annoyed or even surprised.

"I wouldn't put it that way," he said.

"But it's the truth."

All of a sudden the night was too still, even though they could hear the distant music and the laughter of Sheryl's neighbors and friends. All of a sudden what had seemed so right and good was awkward.

Sheryl's hand slipped from his. "It's not like I expected an escort for every day of the weekend, Donovan. So you need to work? No problem. Really."

So, he was Donovan again. Impersonal. Unattached. That was the way it had to be, so why the hell did it hurt?

Somehow he had to explain, but he'd never been good

with words. "I didn't come here for this. I didn't expect—"

"Of course you didn't," she said with a harsh laugh. "You came here for some moldy old papers. Lucky you that you found a woman who was so desperate for companionship that she'd gladly fall on her back and—"

"Dammit!" He grabbed Sheryl's wrist and pulled her up against him. She stayed there, small and strong, warm and as right as anything he'd ever known. "You're twisting around everything I say."

"Am I?" She didn't look up but continued to stare at his chest. "Three people have contacted me looking for those damn files, and you're the only one rooting through them. Did you think if you slept with me I'd give you an exclusive on the junk in my attic?"

"No!"

"Why should I believe that?" She swiped quickly at her face with one hand. "Crap!"

"What's wrong?" The way the moonlight shone on her face, it looked like she was crying.

"Nothing." He could hear the tears in her voice now. He could hear them as if they were stuck in her throat.

"Nothing my ass," he grumbled.

"It's just… This is supposed to be all about sex," she said. "Fooling around without any expectations or commitment would be so easy, so uncomplicated. Why can't I be that woman? Why can't I live the quiet life I want and have a fling that doesn't mean anything? Why do I have to turn into a sniveling girl?"

"You're not sniveling."

"Not yet," she said. "Trust me, I am headed directly for snivelhood. I hate women who snivel!"

They turned onto a narrow side street, and Hawk led

Sheryl to a long wooden bench that sat in shadows under the caves of an out-of-the-way beauty shop. He sat and pulled her down to sit beside him. For a moment she was stiff, and then she put her head on his shoulder and relaxed.

"I was going to be completely detached," she said softly. "A...a free-spirited twenty-first-century woman who doesn't want anyone or anything to tie her down. You're leaving in a few days. Shoot, if you find what you're looking for, you could be gone tomorrow! A sexual relationship without any emotional attachment at all seemed like such a good idea, and here I am sniveling because you'd rather search through those files than take me to a stupid craft fair that I really don't give a fig about."

"I like you, too," Hawk said.

"Sucks, doesn't it?"

He laughed.

"It does suck! If I'm sniveling now, what am I going to be like when you leave town for good?"

Hawk had always known this relationship was tempo rary, but when she said the words they hit home. He'd never felt this way about a woman before. Would he be a complete fool to just walk away? Did he have any choice in the matter? He didn't know how or if he could ever tell her about his abilities. He didn't know if they had anything more than great sex. All he knew was that he didn't want to leave Sheryl behind for good.

"Ever been to Texas?" he asked.

"No," she said shortly.

"Maybe you should think about a visit."

She didn't answer right away. The night was too quiet, and he didn't know what else to say. He'd asked her once. If she ignored him or said no, he wouldn't ask her again.

Finally Sheryl said, "Really?"

Hawk breathed deeply in unexpected relief. "Why not? Even veterinarians take vacations."

"I suppose."

"So, Texas?"

She was quiet. No more sniveling. No more wiping away unwanted tears. "Maybe," she whispered. "Man, Donovan, you really know how to turn a girl's world upside down in a short period of time."

"Hawk," he said.

"I don't know," she said softly. "I mean, you really do look like a Donovan."

"Hawk." He hauled her onto his lap and she squealed. And then she laughed and wrapped her arms around his neck and held on tight.

"Say it."

She laid her mouth against his throat and kissed lightly. Her tongue flicked across his skin.

"Don't change the subject."

She continued to kiss his throat and feather teasing fingers over the back of his neck. He closed his eyes. Hell, she could call him anything she wanted to, as long as she touched him this way.

If she came to Texas one time, they'd be fine. Maybe they'd find they didn't have anything that would last beyond a few days. Maybe the visit would be awkward and she'd be glad to go home when it was over. But if they started regularly traveling back and forth, maybe meeting in Tennessee now and then, he'd have to tell her the truth. He'd have to tell her everything.

Heaven help him, he couldn't do that.

They had tonight, and maybe tomorrow, and maybe a few really great days and nights to come. Maybe they'd even meet a few months down the road, here or in Texas

or in Tennessee. But it would be like this. Hot but temporary. An amazing distraction, not a change of lifestyle. He
didn't dare to think beyond the physical connection they
had found.

Hawk reached inside Sheryl's dress and shifted her
breast so one nipple peeked over the neckline. A stitch
popped, but he didn't care. Neither did she, when he bent
down to rake his tongue over that nipple.

"Someone might—" she began, her voice a husky
whisper.

"No. We're alone, Sheryl."

"But—"

He sucked the nipple deep into his mouth and held it
there, and she quit arguing. Instead she arched against him
and moaned.

While she swayed into him, he slowly shimmied her underwear down and off. Her legs trembled as his fingers
brushed against them.

He wanted her with a sudden fierceness, and he wanted
her now. Here.

He tossed the underwear aside and she straddled him,
body shaking and lips hungry for his. He kissed her, deep.
He slipped his hand between their bodies and found her
damp center.

Her long dress and the shadows covered them, and besides…there was no one out and about on this narrow side
street. No one to watch. There was nothing and no one in
the world that could stop them from taking what they
wanted. He stroked her and she moaned deep in her throat.

"Hawk," he whispered in her ear while he caressed her.

"What difference does it—"

He slipped a finger inside her and she shuddered. "Say
it, Sheryl. Look me in the eye and say, 'I want you, Hawk.'"

She did want him, of that he had no doubt. She moved slightly against his hand, wet and trembling. Her lips parted gently, and then she said it. "I want you."

He moved his thumb against the nub at her entrance and she gasped. "Not good enough."

She let loose with an exasperated sigh. "Did anyone ever tell you that you talk too much?"

He laughed and thrust two fingers into her. "No. Never."

"Fine," she said with a deep tremble in her voice. "I want you, Hawk. You drive me crazy, *Hawk*." She looked him in the eye. "I don't know if you make me become someone I'm not or if you make me become…me."

He had a condom in his back pocket. While Sheryl freed his erection, he grabbed the condom and opened the foil pack. But she took the prophylactic from his hand and sheathed him herself, her hands moving with torturous indolence.

Payback.

While she raked her hands down his length she kissed him, her tongue searching, her lips soft and demanding. She sucked against his lips, teased his tongue with hers, fluttered her fingers over him until he was crazy with needing her. So, who was in control now?

He didn't care.

Finally, she lifted her hips up and then lowered herself onto him, closing her eyes as they came together. She rose up again, descended as if she was savoring every new inch of him. Her movements were so leisurely, so gentle, it was as if she moved in slow motion. Hawk pushed his hands beneath the skirt and held her hips, guiding her.

He didn't close his eyes. He watched Sheryl. Maybe it was the night, the dance, the fact that he was deep inside her, but he thought that maybe he could tell her everything.

All his secrets, all his fears. And she'd understand. She wouldn't laugh or cringe or run. She'd stay beside him no matter what, hold his hand, accept what others found unacceptable.

Sheryl rose up and moved down slowly again, until he was buried in her completely. She moaned low in her throat as if she were about to come apart. Hawk was almost there, holding back, waiting for her to cry out and clench around him.

The demands of his body made him forget everything but the way Sheryl felt wrapped around him.

Chapter 9

It was after three in the morning. Everyone in Sheryl's house was asleep but Hawk. Even Bruce slept on his perch. The house had surely never been this quiet. The only sound was the shuffle of papers as Hawk flipped carefully through yet another file. The dates were all wrong, so he didn't pay much attention to the faded words.

What if he didn't find anything? What if the woman in the pharmacy had been a quack, nothing more than a crazy old woman, just as Cassie had suggested? His trip here had been wasted.

Hawk thought about the woman sleeping in the bed down the hall. No, his time here had not been wasted.

He reached into the box that sat in the middle of the spare room carpet and pulled out another file. He placed it on the floor in front of him and opened it to a page that looked like all the others. Names that meant nothing. Dates that couldn't have had anything to do with his conception or birth. He rubbed his eyes, beyond tired but also unwilling to give up.

"What are you doing?" He turned to watch Sheryl enter the room. She wasn't wearing anything but his shirt. She'd probably grabbed it from the floor by the bed, just as he'd snagged his jeans as he'd left her there sleeping.

"I couldn't sleep," he said.

"I'll help." She yawned as she took another file from the box and sat on the floor a few feet away with her back against the narrow bed and the file in her lap.

"You have to work in the morning."

She closed the file and placed her hands over the stained manila folder. "I am trying to be nice," she said. "Even though I know the sooner you find what you came here for, the sooner you'll leave. Selfishly, I almost hope you never find it. If I didn't like you so much, I would hide the real documents and stuff these folders with something absolutely worthless, like my own files."

"The constant mention of fleas would probably give you away."

"Yeah, well, that's why I'm no master criminal. I don't think ahead."

She reopened the folder on her lap and began to leaf through the pages. Since she'd helped him organize the pages he was interested in, she knew what to look for. She knew the dates, the names that had popped up so many times, the mention of difficulties with various pregnancies.

Hawk opened his own file and began again. There was only one box left. One unopened box that might contain answers hidden for almost thirty years. There was nothing of interest in this folder.

When he reached into the box for another file, two photos fell from between the other pages. Different in size as well as finish, they slipped away and drifted to the floor. One landed by Hawk's knee, the other close to Sheryl's thigh. They both lifted their photos at the same time.

"My keen detecting skills tell me this is a snapshot of a bunch of geeks celebrating Christmas," Sheryl said.

Hawk studied the photograph that had landed near him. "I have a couple of nerds sitting at their desk looking like someone just surprised the crap out of them by taking this candid photo."

Sheryl offered her photo. "Swap. Yours sounds more interesting than mine."

Hawk handed her the photo of two wide-eyed, bespectacled guys in lab coats and took hers.

Christmas. You could tell by the sloppily arranged garland in the background and the wrapped gifts on the desk. The same nerds from his photo were standing by a bowl of punch, but there were others in this picture, too.

Hawk's eyes were drawn to the woman standing at the far right. His heart stuttered in his chest, and he turned the photo to the side so that it caught the light in a different way. He wanted to be sure what he saw wasn't a trick of the light or the aftereffect of not getting enough sleep. The woman— No, she was more a girl than a woman. She looked so much like Cassie! She could be her twin.

The old woman in the pharmacy hadn't been crazy after all. Finding this woman who looked so much like Cassie…it couldn't be a coincidence.

He very hesitantly touched his fingertip to the photo. He'd wondered for so many years what his biological parents had been like, and why they'd given him and Cassie up…and then he'd stopped wondering because it didn't make any sense to make himself crazy with all the questions he would never know the answers to. In anger, he had sworn to himself and to anyone else who asked that he didn't care.

It was a lie. He knew that now.

With the photo in hand, he moved across the room and sat beside Sheryl. He settled in and stretched his long legs out beside hers.

"I'm here to work, mister," she said when he put his arm around her. "Stop trying to distract me."

He held the photo near her thigh so they could both see it well. "See that woman on the right?"

"The pretty one?"

He nodded. "The pretty one. Sheryl, that's my mother."

She had to practically drag Hawk to bed. He carried the photo with him and placed it on the bedside table before crawling under the covers to lie beside her.

"I wonder if anyone around here knows her," he asked, wrapping his arms around her and holding on nice and tight.

"Maybe. You can show a few of the old-timers the photograph and see if they remember anything."

Hawk settled his body against hers and answered with a hum. After a minute he said, "What if she still lives around here? What if I show someone the picture, and they say, 'Oh, yeah, that's Jane Doe and she lives right around the corner.'"

"Is that what you want?" she whispered.

After a short pause Hawk answered. "I don't know what I want. Answers for Cassie, sure, but beyond that…I honestly don't know."

He held her, but neither of them made a move toward anything more. She almost wished he would make a move.

That he would kiss her or touch her in a way that made her forget. But he didn't, and neither did she. Sex was easy, compared to midnight conversations about matters of the heart.

"The people who adopted you," she asked, "were they good parents?"

"The best," he answered without hesitation.

"That's good." She shifted her body against the mattress and the pillow and Hawk's body until everything was just so.

"What about your family?" Hawk asked. "You've never mentioned them."

She smiled in the dark. No, they had swept past the normal part of their courtship and sailed right into the thick of it. "Mother, father, two brothers and a sister. I'm the youngest."

"Of course you are," Hawk teased. "You were spoiled rotten, weren't you?"

"Of course not." There had been a time, before she'd set herself on a career path, before Michael, that she had been a little spoiled. "We're spread all over the country now. Mom and Dad in Virginia, Patrick in Minnesota, Sean in Colorado, and Lisa in Tennessee."

"Halfway," he said.

"Halfway to what?"

"Tennessee is halfway between Texas and here. Do you ever visit your sister?"

"Not very often. It's tough to get away, especially now."

Hawk asked about Tennessee as if he really thought they'd get together after his time in Wyatt was done. And deep down, in a place she tried to hide, Sheryl wanted that to be so. She wanted it more than anything. But who was she kidding? A long-distance relationship would never work. She had her practice; Hawk had his ranch. They were busy people who barely had a moment to themselves. Neither of them had the time to take days off to pursue a relationship.

Whatever they had would die from neglect once they were separated. And knowing that wasn't a problem for Sheryl. All she and Hawk had was sex, anyway. Nothing more.

Then why were they talking about family in the dark?

"You should get some sleep," she said.

"How can I possibly sleep?"

Sheryl raised herself up and looked down at Hawk. She wanted to make everything right for him. She wanted to make sure he ate well, buy him a few new shirts and see that he got enough rest. She wanted all the things that would make this *more* than sex.

She touched her fingertips to a strand of dark hair that had fallen across Hawk's forehead. "You'll sleep because tomorrow is going to be another busy day, and you can't function without at least a few hours of rest. If you go around town looking like a crazed man who hasn't slept in days, then who in their right mind is going to talk to you about your mother? You can't do anything else tonight. So sleep."

Hawk almost had what he'd come here for—and that meant he'd soon be gone. As much as she wanted more, Sheryl knew deep down that Tennessee would never happen.

Hawk walked along the square, the picture tucked neatly into his shirt pocket.

He hadn't called Cassie last night to share the news. When he'd found the photo, it had been much too late to call. He'd planned to telephone her first thing this morning, but with his fingers on the call button of his cell he'd hesitated. Maybe if he waited a few hours, he could give his sister more than the news that he'd found an old picture of a woman who looked just like her. He could give her a name, maybe even an address.

He'd started the day with high hopes, but so far he hadn't had any luck. Sheryl was at the clinic and would be until noon. If he wasn't there by that time, she'd meet him in the square and help him talk to the local residents. After all, talking to people wasn't his thing. He wasn't any better at talking than he was at dancing.

Sheryl was a big part of this, like it or not. He'd tried to push her away, more than once. But somehow she kept creeping back into his life, this woman he hadn't known a full week.

Baby walked beside him, interested in what was going on around her but almost nonchalant about the proceedings. She stayed close, but at least she wasn't as skittish as she had once been. When he'd first found the wounded pup on the road to town, he'd been angry at the way she'd been abused. Now if he could get his hands on the man who had hurt her, he'd very likely kill him. Baby had the heart of a lion and the disposition of a playful puppy, even though her puppy years were behind her. If not for that man, long ago, she never would've known that there was hate and pain in the world. Hawk did his best to make sure she could forget.

Man's best friend. In his case that was the truth. He was more comfortable with Baby than he'd ever been with any human being. She understood him, and he understood her. Until he'd met Sheryl, that fact had never bothered him. Here he was, falling into a relationship, and he had no idea what to say, what to do, how to handle what came next.

If anything came next.

So far it had been a frustrating morning. He hadn't run into anyone who recognized the woman or anyone else from the old photograph. He'd only asked a few people, those he knew were longtime residents. There were lots of folks from outside the area here today, perusing the selection of homemade wooden toys and dolls and pottery and Christmas ornaments. Where could he find the answers he was looking for?

Baby picked up on Hawk's frustration and nuzzled his leg, offering comfort. Hawk ruffled the fur behind Baby's ears and told her not to worry. He'd do enough worrying for both of them.

Everything about downtown Wyatt looked different today, and it wasn't because the normally quiet square was filled with people and booths and laughter. His mother had lived here. For a short while this morning a small, helplessly optimistic part of Hawk had wondered if maybe she still did. That optimism hadn't lasted long, though.

"Hi, there, young fella." Harold Johnston, Sheryl's client who owned the calico cat, gave Hawk a big smile. The old man sat beside Mildred Harris, Toby's owner, at her booth. Mildred had a collection of crocheted doodads for sale. Doilies, pot holders, store-bought towels with crocheted decorations on the ends and more Christmas ornaments, these in the shape of snowflakes.

Hawk pulled the photo from his pocket and passed it to Harold. "The girl on the right, do you recognize her?"

The old man wrinkled his nose. "She does look a mite familiar, but I can't quite place her."

After the first few inquiries had led him nowhere, Hawk had given up hope that someone would direct him to a house down the street. Whoever his mother was, wherever she was, she no longer resided in Wyatt, North Carolina.

Harold passed the photo to Mildred, who lifted the reading glasses that hung around her neck to get a good look at the photograph. Hawk was prepared for another shake of the head but Mildred gave an interested hum instead.

"I remember her," Mrs. Harris said softly. "Let's see, it was... Oh, goodness. Years ago. She joined the ladies club, but didn't remain a member long. As I recall, her husband didn't approve."

"You remember her?" Hawk repeated slowly, in case he had misunderstood. "Do you know her name?"

Again, Mildred thought for a moment. "Donna... No, that wasn't it. Deanna," she said brightly. "Her name was Deanna Payne." She shook her head slowly, and her voice was not very lively when she said, "Poor girl."

Deanna Payne. Hawk clenched his fists and tried to slow the suddenly quick beating of his heart. His mother had a name. She had been here, and someone remembered her. "Why 'poor girl'?" he asked in a calm, steady voice. "What happened to her?"

Mildred passed the photo across the table. "So much tragedy for such a young thing. Let's see... I'll remember the details better if I start at the beginning, I suppose. While Deanna was still a member of the ladies club she got pregnant, I remember."

Hawk's heart thudded. "Twenty-eight, twenty-nine years ago?"

"No," the old woman mused. "Annette Mailer was president of the ladies club when Deanna joined and then left us, and Annette passed away thirty years ago, so it had to be maybe thirty-two years ago. I remember the young woman was so excited about her pregnancy. I did think she'd be a good mother. It was so sad...." Mildred's voice trailed off as her attention was diverted. She lifted her hand and waved to a friend across the square. "Oh, there's Mary Tinker. Last I heard she was sick in bed. She looks very well, all things considered."

Hawk wanted to grab the old woman and make her finish her agonizingly slow tale. He purposely moved between her and the woman across the square. "What was so sad?"

Mildred looked up at Hawk. In the sunshine, every line on her face was starkly revealed. Her lips were thin, her color not so good. But her eyes had a youthful gleam, even as she relived past events that were, in her own words, sad.

"Shortly after Deanna quit the club, she and her husband moved out of town." Mildred pursed her lips. "I never liked Benedict Payne. He was much too controlling and rather sour. Even when he smiled, you would get the feeling that he wasn't smiling on the inside but was putting on a show. There was something about him I just didn't like. And I wasn't alone. Several of the ladies commented that he was, well, odd. Deanna was such a sweet, pretty young girl, I couldn't see— Poor girl."

Again with the "poor girl." "What happened to her?" Hawk snapped.

Mildred's eyes widened slightly, and she almost backed away from him, either offended or frightened, or both. "The Paynes moved into an old farmhouse closer to Henrietta than Wyatt, and I didn't see her after that. I asked about the baby, a few months after they moved, but Dr. Payne said his wife had lost the child and was quite distraught. I asked if I and a few of the other ladies could pay her a visit, but he said the loss of her baby had been very hard on Deanna, and she was no longer mentally stable. He told me he'd hired a full-time nurse to care for her and was afraid he might have to put her in a facility." She whispered the last two words, as if they were poison.

"Dr. Payne," Hawk said. "Her husband was a doctor?"

"Well, not a *real* doctor," Mildred answered. "He worked at a clinic or some such."

"A fertility clinic?" Agnes Payne. That name had come up time and again. Was Benedict Payne a relative? Likely.

"Yes. It closed up after…"

"After what?" Hawk asked when Mildred stumbled.

A soft breeze ruffled Mildred's iron curls. But not much. They had been teased and sprayed into submission. "Well, I don't know all the details, but a few years after they moved away from Wyatt that nasty Dr. Payne killed his wife." She shook her head. "I always knew he was no good."

Hawk's heart nearly stopped. His knees went weak. "Deanna Payne was murdered?"

"Yes."

"I remember that now," Harold said with a shake of one bony finger. "The clinic where the doctor had been working closed up within a matter of days. One day they were operating as usual, the next they were just gone. Had the whole town buzzing for weeks."

"And Payne?" Hawk asked.

"Disappeared," Mildred answered. "I wonder if they ever caught him. I certainly hope so. There wasn't much at all in the newspaper, just a short bit on one of the back pages, and I saw nothing on the television news. Of course, in those days we didn't have so much news on the television, not like we have now. Maybe it was better when we didn't know so much, but I would like to know if they ever caught that awful man."

Hawk pushed down the lump in his throat. It shouldn't hurt. He'd never known the woman who'd given him birth. He'd never expected to know her. But the news that she'd been murdered sent a chill down his spine and made him physically ill.

"Why are you digging up all this old history?" Harold asked. "Who's the woman in that picture to you?"

Hawk hesitated. He'd never been one for spilling his guts, and he wasn't going to start now. "No one. I found the picture and she looks familiar. That's all."

"Well, you got a helluva lot of information," the old man said. "Least you can do is buy something."

"Now, Harold." Mildred slapped her friend's arm lightly. "Don't push the boy into buying something he doesn't want."

Hawk pointed to the largest item on the small table. "What's that?"

"A toaster cozy," Mildred said brightly. "I have them in yellow, green and blue."

"I'll take a yellow one."

She smiled as she selected a yellow toaster cozy, whatever the hell that was, and placed it in a crumpled, hand-me-down plastic bag from the only grocery store in Wyatt.

"The farmhouse where the Paynes lived," Hawk said gruffly as he returned the photo to his pocket and reached for cash to pay for the crocheted item. "Can you tell me how to get there?"

They were almost an hour away from Wyatt, and Hawk hadn't said a word since he'd picked her up at the clinic. She'd asked a few questions when she'd first stepped into the passenger seat and as they'd driven away from town, but he'd brushed them off. For the past forty minutes or so she'd been as quiet as he.

Even Baby, stretched out in the back seat, was restless but silent.

They truly were in the middle of nowhere. This winding two-lane road twisted past fields and deserted barns and one old store that probably hadn't seen a customer in at least twenty years.

Finally Hawk slowed the truck and turned onto a dirt road. At the end of the drive sat a two-story house that had once been white but was now mostly gray, thanks to the peeling paint that revealed weathered boards beneath. The roof was falling in on one side, and the porch overhang looked as if it could crash to the ground at any moment. As Hawk drove slowly closer, Sheryl saw other signs of disrepair. Broken windows, rotting wood, weeds growing through the slats of wood around the sagging porch. Hawk stopped the truck a good distance from the house. He stared at it for a long moment. If she didn't know better, she'd think he had forgotten she was with him.

"Hawk?" she said softly. "Why are we here?"

He rested his forearm on the steering wheel and pointed to the house. "My mother used to live in that house."

"Really?" She smiled and laid a hand on his arm. She was surprised when he shook her off.

"Yeah, really. She was murdered here, too. By my father."

It was a horrible truth to find; a sad ending to the story of his beginnings. Sheryl wanted to comfort Hawk, but she knew he didn't want to be touched. It was clear, by the way he'd shaken her off and by the hard, tense expression on his face, that he didn't want her comfort.

But he did want her here with him. If he didn't, he wouldn't have come by the clinic to pick her up at twelve on the nose. That had to mean something.

"I'm sorry." She scooted closer to him, even though his entire body stiffened when she touched his arm. "I'm so sorry you didn't find what you wanted."

He looked down at her, and he didn't shake her off again. There was such deep pain in his dark eyes, she wanted to throttle whoever had told him the truth!

"I never should've come here," he said, almost beneath his breath. "I never should've started poking around in the past."

"You were thinking of your sister." Sheryl wanted to lay her hand on his cheek, but she knew he'd never accept that touch. Not now, when he was so angry and confused. It was as if he'd drawn away from her, as if they'd never touched or talked or laughed before. "There's nothing wrong with what you've done. You tried, Hawk. You did everything you could."

"Yeah," he said sourly. "And what did it get me?"

Me, Sheryl wanted to say. It got you me.

"We're not finished with the files," she said instead. "There's still one unopened box, and we can go through the other documents again looking for a mention of your mother's name. If that doesn't take us anywhere we'll check old newspapers at the library and maybe the Henrietta courthouse." She realized that Hawk was barely listening.

"Why did Payne move her way out here?" he asked softly. "It would make for a long drive to town, since apparently he was still working at the clinic. Before Cassie and I were born there was another pregnancy. She lost the baby, and it made her crazy. More good news." He ran a hand through his hair, as if he were nervous. Was Hawk Donovan ever nervous? "She had a full-time nurse, and Payne was talking about putting her in a facility...but something must've happened, because Cassie and I were born, and then he killed her.

"But if she had so many problems, why did he stick her

way out here, so far away from everything and everyone?" Anger replaced his agitation. "It doesn't make sense. None of it makes sense."

"Are you sure she's your mother? Just because there's a resemblance—"

"I'm sure," Hawk said gruffly. "I wish I wasn't. It would make this news a whole lot easier if I could make myself believe Deanna Payne wasn't my mother. There's not just a *resemblance*. The woman in that picture could be Cassie. It all fits. The address, the timing, the adoption. It all fits," he said again.

Sheryl rested her head on Hawk's arm and looked at the house at the end of the dirt drive. She wished she could make everything right for him. She wished she could offer him the answers he wanted on a silver platter…give him one final gift before he left town.

"Are we going inside?" she asked.

Hawk put the truck into gear and drove slowly closer. "Why not?"

Chapter 10

Hawk had never imagined that he and Cassie had been put up for adoption for such a sordid reason. In his youth, when he'd allowed himself to wonder about such things, he'd reached for the less painful possibilities. There were financial problems. Their mother had been unmarried and wanted a better life for her kids. Hell, he'd even imagined that maybe she just didn't want children.

He'd always known there was a possibility that his mother was dead, but he had never come close to imagining that she'd been murdered by his father.

The house where she'd died was as neglected on the inside as it was on the outside. There were spiderwebs everywhere, years of water damage on the ceiling and the outer walls, and signs that rodents often nested here. And he hadn't yet left the room he'd entered through the front door—what had once been the living room, he imagined.

Oddly enough, a few pieces of furniture remained. They were old, damaged pieces that no one would want, but they gave the room an odd look, as if it might've been lived in just yesterday. A landscape print, the glass cracked from one corner to the other, hung crookedly on one wall. A side table with three legs was positioned precariously beneath it.

Sheryl reached out and took his hand, her fingers gentle and firm and reassuring. For a moment he let her hold on, and then he shook her loose. She didn't need to get any closer to him than she already had. He was a freak of nature, a damn animal psychic, and on top of all that his mother had been loony and his father was a murderer. Nice genetic icing on top of the other so-called gifts he'd been given.

"I'm sure it was much nicer when your mother lived here," Sheryl said, a false note of confidence in her voice.

"I imagine she chased the rats and the spiders out now and then," he said gruffly.

"She lived here a long time ago, before time and neglect took their toll. I'm sure it was a very pleasant home." Sheryl's eyes swept the room. "There was probably a pretty couch over there by the fireplace, and knickknacks on the mantel, and fresh flowers here and there."

Hawk glared down at the woman who stood beside him. "Don't," he said softly.

"Don't what?" she asked, turning sparkling blue eyes up to him. Great. He really did not need to know that she was holding back tears.

"Don't try to make me feel better."

"I thought maybe that's why I was here," she whispered.

Why had he gone by the clinic to fetch her before riding out to this farmhouse? She couldn't help, she couldn't make him feel better about the reality he'd uncovered. No one could. The truth of the matter was that in a moment of weakness he'd wanted her beside him when he walked into this house.

Weakness… Something he couldn't afford now or ever.

He walked to the center of the living room, looking into every corner as if he expected to remember something. Anything. He tried to see what Sheryl had seen here. He tried to imagine what this place had been like twenty-eight years ago. But his imagination was not that potent. All he saw was decay and neglect. The floor beneath his feet creaked as if it could give way at any moment. Baby hung back, standing beside Sheryl and watching him warily, as if she expected an explosion at any moment.

"I don't know why I even came here," he said.

"I do," Sheryl said softly.

"Please tell me."

She ignored his sarcasm. "In a very basic way, this is where you come from, Hawk. This was once your home. Isn't that what you wanted to find, maybe even as much as you want to find an answer for your sister? You have roots here."

"Rotten roots," he grumbled. More rotten than he had ever imagined.

"It doesn't matter," Sheryl whispered.

He looked her in the eye, challenging her because she was here and he could. "How can you say that?"

"You haven't changed." Again her eyes sparkled as if she was pushing back tears. "You're still the same man. The same good, decent, fine man you were yesterday before you knew—"

He took a long step toward her, his boot heel thudding

on rotting wooden floors. "Don't go tossing around words like *decent* and *good.* You don't know me, Doc. You're a pretty girl, and you were convenient. I hadn't been laid in a couple of months. You hadn't been laid in a couple of years. We rocked each other's world in bed and a couple other places a few times, but that doesn't mean you *know* me. Maybe you convinced yourself that I'm *decent* and *good* because you needed a reason to justify the sex, but the truth of the matter is you know nothing about the man I am."

He waited for her to run, but she didn't. He waited for her to get angry, but she didn't.

"I am your friend, Hawk." Sheryl reached out to touch his face gently.

He couldn't afford to believe that. Not now. *Lover* was easier than *friend.* It came with less demands, less expectations. "No, you're not. You're just a body. A tight, hard, willing body."

Still she didn't run. "Do you push everyone away when they get too close, or just me?"

"What makes you think you're close?" Hawk knew he was near to losing control when Baby cowered, as if she were hiding. Hiding from him.

Go.

Baby jumped up and gratefully ran through the open front door.

"Where's she going?" Sheryl asked, alarmed at seeing Baby move so quickly and so suddenly.

"To chase some squirrels," Hawk said, running his fingers through his hair and reaching for the control that always, *always* ruled his life. Who was he kidding? He'd lost control the moment he'd walked into Sheryl's clinic and seen her standing there.

"How do you know that?"

"I just know."

She didn't question that answer, not this time, but reached out and laid her hand on his chest. "Hawk—"

"If you want to help, if you really want to make me feel better, take off your clothes."

Sheryl glanced around the room, and from the way her eyes widened he knew she saw this awful place for what it was, not what it might've been at one time. "Here?"

"That's what I thought," he growled. "Not such a pretty place now, is it?"

Sheryl hesitated for a moment, then tilted her head back to look him boldly in the eye. For a little thing she had guts. She had heart. Nothing scared her, not even him.

She began to unbutton her blouse. Slowly, without trembling fingers or those tears in her eyes, she unfastened the tiny buttons from neckline to hem of her plain beige blouse. With a shrug of her shoulders she sent the blouse to the floor. She reached behind to unhook the satiny white bra that contained her breasts, and it, too, fell to the floor. Each move was elegant and seductive, and made without haste or fear or anger, even though he had done his best to take his rage out on her.

Hawk didn't budge. He watched. He became mesmerized by the way Sheryl moved as she stripped. Why didn't she run? Why didn't she tell him he was a son of a bitch and take off?

Sheryl unsnapped and unzipped her trousers while she kicked off her shoes. Moving slowly, but without a hint of uncertainty, she pushed the trousers down and stepped out of them. Moments after he'd angrily ordered her to take off her clothes, she stood before him completely, gloriously naked.

How could he look at her and still be angry? How could

he keep his mind in the past, when the present was right here before him, and it was so damned good?

"If sex is all we have," she said, stepping to him and lifting her arms to wrap them around his neck, "then we might as well make the best of it." She rose up on her toes and kissed him, lips parted and tongue teasing. Her bare body rested against him as if it belonged there.

Sheryl was pale and soft, fragile and strong. One kiss, and he couldn't think of anything but losing himself in her.

Hawk closed his eyes and pushed everything but Sheryl out of his mind. He wanted to forget the ugliness he'd found here, and she gave him that. She took him to another place. He touched her while they kissed, his hands gentler than his mouth as they brushed over silky flesh. Her response was genuine and immediate.

The way her body pressed against him, the way her tongue moved and her lips tasted…it was sweet and harsh and beautiful, and dammit he needed her *now.*

His blood boiled; his mind raged. His body responded to hers until there was nothing but the urgent and relentless need to be inside her. He freed himself, lifted Sheryl off her feet and filled her in one long, hard thrust.

She gasped and shuddered and tossed her head back. Holding on tight with her arms and her legs, she was wrapped around him in more ways than one. When her body and her mind had adjusted to the sudden joining, when she found her breath again, she began to ride him. Slowly. Eyes closed, heart racing, skin like fire, she swayed and rocked and ground against him until the room spun and faded and there was nothing but the feel of their bodies coming together.

Hawk didn't move. He stood there, feet planted, and held Sheryl in his arms while she made love to him.

They had always had heat, they had always had passion,

but this…this was primitive. It went beyond the body, beyond the flesh. There was more here than he could fathom. There was comfort, pleasure, spirit.

She lowered herself and then rose up again, and suddenly Hawk felt the blood in Sheryl's veins as if it was his own. Her heartbeat was his, the breath in her lungs was his. He was inside her in more ways than he had known possible, and he experienced the depths of her pleasure and her need and her love.

Love. She'd tried to hide it, not only from him but from herself. She didn't want love any more than he did, but it had found her, anyway. It filled her heart and her mind and her dreams; it made her reach for him when he tried to push her away.

It brought her here, to this place and this time.

She tried to be so tough, so independent, but deep in her heart she wanted this as much as he did. To love and to be loved. To have someone to catch her when she fell. To do the catching when the time came to return the favor. Most of all, she wanted not to be alone.

When Sheryl came, he felt it shuddering all through the length of his body. He came with her, pumping inside her as the final spasms of her orgasm squeezed and caressed him. The physical wiped away everything else for a moment. He didn't remember why he was here; he didn't see or feel or remember anything but Sheryl. She moaned softly and moved one last time.

And then they were still again, spent and sweating. Feeling out of time and out of place. Her heart beat against his, her breath felt warm and real and right upon his neck. Her arms held him tight, and he held her the same way. Close. Closer than any other had ever been. He didn't want to let her go. Ever.

Hawk slowly lowered Sheryl to the floor, uncertain as to what had just happened.

No, he knew what had happened, but it was impossible. He didn't connect with people. Ever.

Love.

Sheryl leaned against him and sighed, one arm drifting around his waist. He could still feel her heart thudding against her chest. Pounding hard, it raced as she fought to catch her breath.

Hawk took her by the shoulders and gently forced her away from him. She was so beautiful, so perfect, especially here, surrounded on all sides by decay and ugliness.

His decay and ugliness.

"Get dressed," he said as he swept past her, headed for the door and zipped up his pants. "We're getting the hell out of here."

This had not been an afternoon filled with wise decisions, and that was possibly the understatement of her life. She'd had unprotected sex with a man who now refused to talk to her, a man she liked more than she should, a man who was determined to push her away. For good this time.

And there was nothing she could do. She wouldn't beg him to stay. She would never plead with any man for anything. Not even Hawk. Had she really been so stupid as to think sex would take away his pain?

She stood on her front porch and watched while he tossed the last unopened box of his damned files into the back of his truck. Most of the documents from the fertility clinic were still stored in the spare bedroom, but he'd taken a few others, along with the final box.

Hawk was leaving, and she would never see him again. Never. He'd mentioned a trip to Texas last night, but now there was nothing. No invitation, not even a hint that there might be more for them. Just cold, detached silence.

"Good luck," she said as he closed the tailgate.

His response was a grunt of some kind. Of course, she had never wanted or expected glib, meaningless conversation from Hawk Donovan. He opened the door to the truck, and Sheryl held her breath. This was it—the goodbye she'd been dreading since the first kiss. But Hawk didn't leave. He reached into the back seat and came back toward her with a crumpled plastic bag grasped in his hand.

"I bought this for you," he said hoarsely, tossing the bag to her.

She caught it easily and reached inside to discover… some yarn thing. "Thank you. What is it?"

"A toaster cozy, whatever the hell that is."

"Oh." She dropped it back in the bag. "Thanks."

He turned away and walked toward the truck, and Baby followed, sparing only a quick glance back to the new friends he was leaving behind. The kiddies were all sitting on the porch at Sheryl's feet. All but Bruce, who had been relegated to his cage after chasing Laverne all over the house and scaring poor Bogie into a corner.

"Hawk?" Sheryl called as he reached the truck and opened the passenger door for Baby.

He looked back at her but remained silent. This was the man who'd walked into her clinic days ago. Dark. Determined. Different in a way she could not explain. He was walking away from her, and he would never look back. A few months, maybe even a few weeks from now, he'd probably have to struggle to remember her name. How could he throw away everything they'd discovered?

No matter how she tried, she couldn't be angry with him.

"I hope you find what you're looking for."

He didn't say a word but slammed the passenger door and rounded the truck.

Sheryl didn't stand on the front porch to watch Hawk leave, but herded the animals into the house and closed the door with a loud, final-sounding thud. She stood there for a moment, though, and listened as the engine fired and the truck pulled away.

As she walked past the living room, toaster cover in hand, Bruce squawked. "He hurts."

There had been a time when she would have been completely taken aback by such an astute observation from a bird. But not today. Maybe not ever again.

"I know," she replied.

Benedict sat in a folding chair outside the door to his motor home. His positioning had two purposes: to enjoy the September evening air and to make sure Janet was not disturbed.

"This Dr. Eldanis, she's a veterinarian," Ricky Driggs said, his British accent horribly out of place. And the way he said *veterinarian* got on Benedict's last nerve. The Englishman always insisted on pronouncing each and every letter of a word.

"Why would a vet be interested in Agnes and Oliver's work?" Benedict snapped. "It makes no sense."

Ricky was not yet thirty, and he took care with his appearance. He was fond of blue jeans and T-shirts, but the jeans were always pressed and the shirts were never faded or wrinkled. His blond hair was always perfectly groomed, and some women might find him attractive, if they didn't mind the pale skin and the longish nose. "Her clinic is located where your sister and her partner once operated. Perhaps she discovered something."

A chill ran down Benedict's spine. Could his late sister have left something of importance behind? Apparently she hadn't been the smart one after all. "Search the clinic first. I know Agnes used to store old files down in the basement. I suppose you could start there."

"I thought of that myself," Ricky said as if he had half a brain. "I could have gone in last night, before you arrived, but I decided to wait. Since the clinic is closed tomorrow, the break-in won't be discovered until Monday."

"If you find nothing there, you'll have to pay the vet a visit at her home," Benedict said in a lowered voice. There was no one else around to overhear the conversation. There were other RVs in the park, most of them in the more desirable positions near the river. He had chosen this spot because it was so far away from the others. As they'd arrived, the other campers had eyed his large motor home with interest, of course, but no one came near. Benedict made it clear that he and his "wife" were looking for solitude, and the campers gave it to them.

"I know where she lives," Ricky said proudly. "I even got a look at her this morning. Quite a looker, for a veterinarian. I was rather expecting an older woman with gray hair and combat boots, but Dr. Eldanis is quite dishy. She won't be a problem, I promise you that." Ricky gave Benedict a telling wink. "Before I'm done with her she'll tell me everything."

"I want to know why she's been poking around where she doesn't belong."

"Don't you worry, boss. I can make her talk."

Since Ricky continued to comment on how attractive the vet was, it was clear what methods he'd call upon when he finally confronted the woman. Benedict didn't care what method he used, as long as he didn't raise an unnecessary stink. "Be discreet if you can," Benedict said with great patience. "I don't care how you get the information I want, but remember, there's no need to draw attention to ourselves."

He didn't care about Ricky, but if the man led authorities here…well, that was another matter.

"Maybe Janet can whip up a batch of her special drug and we can have a go at the Eldanis woman that way," Ricky suggested.

"I don't think that's wise, not until we've established without question why Eldanis is nosing around. If there's a simple explanation for the Internet search, we'll walk away as quietly as possible." He looked the younger man in the eye. "Are you capable of walking away without creating a scene, Driggs?"

"Just a suggestion," Ricky said, not at all pleased with the prospect of walking away quietly. "It might be a nice little experiment, and I wouldn't mind having a woman around who'd do anything I asked in order to get her next dose." Again, he winked.

The man was a cretin.

"I'll think about it," Benedict replied, his tone indicating that the meeting was over.

When Ricky had finally gone, Benedict closed his eyes and took a deep breath of the fresh air. In an odd sort of way he had liked it here all those years ago. He had enjoyed being close to the ocean, but not too close. If the wind was just right you could smell the sea. He'd liked the thick stands of trees and the solitude and the people. Some of them, anyway.

It did no good to look back. Perhaps if he hadn't indulged in a small social life while he'd lived in Wyatt all those years ago, he might not have to worry that if he went to town someone might recognize his face. He hadn't changed all that much, he thought with a squaring of his shoulders. He kept himself fit, and he still had all his hair, even if it had turned silver a few years back. While he had a few distinguished lines on his face, and his goatee was as silver as the hair on his head, he was still an attractive man.

If he could be absolutely positive that no one in town would recognize him, he'd pay the vet a visit on his own. But it was best to remain here, a few miles away from town. Just in case.

Benedict walked into the trailer and closed the door firmly behind him. The lock was a sturdy one; he couldn't afford to have a less-than-state-of-the-art security system on this vehicle. From this vantage point, the interior of the RV looked perfectly ordinary. There was a small kitchen, a seating area and table, a bed and a bathroom.

Beyond the door at the rear of the RV, the vehicle was unique.

He opened that door and found Janet hard at work in her mobile lab, her head bent over her task. She was so intently focused on her work she did not even know he had arrived.

When Janet took off her glasses and let her hair down, she wasn't a bad-looking woman. She didn't often take off her glasses or do anything with her dark hair, which was showing a few strands of gray these days. She wouldn't worry about the gray, like so many women her age would. Dr. Janet Sheridan's mind was most definitely occupied with more important matters.

"How's it coming?" he asked.

Her head snapped up. With her hair in that little bun and her glasses slipping down her nose, she looked a little bit older than forty-nine. Not that he cared.

"What?" she asked, her voice thick as if she were in a daze.

"How's it coming?" he asked again.

She frowned. "Slowly."

"We can't have our subjects dying on us before we're finished with them, Janet. Fix it."

"They don't die all the time," she argued. "And I am trying to fix it. I've tweaked the formula here and there. In a couple of days I'll be ready to test it again."

He could not afford to risk the lives of those he was searching for. Not yet, at least. Not until he had the answers he sought. "Guinea pig or genuine target?" he asked.

"Guinea pig," she answered.

"How about Ricky?" The Englishman had been getting on Benedict's nerves of late, thinking himself more important than he would ever be. Ricky Driggs was, and always would be, a lackey. Worse, he was getting sloppy, and Benedict could not abide carelessness in his employees.

Janet nodded absently and then returned to her work. Benedict remained in the doorway, watching.

It was possible that he had found the perfect woman in Dr. Janet Sheridan. She was quite eager in bed, and she didn't ask for much in the way of attention outside their encounters in the bedroom. Nine years younger than he, she was his lover and his most trusted employee. They had sex; they did not make love. And like so many other gullible women might've done, she never fooled herself into thinking otherwise.

Janet was surprisingly fit, lifting weights in her spare time and eating healthily. Perhaps she wasn't pretty in a conventional sense, but she had a body many younger women would kill for.

Beyond the bedroom she was an absolutely brilliant

scientist. Janet Sheridan never let scruples get in the way of her ambition.

Benedict told her, "I'll get a strand of Ricky's hair next time I see him, so you can extract his DNA for the formation of the drug."

"That won't be necessary," she said in an offhand manner. "I have a sample of his DNA stored here in the lab."

Benedict smiled. "You do?"

"I thought it wise, in case such a circumstance should arise."

He wouldn't be sorry to see Ricky on the wrong end of Janet's needle. The sometimes-useful hoodlum would either end up addicted to a powerful drug designed specifically for him, or dead.

Benedict had a feeling Ricky was going to end up dead, one way or another. Janet would end up dead herself one of these days. She knew too much, and that made her a potential threat.

For all he knew, she had a sample of *his* DNA stored in this lab of hers.

But Janet was safe for now. He needed her. He needed her genius and her cold detachment and her willingness to do anything to succeed.

Chapter 11

After working and living at Sheryl's house for the past few days, Hawk found the hotel room seemed too small. Even Baby was unhappy with the new arrangements. She missed her new friends; she missed Sheryl. Baby curled up on the bed and moped as if Hawk had taken away her favorite toy.

"We'll be home before you know it," he said as he squinted to read a scribbled notation in the margins of some woman's medical files.

Baby whined, but just a little.

The Wyatt Hotel had large guest rooms, compared to more modern hotels. Of course everything in the room—the bed, the television, the table and chairs, and the love seat—were all antiques. They weren't show-off antiques, they were just old. The love seat, which was covered in a pattern of faded roses, had a musty smell that kept Hawk in one of the ladder-back chairs by the small walnut table. His eyes were often drawn to the window, which looked down on a quiet, narrow side street. Darkness had fallen a while back.

This had surely been the longest day of his life.

When the walls started to close in on Hawk, he left his work and Baby behind and headed for the restaurant downstairs.

The hotel was an old, five-story brick building a block from the town square. It had once been a fine hotel, though why anyone would build a fine hotel in Wyatt was beyond Hawk. In any case, it hadn't come anywhere close to fine in many years. Like his room, the hallway showed the place's age. The carpet was faded; the tables sporting silk flowers were dented and scuffed.

Like everything else in this place, the elevator was old and creaky. Hawk took the stairs from his third-floor room and came out of the stairwell into the lobby, just a few steps away from the hotel restaurant.

Bethany, or so her name tag implied, gave him a grin as he approached. The restaurant was small, and she served as both hostess and one of two waitresses. She'd been working last Tuesday, when Hawk had brought Sheryl here for supper, but she hadn't smiled quite so widely then.

"Hi, there," she said, that bright smile staying in place. "Table for one?"

"Yeah."

"I'll put you over here in my station," Bethany said, casting a glance back as she led the way with a swing of her hips. "I'll take good care of you tonight. Promise."

Hawk might not socialize much, and he might not be able to read people the way he did animals, but he was smart enough to know when a woman was flirting with him.

He sat in the booth where Bethany deposited the menu. "What can I get you to drink?"

"Beer."

"Sure thing. You look at the menu and I'll be right back." Bethany scampered off in a hurry, but she did cast him another of those come-hither grins, and there was a suggestive wiggle in her hips.

If everything he'd said to Sheryl this afternoon was true, then he could prove it here and now. Bethany was willing, she was pretty. While she didn't have Sheryl's compact, strong body, she had curves in all the right places and she wasn't at all hard to look at.

If he said the word she'd be in his room in a flash.

But he didn't want Bethany. He couldn't imagine inviting her back to his room.

"Here you go." She placed a cold bottle of beer before him. "Have you decided?"

He hadn't even opened the menu. "Cheeseburger and fries. Make that two cheeseburgers." Maybe a burger would make Baby feel better.

Bethany wrote his order down slowly, her hip cocked. Her eyes flickered to him too often, and she licked her lips more than once.

"The burgers here are pretty big. Sure you can handle two?"

"One of them's not for me."

She licked her lips again, and this time she left the tip of her tongue waiting there at a corner of her mouth just a little bit too long before she said, "Hey, where's that woman you were with the other day? The vet."

"Home, I guess."

"I thought maybe you two were…" She waggled the fingers of one hand suggestively.

"No."

Bethany nodded and breathed deeply, all but thrusting her breasts in his direction. "She's kinda the brainy type, and you don't look to me like the kinda man who goes for that sort, you know? Brainy types just aren't a whole lot of fun. I know, because I dated a smart guy once, and he just wanted to talk all the time." She rolled her eyes. "Can you imagine? I can definitely see where hanging out with a brainy woman might get on a *real* man's nerves after a while."

"Actually," Hawk said tersely, "it's the talkative type that gets on my nerves."

Bethany wasn't completely stupid. Her grin finally faded.

"Make my order to go. I'll take it up to my room."

"Whatever," Bethany said as she slapped his check on the table and walked away. There was less swing in her hips this time.

It was official. Sheryl Eldanis had ruined him. In the past, Bethany would have been exactly his type. Not too bright, willing to get busy for the night without demands for tomorrow. All she wanted was someone to make her feel good for a while, and he could do that. There wouldn't be any talk about the past or the future. Once they got past a certain point, there wouldn't be any talk at all. Hawk had known his share of women like that. The world was full of Bethanys.

Not too many Sheryls around, though. Not that it mattered.

He could leave town tonight, taking the last of the files with him. It's not like he was going to sleep. He had what he'd come here for—the fertility clinic files and a name for his birth mother—and he wasn't going to find anything else.

But he wanted one last look at the house where his mother had died. No, where she'd been murdered. Not tonight, in the dark, but tomorrow, by the light of day. When that was done, he'd be gone.

She could go out for the evening, showing Hawk and herself that she didn't care that he'd dumped her. She was too old to get her feelings hurt because a guy she had always known was going to leave had actually left. There was no dance tonight, but the festivities were not yet over. What was scheduled for tonight? A speech by the mayor. An announcement of who won the pie and the pickle contests.

Nah, she'd rather stay home with her kiddies and her misery.

Sheryl made dinner, ate too quickly, cleaned up the kitchen and did some laundry. She even placed the cozy over her toaster, even though she didn't much like it. It was much too froufrou for her. She didn't do froufrou, and Hawk should've known that.

At least the color was right.

Laverne was restless tonight. So were the other animals. Instead of settling in as they usually did, all three of the cats and both dogs paced restlessly. Bruce cussed up a blue streak, and then settled into an unusual silence that seemed very much like a pout. They missed Baby. They missed Hawk.

So did she.

Sheryl changed into her flannel sleep pants and a cotton T-shirt that had shrunk in the dryer, and soon found herself in the spare bedroom. There should be something here to help Hawk with his search. Something that wouldn't hurt him so much.

He hadn't found anything in these nasty old boxes other than that one photograph. Odds were she wouldn't, either.

But she looked anyway. She leafed through discarded files looking for the name Deanna Payne. She wished so deeply for something, anything, that would heal Hawk's pain a little. It was a frustrating search; she found nothing at all.

Sheryl finally had to give up on her search of the documents. No wonder Hawk was so frustrated! Searching through the stupid files was like swimming through molasses. She wasn't getting anywhere.

It was past her normal bedtime, but Sheryl knew she wouldn't get a wink of sleep if she went to bed now. So she sat down in front of her computer, signed on and went to her favorite search engine. She hesitated a moment, then typed in Deanna Payne.

He hadn't given the old farmhouse a thorough search this afternoon. It was damned hard to follow someone on a deserted road and not get caught, and when the two he'd been tailing had left the house, Anthony had been more interested in following them than poking around an obviously deserted old house.

Anthony stepped through the broken front door of the house in question, the flashlight in his hand casting a bright light across the room. Obviously, the place had been deserted for a long time.

Goose bumps rose up on his arms as he stepped deeper into the house. His stomach knotted, and he wasn't sure why. It wasn't as though this was the first place he'd sneaked into in the dead of night. He took a few more stealthy steps, and the boards beneath his feet creaked. Rodents scurried. No one had lived here for a very long time.

There was something familiar about this place, but it was as if everything had shrunk. The walls were too close, the ceiling hung too low. The few pieces of furniture that had been left behind were too small.

His stomach lurched inexplicably as he passed a less than structurally sound flight of stairs and entered the hallway off the main room. The walls threatened to close in on him, but he continued to move forward. Why? What drew him in this direction, and why did the hallway feel so damned tight and narrow?

He stopped in the doorway to what had once been a bedroom, and his heart crept into his throat. Images he didn't want or need flashed into his mind, almost making him step back away from the small room. The past didn't creep up on Anthony; it bombarded him with a thousand images at once, making him dizzy and sick to his stomach.

The bedroom had been much nicer then. It had been a pretty place, and the bed had been soft, a place to cuddle with his sisters and his mother when the storms came or early in the morning when it was still dark outside. He had loved that bed….

His head snapped around and he saw it. Door standing open, insides dark as an airless cavern.

A closet. *The* closet. They'd hidden there. They'd cowered and cried…

He turned and fled the room, but it was too late. He remembered. He remembered everything. She'd told them to hide in the closet, and they had. But they could hear the screams, and those screams had made Anthony creep out of the closet toward the living room. Watched his father wrap his hands around his mother's throat. The bastard had killed her. He'd choked her until she didn't have any breath left. He'd taken her from them.

Anthony stopped in the main room. He was back in the present, but the past remained with him. His mother had tried to make this room pretty and warm and safe, like the bed where she had cuddled her children and laughed.

She had died here.

His father had killed her.

Everything that had been happening to his family suddenly began to make sense, in a clear and sickening way. His father was the man who had become a danger to them all.

Anthony ran again, this time escaping into the night.

"You're sure there was nothing in the building?" Benedict snapped.

"Positive." Ricky smoothed back an imaginary stray strand of his short blond hair. "I tore the dishy veterinarian's clinic apart, boss. I even took a sledgehammer to the walls to make sure there was nothing hidden thereabouts."

So much for keeping a low profile.

Ricky was obviously annoyed at being summoned so early on a Sunday morning. As far as Benedict was concerned, that was yet another sign that Driggs's usefulness was coming to an end. His employees came when he called, without question, even if the sun had not yet risen. If they felt annoyance, they did not dare to show it.

"And the woman?" he asked. "You spoke to her?"

"Well, no. You see, there's this fellow," Ricky said. "He's rather a big fellow and he's always hanging about. I thought perhaps I'd wait a few days and see if he'll go away."

Benedict sighed. "A big fellow."

"Yes. Apparently he's shacking up with the veterinarian, and he often fetches her from work. But he has Texas plates on his truck, so I believe he's just visiting. I imagine he'll be out of the way soon, and I really would prefer my time with Dr. Eldanis to be uninterrupted."

Benedict wondered if Ricky would feel the same way if the vet was seeing a *small* fellow.

There was nothing of note in the clinic itself. The most likely scenario was that Eldanis had run across a tidbit of useless information and her curiosity had gotten the best of her. That would explain away the Internet search. Blasted curiosity.

He wondered if the vet had heard the old saying about curiosity killing the cat.

Benedict allowed his anger to fade away when Janet exited the lab at the rear of the RV. Ricky's efforts had proved to be less than satisfactory, and Benedict was annoyed that he didn't have the answers he wanted. But there were more interesting concerns for today.

Janet was careful to close the door behind her—and to cleverly disguise the syringe in her hand by keeping it palmed and low. Ricky reacted to her entrance in a subtle but telling way. He smiled and straightened his spine. He got the same odd sparkle in his eye as when he spoke about the pretty vet and his plans for her, even though Janet was old enough to be his mother. Apparently the boob actually liked Janet.

That wasn't likely to last.

"Dr. Sheridan," Ricky said. "How are you this morning?"

"Very well," she said calmly.

"You've been hard at work the past couple of days."

"Yes, I have," she answered. "As a matter of fact, I have something to show you. Please have a seat." With her free hand, Janet gestured to the chair at Ricky's right. He obediently moved there and sat. The man looked like a puppy, all eager and innocent. Driggs had been eager on occasion, but innocent? Never.

Ricky sat there, his hands in his lap, while Janet approached. He didn't know what was coming until the needle was thrust into his neck and the woman he admired depressed the plunger with her thumb.

The reaction was immediate and severe. Ricky's body stiffened, his eyes rolled back in his head and he gasped for breath. His body convulsed, once and again. His hands clutched at the air, trying to grab hold of something. Anything. Those flailing fingers were rather pathetic, especially when his flailing hands fell on Janet's arm.

"There now," Janet said gently as she removed the needle from his neck. She reached out to stroke his hair in an oddly caring fashion. "You'll feel better in a moment, I promise."

Benedict found the process fascinating. Just as Janet predicted, very shortly Ricky's stiffened muscles relaxed, his eyes closed, his breath came easy once again. After a moment his eyes opened. Halfway, no more. Not understanding what had happened to him, he smiled and uttered a soft, "Smashing."

Ricky would enjoy these first few moments. He was high, as he might be from using any other addictive drug. But in a few hours he'd need more to take away the pain. And the only way he'd get what he needed was to do as he was told.

"So far, so good," Janet said softly as she stepped away from her latest guinea pig.

"He's still alive," Benedict said. "That's an improvement." He watched Ricky closely. Yes, the man was feeling no pain. Tomorrow would be another story. "When will he need more?"

Janet shrugged. "That has proven to be a variable. Given his body weight and metabolism, I surmise he'll crave a second dose in twelve hours. After twenty-four to thirty-six hours, he'll be useless without an injection."

"Good. Are you ready with the second treatment?"

"Of course." She sounded almost insulted that he'd suggest she was not prepared.

Together, he and Janet watched as Ricky's body adjusted to the invasion of TitanVX103, the drug Benedict had named for himself. For his new self, with his new name. It was only fitting, after all. Yes, he had once been Benedict Payne, but Titan was the man he had become.

The Englishman closed his eyes, shuddered and mouthed another, "Smashing."

The process was fascinating. The possibilities were limitless. Benedict smiled. As soon as the formula was perfected, no one would be able to stop him. No one. With the smallest sample of DNA, he could control anyone. He'd have the world at his fingertips.

"Are you ready to conduct another test?" Benedict asked as he watched a limp Ricky begin to drool.

"So soon?" Janet sounded more intrigued than surprised.

"Perhaps. If our experiment with Ricky proves to be a failure, or if he simply disappoints us, then we might have to turn elsewhere for the information we seek."

"Please be specific, Ben," Janet snapped. "I do so hate it when you ramble."

He glared at her. No one else dared to insult him. No one but her. And she knew she was safe because she was invaluable. For now.

"Dr. Eldanis apparently has a lover. A large man, according to Ricky. If she tells too many people about what's been happening at the clinic, someone might put two and two together. We can't allow that to happen. As soon as we have the information we came here for, she must be disposed of."

Janet nodded.

"I know Ricky will be disappointed," Benedict said. He turned his eyes to the drugged man who was currently so out of it he didn't realize where he was. Apparently he hadn't yet realized what he'd been given. He knew what the designer drug could do, and yet he showed no concern for his own well-being. Not yet, anyway. "He has plans for the girl. But it makes more sense to handle her another way. If she's accosted and murdered by a stranger, a lot of curious eyes will turn this way. But if she's the victim of an unfortunate domestic situation, no one will look our way. We'll use the drug on the vet's lover and have him kill her and then himself. Murder-suicide." He smiled. "Happens every day."

"I'll need his DNA."

"I'll get it for you myself."

Unconcerned about the details of the next test, she turned her attention to Ricky, studiously attentive to his reactions to the drug.

The damn place didn't look any different today than it had yesterday. It didn't look any nicer, or any safer. But as Hawk stood in the center of the living room, on the very spot where he and Sheryl had come together for the last time, he realized that something was different.

Thanks to her, there was more than the past in this room.

He wished there was something here that might remind him of a happier time. Something that would prove to him his mother had been more than a crazy woman who'd been murdered by an abusive husband. He wanted her to be happy. He wanted her to be normal.

Who was he kidding? There was nothing normal about him, and there had likely been nothing normal about his mother, either.

Baby stood beside him, her eyes turned up anxiously. She was as ready to go home as he was, and they were on their way at last. He'd checked out of the hotel. The last of the useless files and his suitcase had been tossed into the back seat. If he could manage it, he wouldn't even stop in Tennessee to spend the night but would drive straight through.

And still he stood there, expectant and curious and at a loss he could not explain. Every instinct he possessed told him there was something in this house. Something of her.

Baby growled.

"What is it, girl?"

Hawk couldn't sense what was bothering the dog. His mind was too filled with other things today to concentrate.

But something was bothering Baby. She pranced and growled; she twitched her tail.

Baby knew, as well as Hawk knew, that what he wanted was somewhere in this house.

He could tear the place up looking for it, but surely anything his mother had left behind was long gone.

It wouldn't take much to find out.

He started in the kitchen. It was a woman's place, right? That was a thought that could get his ass kicked if Sheryl ever heard it. Not that she ever would. He found nothing of interest. Not a teapot or a dish. Not a clue as to whether Deanna Payne liked strawberries or blackberries, green beans or carrots, red or yellow. The dining room was no better.

He ran up the stairs, ignoring the warning scream of old steps. There was less above stairs than below. The rooms here had been cleaned out completely, and there was nothing in the walls or the doors or the rotting floors to remind Hawk of previous residents.

By the time he worked his way back down the stairs and into the living room, his frustration and anger had grown. He'd come all this way for nothing. Worse, he wished he didn't know the truth. How could he tell Cassie what he'd discovered? He certainly couldn't deliver the news over the phone. Maybe it would be best if he told her he hadn't learned anything about their biological parents. In this case a dead end would be a more satisfying answer than the truth.

As if he could hide the truth from Cassie. He could try, but she'd know. Somehow she'd know.

Hawk kicked at a broken chair, catching a wobbly leg and sending it tumbling across the floor. He turned over the table with three legs, and it crashed into the floorboards with a splintering crack. His booted foot came down with such force he put a hole in the rotting floor.

It felt good to lose control. To let go completely and allow himself to express the anger he could no longer hide. But as always, he was not alone. Baby howled. Above the house a falcon screeched. A twittering squirrel escaped from its home in a hole in the wall and ran out the front door. Baby didn't even think about giving chase.

Hawk kicked at the wall, punching a hole in the old sheetrock. He kicked again, and then he took an old picture, an ugly landscape, off the wall and tossed it. It sailed through the air like a big, square Frisbee and landed with a crash. Broken glass went everywhere, flying up and out as the frame skidded across the floor. When Baby headed in that direction, Hawk pulled himself back from his rage.

"No, Baby. Stay. You'll get hurt." He'd worked up a sweat taking his anger out on this house, and his breath came hard. His lungs burned, his heart pounded. Above the house another bird shrieked. In the forest near the old house, he heard the rustle of animals that had been disturbed by his anger. Deer fled. Rabbits hid.

Baby didn't back away from the ruined picture, but stood at the edge of the destruction and growled. Broken glass sparkled in the sunlight.

And then Hawk saw it. Peeking from beneath the destroyed frame was one corner of a manila folder. Just a single corner, but the sight was enough to give him chills.

He picked his way across the room, ordering Baby to stay back, away from the broken glass. The shards crunched beneath Hawk's boots as he turned the frame over.

The thick manila folder had been taped to the back of the frame. When the frame had scooted across the floor, some of the old, dry tape had come loose, and that was why the manila folder now peeked out as it did. Hawk very carefully pulled the rest of the old tape away, blew off a few bits of broken glass and opened the folder to discover a five-by-seven black-and-white photograph of his mother.

Hawk placed his hand over the photo. She had been so young, so pretty...

And the file was so thick.

He wasn't going home empty-handed. This was what he'd come to Wyatt searching for.

Chapter 12

Sheryl smiled and said hello to the clients who greeted her as she walked the square. The walls at home had been closing in on her all morning. She usually enjoyed her quiet Sundays at home, but today she would have welcomed the opportunity to go to work. She could lose herself in work, as she'd done in the past.

But instead of heading to the clinic to rearrange files and clean, she'd come here to the town square for the final day of the Fall Festival. There were baked goods galore, but she had no appetite. She had bought a small cup of the apple cider, but hadn't been able to finish it.

Not even Laverne was with her today. The cat had picked up on Sheryl's restlessness and opted to stay at home where she could sleep and harass the others in peace.

Sheryl felt as if she'd never know peace again.

"Yoo-hoo!" a high-pitched voice called.

Sheryl turned her head and found herself almost face-to-face with Mildred Harris, who sat at her booth with Harold Johnston at her side. The table before the couple was filled with neatly arranged items for sale—including toaster cozies.

"Beautiful day, isn't it?" Mildred said.

"Yes, it is." Cool, clear, crisp—lonely.

"Where's your friend?" Harold asked.

I don't have a friend. "On his way back to Texas, I imagine."

Mildred's smile died, and Harold grunted, obviously embarrassed. Did the entire town know she and Hawk were involved? Of course they did. Secrets were hard to keep in a place like Wyatt.

Sheryl moved toward the table. She could just keep walking, she imagined, but as she'd meandered around town and tortured herself about everything that hadn't happened and everything she hadn't said, an idea had begun to blossom. Hawk was so certain he didn't need anything more in his life, just as she'd been certain she didn't need him or any other man. She wasn't enough for him, but more than that, what he'd discovered here wasn't enough.

"Did Hawk ask you about his mother?"

Mildred's eyes went wide.

"His mother?" Harold asked sharply. "He never said Deanna Payne was his *mother.*"

"Yeah. I tried to do an Internet search on her last night, but I didn't find anything at all." It had been an incredibly frustrating attempt.

"Oh, dear," Mildred said softly. "I would have handled his questions differently if I had realized. He didn't even know her name, so it never occurred to me... He said he was just curious about an old picture he found interesting.

Oh, dear. And he's already left town? I feel like I should make amends somehow."

"Did you know Deanna Payne?" Sheryl asked.

"Not very well, I'm afraid."

"Is there anyone in town who knew her well?"

Mildred pondered the question for a moment. "Wilma Preston and Deanna were about the same age. I don't know if they were great friends, but they did spend some time together. They had lunch after the ladies club meetings on occasion, if I remember correctly."

Sheryl didn't know any Wilma Preston, which only meant the woman didn't have a pet. Or else she'd moved away years ago. Or else she was dead.

There was only one way to find out.

Hawk sat on the front porch and opened the thick file. The house hadn't changed in any physical sense, but it did feel different to him. More peaceful somehow. Today he noticed the way the sun shone onto the porch in streaks of brilliant light, not the decay of the boards. He noticed the wildflowers that danced in the wind, not the weeds that had attempted to take over the yard. Maybe Sheryl had been right when she said this had been a nice place once upon a time.

He leafed through the pages in his lap, much as he had leafed through the files from the old fertility clinic. He moved much more slowly this time. There was a lot of information here, and he tried to soak up what he could as he quickly studied page after page.

Donor sperm. The words popped out at him as if they were bolder than the others. The man who had murdered his mother wasn't his biological father. The force of the relief that rushed through him almost took his breath away.

The murderer had been his legal father, perhaps, but at least he and Cassie didn't carry those damaged genes. Cassie's baby wasn't the grandchild of a killer, and if he ever had kids...

No, that wasn't for him. Cassie could have babies, and he'd be a great uncle. But father? No way.

At first he was confused by the discrepancies in the dates, and then he realized that there had been more than one successful pregnancy for Deanna Payne.

The word *triplets* was typed and handwritten again and again, in these files. Not twins. *Triplets.*

A breeze kicked up and ruffled the pages, so he laid a hand there to keep everything in place. He didn't want to lose a single sheet of the massive file.

A word caught his eye as he tried to absorb the information before him. *Seizures.* He read the notations on that page with an interest that made him hold his breath, and he sighed with relief and even grinned when he got to the bottom of the page.

The wind kicked up again, and he closed the file. He'd have to study the rest of this later, when he didn't have to worry about the wind taking it from him.

He had a feeling he'd be studying these pages again and again.

He grabbed his cell phone and hit the speed dial. There was a lousy signal out here in the boonies, but this couldn't wait.

Cassie answered on the second ring.

"Write this down," Hawk said.

His sister laughed. "No 'hello, how are you, what's happening'?"

"Hello, how are you, what's happening. Write this down."

He waited a moment while Cassie got a pen and paper, and then he gave her the ingredients for an herbal tea their mother had used to treat the symptoms Cassie was having. Deanna Payne had suffered from something similar, though there was no note of the flashes of precognition. Still, if the herbal tea helped Cassie deal with her new problems, this trip was worthwhile.

He didn't tell her that their mother had been murdered. That wasn't news that should be shared over the phone.

"Where did this so-called remedy come from?" Cassie asked.

"Our mother had the same problem you've been having," he explained.

There was a long moment of silence that had nothing to do with the bad connection. Finally Cassie said, "You found her."

"I'm coming home. I'll tell you all about it when I get there."

"I don't think so!" A crackle buzzed in Hawk's ear. "You can't tease me like this and not tell me *everything!*"

No, he couldn't. "I didn't actually find her," Hawk explained. "She died a long time ago, when we were babies."

"Oh." She sounded disappointed. God, he hated the idea of telling her everything.

But it wasn't all bad news.

"I found a couple of pictures. You look just like her."

"I do?"

"Yeah. And do you remember when we were kids and when I did something that annoyed you, you'd say, 'My other brother would never be mean to me. My other brother would play dolls with me.'"

"My imaginary other brother," Cassie said softly, her words almost lost over the bad signal.

"Not so imaginary after all," Hawk said.

The cell signal got worse. Cassie's response was broken and distant.

"I'll call you later when I have a better signal," he said, rising with the file in one hand and the phone in the other. "Make that tea and give it a try."

"Don't forget to call me back," Cassie said urgently.

"I won't."

Hawk opened the truck door for Baby, who leaped in and took her place in the passenger seat. He then placed the file on the floor of the back seat, in a secure position where it wouldn't move around too much.

He was glad to leave the old farmhouse behind. Even though he couldn't possibly remember living there, the place gave him the creeps. Maybe if it had been lived in over the years, he'd feel differently, but spending time in that house was too much like meandering through a graveyard.

"We're going home, Baby," he said as they pulled off the dirt drive and onto the road.

She answered with a very uncertain growl.

"Don't give me that," he said as he accelerated. "You knew when we came here that we weren't going to stay."

The sound that emitted from Baby's throat was very much like a whining complaint.

"It's better this way," he answered. "A clean break for both of us."

Baby barked once, then stuck her head out the window.

"Fine," Hawk said softly. "Ignore me. Don't talk to me. Tell me I'm an ass. You're not the first one to say that, and you won't be the last."

Hawk braked at a stop sign. If he turned right, he'd be headed for the interstate. If he turned left, he'd be on that winding road that led to Wyatt.

A clean break really was for the best. Yeah, there were things he wanted to tell Sheryl that he hadn't found the time to say, but what difference did that make?

Baby pulled in her head and stared at him. She waited, just as Hawk waited, for the decision to be made.

A car stopped behind the idling truck, and after a moment the driver honked his horn impatiently. Hawk glanced in his rearview mirror. With the afternoon sun on the windshield, he couldn't see the driver's face, but a black-clad arm hung out of the open window.

The driver honked again, and this time that black-clad arm raised up and the frustrated driver gave Hawk the international hand symbol for "Where the hell did you learn how to drive?"

"I'm an idiot to the core," Hawk said as he turned, ignoring the finger. Baby stuck her head out of the window and smiled as the wind brushed back her ears and her blond hair.

Sheryl sat at the kitchen table and wrote as quickly as she could, afraid that she might forget something if she didn't get it all down now. She didn't know Hawk's address, but she did remember Greenlaurel, Texas. The letter would find him. If she mailed it first thing in the morning, it should get there shortly after Hawk got home.

She shouldn't care, but she did, dammit. She had a vested emotional interest in that annoying, stubborn, impossible man, and she didn't want to see him hurting the way he did. She couldn't fix his life, she couldn't give him everything he wanted. But she could give him this.

Laverne came to the table, pacing and mewing.

"I've already fed you," Sheryl said. "You don't need another bite."

After a few minutes of pacing and switching her tail, a very antsy Laverne bolted from the kitchen. Funny, the only other time Sheryl had seen the cat act this way was when—

She jumped up from the kitchen table and walked slowly to the front door. Bruce, who was in his cage once again, began to squawk.

All three cats and both dogs were waiting in the entryway, eyes anxiously on the door, bodies absolutely still. They didn't turn to look at her, they didn't acknowledge one another in any way. She had never seen them all so unnaturally still, so deeply and completely expectant.

Sheryl knew what was coming, and when the doorbell rang she still jumped out of her skin. Not that she didn't know exactly who was standing on her front porch.

She hesitated, and the doorbell rang again. Twice. Laverne looked back at Sheryl and mewed loudly.

"If you're so anxious to see him, you open the door," Sheryl said softly.

"Come on, Sheryl," Hawk called. He didn't ring the bell again, but he knocked loudly. "I know you're here."

Of course he knew. And she should have known better than to think Hawk Donovan would walk away quietly because—hint, hint—she wasn't answering her door.

The animals parted when she moved toward the door, and the knocking stopped. Was Hawk leaving, or had he heard her soft step on the floor?

She opened the door, taking a deep breath as she tilted her face up to look into the eyes of the man she had never thought she'd see again.

Something had changed. She saw the change in those dark eyes, and in the set of his mouth. His anger was…not gone, exactly, but faded. Controlled. No, she could not say that he was happy, but neither was he frustrated.

"I found it," he said, holding up a thick sheaf of papers precariously caught in a manila folder.

Sheryl smiled. "In that last box?"

He shook his head. "At the farmhouse. It was hidden behind a picture. I think my mother hid it from him. My father. Not my father, actually," he added quickly. "Legally, maybe, but not...not. And I found what Cassie needs, I think. I've already called her. Since you were such a help to me, I thought maybe you'd like to know."

"Thanks."

Sheryl looked him in the eye, unafraid. She wasn't the kind of woman who would turn away just because there was an uncomfortable strain in the air, just because there were so many things that could not be said.

Had she fallen in love with his eyes first? Maybe so. They were so dark, so mysterious, and yet when he gave nothing of himself in any other way, she saw the emotion in those expressive eyes. Everything he'd never say to her was there.

He turned away and started walking toward the truck, which was parked at the curb. Baby followed.

Sheryl stepped onto the front porch. "Hey!"

Hawk stopped on the walk and turned to face her.

"That's it?" she said. "You came to my house just to tell me that?"

"I thought you'd want to—"

"Of course I want to know," she interrupted. "But you could have called or written me a letter. You didn't have to come all the way back here just to give me an update."

"Seemed like the thing to do at the time."

He'd wanted to see her again, whether he would admit it or not. And heaven knows it was good to see him. More than good. It was necessary, like coming up out of the deep water and taking air into her lungs.

"Thanks for the update, but I want to know more. I want to know everything. How about letting me have a peek inside that file everyone's so anxious to get their hands on?"

For a moment he didn't say a word. "Are you sure you're interested?" he asked.

Sheryl smiled. "Of course I'm interested. I might actually have something to add, if you have the time to sit for a few minutes."

"Sure," he said casually.

Even though there was nothing casual about this.

He came inside, greeted all the animals, and then left Baby to entertain her friends while the two of them went into the kitchen. Sheryl moved her letter off the table and made room for Hawk to lay out what he'd found. He was so excited about his treasure that he didn't even notice when she slipped the letter into her pocket.

"There's so much here, I don't know where to start," he said. "This is her." The photo was larger than the snapshot they'd found buried in the fertility clinic files. Sharper and clearer.

"There's definitely a family resemblance," she said.

"She looks just like Cassie."

"And more than a little like you."

Hawk shrugged that comment off as if it didn't matter, but she suspected it did matter. Very much.

"Most of this is technical jargon I don't fully understand," he said as he flipped through the pages, "but I understand things now that have been mysteries to me all my life. Things like—" He hesitated.

Maybe he was overwhelmed by what he'd found. Maybe it was too much. But she was so glad he'd found his answers. He deserved that much.

"It must've been difficult, not knowing who your parents were."

"It's more than that." He closed the file but kept his hand over it as if the entire thing might fly away if he didn't hold it down.

Whatever it was he didn't seem inclined to share, so Sheryl took from her pocket the letter she'd been writing and laid it on the table before her. "I found a few interesting details myself this afternoon."

"Such as?"

She looked down at the words she'd written. "Your mother came from Romania." She glanced up briefly. So, that was where those gypsy eyes had come from. "She married Benedict Payne because she needed a green card, but she wasn't married long before she knew she'd made a mistake. But she'd made a promise and she decided to make the best of her situation. She—"

"How do you know this?"

Sheryl lifted her head and looked Hawk in the eye. "I asked a few questions of my own this afternoon. My questions were a little different from yours and I talked to different people. People who knew her. Do you want to know more?"

He nodded slowly, and Sheryl returned her gaze to the paper. "Deanna Payne loved gardenias and chocolate pie and made a kick-ass spicy stew. She wanted very much to fit into her new life in Wyatt, but was never truly comfortable here. She always felt like an outsider, though she did try to adapt. Even though she didn't love her husband, she wanted children very much. She believed that they would fill the void in her life, that maybe they would even cure the ills of her marriage."

Hawk was so still, she wasn't sure he was even breathing. His gaze was pinned not to the note in her hand, but to her face.

"She liked the color blue," Sheryl continued, "and sunsets, and a framed print she found at a flea market that looked very much like her native Romania."

"The one that was hanging in the farmhouse."

She glanced up. "Maybe."

"It's where she hid this." His fingers brushed the file.

"Her husband took her away from the friends she was starting to make here in Wyatt. He rented that farmhouse from the landowner, who'd built a new and better place up the road. The farmer didn't care for Dr. Payne, but he did take a liking to your mother. After she was killed there, he couldn't bear to rent the house to anyone else. It's been sitting empty ever since."

Sheryl didn't need to read the rest of her incomplete letter. "She was a good person, Hawk. I don't know exactly what happened to your mother after she left Wyatt, but I know she loved you."

"How do you know that?" he asked brusquely.

"How could she not?" She handed him the letter, and he took it.

He didn't add her letter to the thick file, but folded it and tucked it into his shirt pocket. "Thanks. This means a lot to me. It'll mean a lot to Cassie, too."

He reached out and touched her face, looking very much as if he wanted to say something but wasn't sure if he could…or if he should. There was a light in his eyes, a light she knew. He hadn't come to Wyatt looking for her, but by golly he'd found her. What were they going to do about that?

Hawk's hand on her face was gentle and strong. Like him. He hid the gentle side of himself. It was possible she was the only one who had seen it, but it was there. It was hers. Why couldn't she just tell him that she needed him? Why couldn't he admit that what they had was much more than they'd expected or wanted?

He leaned forward slightly, as if he were thinking of kissing her, but all of a sudden the quiet was broken by barking, mewing and Bruce squawking, "Holy mackerel!"

Since the commotion might've been started by something as simple as a squirrel spotted through the living room window, Sheryl was not concerned. It was the fact that the barking and mewling didn't stop that bothered her.

She went to investigate and Hawk followed her.

"Holy mackerel!" Bruce called again.

"Did you teach him to say that?" Sheryl asked.

"Yeah," Hawk answered. "Seemed preferable to his usual colorful comments."

"Definitely."

The pets showed no sign of calming down, but ran in circles and made all sorts of noise. Hawk squatted down in front of Baby, who could not keep her feet still, and laid his hand on her head. Immediately the yellow dog froze, and so did the others.

The quiet was more disturbing to Sheryl than the commotion had been.

Hawk stood quickly. "Someone's prowling around the house. A man who doesn't belong here." He headed for the front door, and Baby followed.

"How do you—"

"Stay," he said, and Sheryl, along with Baby, came to a dead stop.

Had he been talking to her? Had he ordered *her* to stay? She should be insulted.

As Hawk went out to investigate, Sheryl came to the conclusion that Debbie's brother-in-law might be out and about. Or the kids down the block cut through her yard again, the way they sometimes did.

She still had her money on squirrels.

A few minutes later, Hawk came back in through the front door. He had the oddest expression on his face, as if he were worried and puzzled, and he rubbed the back of his neck.

"Find anything?" she asked.

"No, but..."

"But what?"

Hawk dropped the hand that had been massaging the back of his neck. "Did you ever get the feeling that someone was watching you?"

"Sure, a time or two."

"It was the oddest thing. While I was walking around the house, the back of my neck prickled, and I got this twisting knot in my gut. I swear, my knees even went a little wobbly."

"Did you have lunch?" she asked.

"No, but—"

"Breakfast?"

He shook his head.

"Then you're hungry. I'll make you a bite to eat. If you want to stick around awhile, that is."

"I really should get on the road," Hawk protested. But not very enthusiastically.

It would be stupid and girlie and pathetic of her to try to change his mind, wouldn't it? Hawk didn't want to stay. Whatever they'd had was over. They had known from the beginning that what they had was temporary. "You could stay the night and leave early in the morning." She tried not to sound too pushy or needy. Her suggestion was simply practical. "It's too late for you to get very far today. Right?"

"True enough," he said. "And I am hungry." He seemed to accept the explanation for his weak-kneed symptoms readily enough.

They walked into the kitchen, and as soon as they entered the room Hawk came to a dead halt. "Where is it?" he asked softly.

"Where's what?"

"The file!" He spun on her. "What did you do with it?"

She looked past him to the round oak table, where the file he'd found at the farmhouse had been left when the animals' uproar had called them from the room.

The tabletop was bare.

Chapter 13

It had been simple enough to slip the lock on the kitchen door, walk inside and swipe the documents Eldanis and her friend had been going over with such interest.

Anthony was miles away from Wyatt before he pulled the car over to the grassy shoulder and snagged the file from the passenger seat. It had been an exciting day. The man in the pickup with the Texas plates had almost caught him earlier in the afternoon. Anthony couldn't think of any reason for the man to sit at that stop sign for such a long time, unless he'd suspected that someone was tailing him. But in the end, the Texan hadn't been suspicious at all, just indecisive.

His heart was beating too fast, and he wasn't sure why. This hadn't been his most dangerous job, not by a long shot. Even if the Texan had caught him, it wouldn't have mattered. He would have escaped. He would have slipped through the Texan's fingers.

Anthony rubbed the back of his neck with one hand while he opened the file with the other. He tried to chase away the odd feelings that had come over him while he'd been in that farmhouse and again while the Texan had been chasing him.

After a restless night's sleep, he'd almost convinced himself that last night in the farmhouse he'd suffered some sort of hallucination. But then again this afternoon he'd gotten chills as he'd escaped from the Eldanis woman's house. Chills and wobbly knees and a twisting in his stomach. Maybe he was coming down with a cold, or had eaten something bad.

The picture in the file ended all curiosity about the odd sensations he'd suffered in the past twenty-four hours. He wasn't suffering from hallucinations; he didn't have a cold; there had been nothing wrong with the food he'd been eating.

It was her. His mother. Seeing that face brought so many memories back, memories that hit him like a ton of bricks and left him winded. In a way he wished he hadn't found this file, because anything that caused this sort of weakness was unwanted. In his business, weakness was more than a character flaw; it was potentially deadly.

But it was already too late to take back what he'd found. Closing the file and trying to forget wouldn't erase the memories that had escaped.

Anthony laid a finger over the photo, caressing his mother's cheek. Their father had killed her and then he'd disappeared.

The son of a bitch was back.

Hawk wasn't a talkative man, but she'd never seen him so still and quiet. Something was wrong, something beyond the loss of the file. Sheryl suggested that they sit on the porch, and he followed her without argument. Only Baby came with them; the other kiddies stayed in the house. Baby placed herself beside Hawk's rocking chair. Her sharp eyes swept the street once, and then she put her head down and closed her eyes, drifting off to sleep.

"I'm sorry," Sheryl said again. How many times had she apologized? "I really did think the kitchen door was locked."

"Nothing to be done for it now," Hawk said without emotion.

"At least you found the treatment for your sister," she said, trying to put a note of cheer into her voice. "That's something, right?"

He didn't answer. His chair began to rock, and he watched the street as suspiciously as Baby had. Sheryl wanted to climb onto his lap and stroke his hair and cry for him, since he refused to cry for himself. Every feminine instinct she possessed told her he didn't want that comfort. But dammit, he needed it. He touched her.

Finally he spoke. "I didn't tell you everything about me."

She wasn't surprised. Hawk wasn't the kind of man who shared himself easily. Sexually, sure. But in his heart? No. "There hasn't been time."

He quit rocking and turned his head to look her in the eye. The sun was setting, but there was plenty of light left to illuminate his hard face, the unforgiving eyes. "I grew up on a horse ranch, so it's only natural that when I was a kid, I got involved in the rodeo. Calf roping at first, then when I was older and bigger I got into bull riding."

It wasn't much, but it was personal. Hawk was voluntarily sharing a part of his past with her. That had to be a good sign. Right? "Do you still ride?"

"Not since I was nineteen." A strange stillness hung in the air for a few moments, and then he continued. "That night I drew the toughest, meanest bull in the competition. The bull no one wanted. The one that assured me either an exciting win or a nasty loss."

That night, he said. Not one night, but *that* night.

"When it was time, I got on his back, grabbed the rope good and tight, and nodded my head to signal that I was ready. The gate opened, and the bull leaped into the ring and bucked hard." His eyes went dark.

"Everything faded. There was no crowd in the arena with us. No cheering, no judges. Just pounding hooves and rage." His voice was low, but deep and clear. "I felt it, Sheryl. I felt that rage as if it were my own. I knew that bull's fear and anger, I felt the heat of his blood and the beat of his heart."

"Hawk—"

"Let me finish," he said sharply. "I've never told this to anyone before, so I'm not quite sure how to do it. If I stop I might not finish."

She nodded silently.

"It hurt," he said softly. "I was inside that damn bull for what seemed like forever, and it freakin' *hurt*. Turns out my forever was fifteen seconds. More than long enough for a win, more than long enough to change my life. I didn't realize it at the time, but the rodeo clowns were there trying to help me off and out of the ring, once my eight seconds were up. Later on they said it was like I was in another world, like I didn't see or hear them or hear the buzzer when it sounded. And I didn't."

He laughed harshly. "Okay, no more beating around the bush. No more subtle hints. I can— Crap, if I tell you I can talk to animals, you'll start calling me Dr. Dolittle. If I tell you I can read their thoughts, you'll think I'm some wacko pet psychic who belongs in a loony bin. You don't have to tell me that it doesn't make any sense," he said before she could respond. "I already know that."

"Can I talk now?" Sheryl asked when he'd been silent for a few moments.

"Sure." The way his jaw was set and his eyes narrowed, she imagined he was expecting her to tell him she thought he was nuts. She didn't.

"I can't explain what you've just told me, but I'm not going to call you a liar or a nutcase. You experienced something that's tough to explain, but…"

"But what?" he snapped.

"You can't just toss this at me and expect me to accept it without question. There has to be a logical explanation. I can't deny that you have a very special gift with animals, but to ask me to believe that you're a—a—" She found no proper word. "I need fact, Hawk. I need something concrete before I can wrap my mind around what you're telling me."

"I think I can make better sense of it now," he said softly. "Finally. It's been nine years since that night in the ring, and I never ran across anything even resembling an explanation. After looking at those files…" He shook his head and looked out to the deserted street again. "You have to understand, it's more than me. Cassie has always had dreams that, well, they were more than dreams. Sometimes they came true. Now that she's pregnant, she's been having seizures."

"I know."

"What you don't know is that she's been seeing into the immediate future right after she has a seizure. Just a few minutes, but—" A wry smile twisted his lips, and the sound that burst from between those lips might've been a kind of humorless laughter followed by one of Bruce's favorite words. "Of course. Why didn't I see it? She knew. She must've known."

"What are you talking about?"

"My name is Hawk, and I can connect to animals in a way that is, as far as I know, unheard of. Cassie's name is actually Cassandra, like the mythological psychic no one would listen to. That can't be coincidence. When she named us, our mother must've known what our special talents would be."

Psychics. Talking to pets. It was definitely a leap of faith for Sheryl to believe what she was hearing. And yet, she didn't believe Hawk would lie to her. Not about this; not about anything.

"There's something else," he said, his voice so low Sheryl had to strain to hear. "Something you really need to know."

"I'm not sure I'm ready for more," she said just as softly.

He hesitated, but then he continued as if she hadn't interrupted. "Yesterday, in the old house—"

Baby woke suddenly and began to growl, her eyes trained on the side yard

"What is it, girl?" Hawk laid his hand on Baby's head, and almost immediately his expression changed. "Someone's here."

At the same moment Hawk's cell phone began to ring He ignored it, then snagged the phone from his belt and checked out the caller ID. "It's Cassie," he said. He tossed the phone to Sheryl. "Take a message for me. I'll be right back."

Baby and Hawk leaped off the porch together, and that

was when Sheryl saw the man racing across her neighbor's backyard.

She answered the call, "Hello?"

Benedict ran. Hawk was giving chase and gaining. That damn dog who'd given him away was at Hawk's side.

If running wasn't such hard work, he'd smile. He'd gone to the house to collect a DNA sample—a strand of hair with a follicle or a toothbrush, most likely—but he'd come away with so much more. He'd overheard everything.

Cassie was the one he wanted. Cassie and her baby.

Benedict ran hard, but Hawk drew closer with each step. He didn't have any use for Dr. Dolittle at the present time, and he wasn't capable of taking the big fella on his own. Not without shooting him. The supple branch of an overgrown bush brushed across his face, and something with thorns grabbed at his trousers and then tore free.

He'd really rather not shoot Hawk. If he killed the boy, what a waste that would be. And if he only wounded him, he might be like a wounded bear, angrier and more determined. The knee—maybe that would stop him. But Benedict's shooting skills were not particularly sharp, though he did engage in target practice on occasion and he was certainly a better shot than most. He needed a slightly bigger target than a moving knee, though.

Benedict had men to do the dirty work for him; he rarely pulled the trigger himself.

Besides, he wanted the boy healthy and whole. Undamaged. Now that he knew where and who Hawk was, and what he could do, Benedict could have him collected at any time.

But not if the boy caught him.

Benedict left the overgrown yard and leaped onto a side street. Out of breath and excited about the days to come, he stopped in the middle of the pavement. His car was another block over; he couldn't allow Hawk to see his car and report a description to the authorities. He had the boy's license plate number, so getting a full name and address and then tracking down Cassandra would not be a problem. All he had to do was make a clean escape.

That might not be easy. Hawk and the dog were close, and now not too far behind them the Eldanis woman frantically shouted Hawk's name. She wasn't able to catch him, though.

The boy moved fast, he'd give him that.

Benedict caught his breath and smiled. No, not a boy anymore. A man. Not a squalling baby, but the fully grown evidence that his experiments had been a success.

Suddenly he knew how to win this round; he knew how to stop Hawk. He drew his gun and spun on the man and dog who burst into view, skirting overgrown shrubs and a pecan tree in the corner lot. With cold determination, he took aim and fired.

Hawk heard the shot, felt the sting, felt his heart drop out from under him. His feet stuttered to a stop on the pavement as the man he'd been chasing turned away and cut through yet another heavily wooded yard.

He turned back, moving in slow motion. His muscles wanted to freeze, his breath wouldn't come.

"Baby?"

The dog Hawk had found years ago on the side of the road, frightened and starving and abused, was lying on the street, whimpering and twitching and bleeding. He dropped to his knees as the man who'd been prowling around Sheryl's house, the man who had surely stolen the file on Deanna Payne and then returned to look for more, made his escape.

Hawk didn't feel the pain of the bullet, not anymore. The bullet hadn't come anywhere near him. The man he'd been chasing had deliberately taken aim at Baby.

He heard Sheryl calling his name, heard her fighting against the same overgrown brush he and Baby had run through. She burst onto the street, white-faced and holding his cell phone in her hand.

She dropped down and examined Baby's wound. "Your sister said this would happen," she whispered. "She was so frantic I didn't understand her at first, and she didn't want to talk to me at all. She wanted you. But she kept saying, 'Baby. Baby,' and finally I got the message. I tried to call you back to warn you, but it was too late." Sheryl handed him the phone, freeing both her hands for Baby. "She's going to be okay," she said firmly. "Give me your shirt."

Hawk whipped his shirt over his head and handed it to Sheryl. She quickly and efficiently bound Baby's flank with the shirt to slow the bleeding. Baby, not understanding what had happened, whimpered and shook.

"Let's get her to the clinic," Sheryl said in a calm voice that trembled just a little.

Hawk very gently lifted Baby from the ground, being careful of her injury. He was angry and worried, shaking deep down and almost shell-shocked by the suddenness of the attack. What kind of a man would shoot a dog? He would've understood if the man had taken aim at him, but to deliberately shoot Baby… It was wrong. All wrong.

He had promised Baby that no one would ever hurt her again.

They walked toward the corner, Baby in Hawk's arms, Sheryl leading the way. The sound of the gunshot had called out all the neighbors, but no one could help them. He would carry Baby to the truck, and they'd drive to the clinic. No one but Sheryl could help him now.

"He should've shot me."

"Don't say that," Sheryl said.

It was the truth. It would have made more sense. How had the man known that shooting Baby would stop Hawk in his tracks?

Holding Baby close, he felt her confusion, her pain. But he also felt her strong heart and her will to live. With Sheryl's help, he told himself, she'd heal.

Hawk had seen the shooter well, and he committed the man's face to memory. If he ever saw that man again, the bastard would wish for someone to shoot him and put him out of his misery.

"Oh my God!" Sheryl moaned as she turned on the light in the clinic waiting room.

Everything had been turned over. Everything! There were huge holes in the walls, the phone was off the hook and making that awful off-the-hook noise, and her plants had been upended. Dirt had been kicked all over the floor.

It was a shock she could do without, considering the circumstances, but Sheryl knew she'd have to deal with this mess later, after she'd removed the bullet from Baby's flank and dressed the wound properly. She could only hope the examining rooms were in better shape.

They were, but not by much. She quickly prepared the least demolished of the rooms, and when she was ready, Hawk very gingerly placed Baby on the examining table.

There was blood on his arm and his torso, and the deepest pain she'd ever seen in his eyes. If she knew nothing else, she knew there was no way she could take care of Baby with Hawk standing over her.

"You should go to the waiting room," she said.

"No." There was no room for argument in that answer, but she argued anyway.

"You can trust me."

"It's not a matter of trust, Sheryl."

"Yes, it is."

When he didn't move, she told him the whole truth. "I can't do this with you watching. Right now I'm as worried about you as I am about Baby, and she needs my full attention. Please, go sit down in the other room so I can take care of her."

"I won't get in your way."

"Please," she said one last time.

Reluctantly he headed for the door.

Hawk would be okay, Sheryl thought as she stroked Baby's fur and whispered encouraging words. He would be fine in the lobby, out of sight if not out of mind. He wouldn't be completely out of the loop during the surgery. She had a feeling he would know immediately if anything went wrong.

Benedict stood over a sweating, trembling Ricky Driggs. The man was such a disgusting specimen. Addiction would do that to a man.

It had been a mere twelve hours since he'd received his initial injection, and yet Ricky's once-careful appearance had already suffered. His hair was mussed, and his blue jeans had a small tear in one knee where he'd fallen while making his way to the RV. His T-shirt was stained and wrinkled, and he didn't seem to notice, much less care.

It was disgusting and yet somehow entertaining.

"I'm going to leave you here in Wyatt for a few more days," Benedict said, as if he were talking to a child.

Ricky nodded, his head jerking. "And you'll leave me with a sufficient supply of the drug, right?"

"Of course I will," Benedict said with a smile. "But you must pay very careful attention to my instructions. If you don't do as I ask, there will be no more of the drug for you."

Again that sweating head bobbed.

"The man, the big fellow you've seen in Dr. Eldanis's company, he is not to be harmed," Benedict explained. "Eldanis you may do with as you please, but I want Hawk left alive."

"Hawk?"

"The big fellow," Benedict said slowly.

"Of course." Ricky nodded his head quickly.

"I doubt he'll be leaving Wyatt anytime soon. I shot his dog."

Ricky jerked a little, and a pained expression flitted across his face. As if the Englishman had any scruples! He'd killed a number of men, in his time with Benedict and before, and his plans for the Eldanis woman were certainly not benevolent. And yet he flinched because a flea-bitten mutt had been shot.

"If it looks as if the big fellow is planning to leave town, I want you to stop him." The last thing Benedict needed was Hawk getting in the way of Cassandra's capture. Cassandra was the one he wanted, the one he'd been searching for. She and the child she carried would be his salvation.

"How can I stop *him?*" Ricky laughed nervously. "I mean, if he wants to leave town he's going to—"

"Stop him," Benedict said sharply. "Do I have to do

your thinking for you? Hawk's departure will be likely delayed for several days at the very least, thanks to the death or injury to his dog. I imagine he would also be delayed by the death or injury of his girlfriend. Remember, she is expendable. He is not."

And if Hawk caught and disposed of Driggs in a violent fashion, as he was likely to do if the Brit had his fun with the girl, all the better. He wasn't worried about Ricky talking before he died; the lackey knew nothing of importance and would likely be a drooling moron before Hawk ever laid hands on him.

Ricky nodded. "I got it. Kill the girl and he'll stay, right? Can I have my shot now? I don't feel so good."

Benedict nodded to Janet, who opened a small leather case and withdrew one filled syringe. There were nine others in the case, most of them filled with the drug Ricky needed. A few were nothing more than colored sugar water.

Ricky's need for the drug would likely escalate quickly, so his supply of the drug would only last a few days. Perhaps a week. A week should be sufficient time to grab Cassandra and get a head start. Janet could, of course, concoct and administer an antidote, but why waste the time and effort on this poor specimen when there were so many other wonderful possibilities on her agenda?

Janet administered the shot to an offered vein in a trembling arm, and the reaction was immediate. Ricky relaxed, his breathing slowed and a touch of color came back to his pasty cheeks.

"From now on, I want you to limit yourself to one injection a day," she said, using the same slow, careful voice Benedict himself had chosen to use with the damaged Englishman.

"Only one?" Ricky asked, his voice thick.

"Yes, that would be best."

He smiled up at her, but the smile was crooked and shaky. "After the boss leaves town, how about I take you to dinner?"

Janet's eyes widened; she was obviously amused. "Wouldn't that be lovely."

"Lovely," Ricky repeated, and then he closed his eyes.

"We have a name and an address," Janet told Benedict as she turned away from the Englishman.

As soon as Benedict had driven a few blocks away from the scene of the shooting, he'd called one of his associates with Hawk's license plate number. He'd expected that he might have to wait a few hours for an answer. This speedy response was an unexpected bonus; they could leave tonight.

"Wonderful."

"Hawk Donovan," Janet said, keeping her voice low. Ricky didn't seem to be listening; he was lost in his own world, savoring the sensation of the drug entering his system and the relief it provided, contemplating a *lovely* dinner that would never take place. "He lives on a ranch near Greenlaurel, Texas. His sister Cassandra lives at the same address, according to her driver's license."

There was little true excitement in Benedict's life these days. Little true joy. But this… He was so close to his goal, the possibilities gave him an unexpected thrill that touched him to the core. Every fiber in his body tingled.

He'd have to give Janet a proper lovers' goodbye this evening, before they parted ways.

"How will I find you when I'm finished here?" Ricky asked, lifting his head slowly and with obvious difficulty. He licked his lips as if the drug coursing through his veins tasted good. He was interested in what was going on in this organization but not overly concerned.

When he ran out of the drug and couldn't contact Dr. Sheridan or Benedict, then he'd be concerned.

"I'll call you on your cell phone once we're situated," Benedict said.

The answer was enough for Ricky, who nodded less frantically than before and then settled back in to enjoy the rush in his blood.

Benedict turned his attention to Janet. He smiled at her and brushed the back of his hand against her cheek. "Bring her to me, darling," he said softly. "She's everything we've worked so hard for."

Her eyebrows lifted slightly. "You're not coming with me?"

"Of course not. I have preparations to see to, as you can well imagine." She should know better than to expect that he'd get his hands dirty with something so common as kidnapping.

Of course, collecting Cassandra wasn't kidnapping, but rather the recovery of something that belonged to him and him alone. The retrieval of something he had lost a long time ago.

Cassandra was his to do with as he pleased. As were all his children.

Chapter 14

Hawk grabbed a broom from the hallway closet where Sheryl stored the cleaning supplies and began to sweep the trashed lobby, primarily because he could not bear to sit still a moment longer. Sheryl might not know it yet, but her clinic was going to be closed for a few weeks. Someone had done a lot of serious damage to her place.

Someone, hell. The man who had done this to Sheryl's clinic was surely the same someone who had pretended to be a building inspector, stolen the file from her kitchen and shot Baby. He should call the police, but the man who'd shot Baby was long gone. Besides, Hawk wanted to catch the man himself.

When he stood very still, closed his eyes and concentrated, he knew Baby would be fine. The injection Sheryl had given the dog had her out like a light, but her heart remained steady and the injuries were relatively minor.

Minor compared to what they might've been.

Hawk swept harder, pushing unfamiliar emotions deep. He was a complete idiot to get so freakin' sentimental over a dog. There were other mutts out there, lots of them. Many of them needed good homes, and if something went wrong and Baby didn't make it, then he'd just get another dog. Right?

So why were there tears in his eyes? Why did he keep imagining the worst when logic and his gut and the connection he shared with Baby told him everything would be fine? Dammit! He had to get this bizarre struggle with his emotions taken care of before Sheryl was finished with the surgery. He didn't want her to see him this way. What a lousy way to end a pretty decent relationship. Him crying like a baby and her saving the day.

He was almost grateful when his cell phone rang. The home number popped up on the caller ID.

"Hi," he said, pushing his distress down so his sister couldn't hear or see it.

"Why didn't you call me?" Cassie asked frantically. "How's Baby?"

"She's in surgery, but she'll be fine." Fine, fine, fine. He continued to tell himself that. "The bastard shot her."

"I know," she whispered.

He didn't ask Cassie how she knew. The timing of her earlier phone call told him all he needed to know. It hadn't been a dream that warned her, but one of those flashes she'd started having. He should've taken that call instead of tossing the phone to Sheryl. Everything would be okay if he'd handled that one moment differently. If he'd known of the danger, he would have told Baby to stay and chased the man on his own.

There was no going back, though. He had to live with

that decision, just as he had to live with so many others. He had to live with putting Baby in the path of a bullet, dragging Sheryl into his sordid little excursion into the past and letting himself get much more involved than he'd ever intended.

"Are you okay?" he asked.

"Great," Cassie said, a touch of false cheer in her voice. "I'm making the herbal tea now, and I'll have a cup after supper."

"I hope it works." Otherwise this—Sheryl, Baby, all of it—had been for nothing. "Listen, I'm going to be held up here for a few days while Baby recuperates."

"No problem. The horses miss you, but everything is running smoothly."

"Good."

"I miss you, too," Cassie added almost reluctantly.

"I'll be home soon."

There was no rush to get back to the ranch. He almost wished there was, because then he'd have an excuse to run away from Wyatt. And Sheryl.

Baby was sleeping. Hawk was still fuming. And Sheryl felt as if her bones were about to turn to butter. Hawk had a way of doing that to her, with a look or a touch, but this was different.

She was furious, she was confused, she was hurt. About Baby, yes, but also about the destruction of her clinic. Who would do this? It would cost a small fortune to make the necessary repairs, and she didn't have a fortune handy, small or otherwise. Insurance would cover most of it, but in order to save on premiums she had a huge deductible on her policy. She'd never imagined that something like this could happen.

Sheryl sat in the chair next to Hawk and rested her very tired head on his arm. She really should try to find him something to wear! She'd thrown away his blood-soaked shirt, and even if she did have an old T-shirt around the place, it certainly wouldn't fit him. At least he'd cleaned the dried blood off his skin, while she'd had Baby in surgery.

"Baby's going to be fine," she said, trying to reassure him.

"Thanks." He put his arm around her. "Thanks is not enough, but at the moment it's all I have."

She nodded.

After everything that had happened, she couldn't deny that what he'd told her was true. Dr. Dolittle. Psychic sister. A mother who had apparently been psychic, as well, at least to some extent.

"You said there was something else," she said tiredly. "Before we were interrupted, you said there was something about yesterday, in the farmhouse, that I should know."

With his legs thrust out and his bare arm draped around her, he seemed even longer than usual. Bigger. Sometimes when she was next to him she felt so small. Fragile. No one made her feel fragile, not anymore. But this was different. She knew Hawk would never hurt her. Not only that, he would do everything he could to protect her from those who would.

Why did she think that way when she knew he was temporary?

"It doesn't matter," he grumbled.

A shiver crawled up her spine. "I think maybe it does."

He didn't answer for a moment, and then he pulled her a little bit closer. "After I discovered what I could do that night at the rodeo, I ran. Joined the Army and got as far away from ranches and rodeos as I could. But of course it wasn't quite that easy. There are animals everywhere, and the genie was out of the bottle. No way to put it back. I learned to control my abilities, but I couldn't turn them off. Not permanently, anyway. There are animals everywhere. Birds. Pets. Wild animals. They are a part of the earth, just like we are, and I couldn't run away from them. Or from myself."

He paused a moment, as if to clear his head, order his thoughts. "There was a girl…"

"You were nineteen!" Sheryl protested with a small laugh.

"Yeah, I was young, but it felt like the real thing at the time."

Love. He didn't say it; neither did she. "While I was in the Army, Sara and I wrote letters for a while. But I couldn't tell her what was happening to me, and she didn't understand why I had pulled away from her."

"You do that. When things go wrong you shut down." She wished with all her heart that he would fight instead of turning away, and she knew there were things he would fight for. She just wasn't one of them.

"I know." He shifted his weight slightly, as if the observation made him physically uncomfortable. "Sara's letters got shorter and less frequent, and so did mine. Finally they just stopped."

"She didn't wait." Sheryl whispered.

"No, and I can't blame her. I can see into a dog's heart, a horse's mind, through a bird's eye, but when I touched a person there was nothing. No connection. No insight. I felt…blinded. It was like my senses were dead where people were concerned."

Sheryl laid her hand on his bare chest. Yeah, he was

tough as nails, hard and harsh. But he was not uncaring; he never had been.

"Yesterday, when I was inside you, something changed."

She shivered again. A few words and she was back there in that shabby farmhouse with Hawk inside her and the world spinning out of control.

"I touched your mind and your heart," he said. "For an instant, maybe two, I experienced a connection that's so hard to explain. I experienced it with you."

Sheryl turned and lifted her head and kissed Hawk's stubbly jaw. "Love'll do that to you, or so I hear."

He didn't say anything, but the tension in his body certainly increased. All of a sudden he was tight as a drum.

Finally he gently set her aside and stood. "I'm going to sit with Baby."

"She won't even know you're there," Sheryl protested.

"Yes, she will," he said softly.

Hawk glanced over his shoulder as he left the waiting room. She'd be angry with him for brushing her off, if she didn't see the pain in his eyes so clearly.

Hawk was alone with Baby for at least half an hour, sitting in a chair at the dog's side, before Sheryl joined them. She checked on her patient first, then, satisfied with what she found there, she perched on his knee.

He didn't mind.

"I made a few phone calls," she said, calmer than she'd been earlier. "Doc Murdock is going to reopen his practice until I can get this place fixed." She sighed. "*If* I can get it fixed," she added softly. "Maybe I should just—"

"I'll handle everything," Hawk said. He hated the way she sounded, dejected and without hope. "This is all my fault, and I won't leave you hurting because of me."

She looked him in the eyes, and he knew what she was thinking. *Too late.* He didn't know what she was thinking because he had been genetically altered before birth. He wasn't reading her mind. He knew it because he knew her in a way he had never known anyone else. Or ever would.

"This is not your fault," she said.

"Yes, it is. I brought trouble with me when I came."

She sighed and placed her hand on his cheek. That was when he knew she was putting on a show for him. Her fingers trembled, very slightly. "Trust me, trouble was already here."

Sheryl kissed him on the temple. It was an odd place for a kiss, not sexual, not sensual. But intimate, just the same. Then she slid back in his lap and rested her head against his. She didn't say anything; she didn't try to pump him for information about what he could do; she didn't chatter. She just sat in his lap and held on, and he liked it. It felt right, and in an odd way he was as connected to her as he'd been yesterday, when he'd been deep inside her and their hearts had pumped as one.

"You're not the only one who has a past, you know," she said.

He didn't answer but threaded his fingers through her mussed ponytail.

"There was this guy, a few years back. I was actually going to marry him."

Michael, the one Debbie had been afraid had come back. Sheryl had never mentioned him; Hawk hadn't asked. "What did he do to you?"

For a minute she didn't answer. He wouldn't force her if she decided not to go further. Sharing secrets was never easy. Not for him, anyway, and apparently not for Sheryl, either.

"I thought I loved him," she said softly. "Actually, I fell in love with the man he pretended to be. When he hit me, I saw the real man. It was so…startling, like the face I loved had been a Halloween mask and he finally decided to rip it off."

Hawk couldn't get past a very small portion of that confession. The same kind of blind anger that had rushed through him when he'd turned and seen Baby lying in the street rushed through him now. *When he hit me.* He touched his hand to Sheryl's face and brushed his fingers across her cheekbone. He sucked up her body heat and at the same time offered his own.

She laid her hand over his. "How did you know?"

"Know what?"

"This is where he hit me. The bastard slammed me in the face with his fist."

Hawk experienced that rush of anger all over again. "Tell me where to find him, and I'll make him pay."

"No." Sheryl rested her head on his shoulder and relaxed.

"Then give this Michael a last name and I'll find him myself."

"No," she said again. Her fingers played with the hair at his nape. "That's not necessary anymore. He's not important. He's not worth the time and trouble it would take to find him."

"That's a matter of opinion," Hawk said gruffly.

Sheryl kissed his neck. "You don't get it. A couple of weeks ago I was still hiding from one insignificant little man. And that's what he is, Hawk. Little and insignificant. I'm not going to let one mistake ruin my life." She raised her head and rested her forehead against his. "Thank you," she whispered.

"I didn't do anything."

"Yes, you did. You helped me to put Michael in the past, where he belongs. You helped me to realize that I don't need to be afraid anymore. He's not that important."

Hawk didn't know what to say to that, so he said nothing. He held her. Maybe that was enough.

After a while she raked her fingers through his hair. "Let's take Baby home."

For two days, while Baby healed, Hawk slept with Sheryl. Technically, at least. He didn't touch her; he didn't offer explanations for the past or muse about what might come next. He didn't talk about much of anything. The silence was almost complete, as if he'd drawn into himself and had nothing to say to anyone. Not even her.

She didn't mention Michael; he didn't mention his uncanny ability with animals. And with her.

As soon as Baby was able, he'd be heading back to Texas. End of story. Nice knowing you. So long.

But it was good to sleep with him at night. While Hawk slept, Sheryl curled up against his back. She took comfort from the fact that he was with her, at least for a while.

Finding repairmen to fix her clinic was a challenge. There was a handyman in Wyatt, but he was always booked and, to be honest, he wasn't very good. Sheryl made phone calls to her insurance company and to contractors in nearby towns. It wasn't as if the animals of Wyatt were suffering; Doc Murdock had gladly reopened his practice, and there was always Micky Darman, who was perfectly willing to see a few domestic pets along with the farm animals he usually treated.

Late Tuesday afternoon, while Sheryl was going through her pockets and getting ready to do a load of laundry, she ran across the piece of paper where she'd scribbled Dr. Faith Winston's name and phone numbers. The woman had seemed nice enough. She hadn't pushed, and she hadn't gotten angry when Sheryl had told her there were no files.

Hawk was sitting in the living room with Baby and the other animals. They were all drawn to him, especially now when he needed comfort. Even Bruce had been well behaved this week. Why did Hawk allow *them* to comfort him but not her? She was actually jealous of her own pets, because they touched Hawk in a way she never could.

Sheryl went to the kitchen phone and dialed the first number she'd written down. After two rings, a frantic woman answered with a breathless, "Faith Winston."

Sheryl immediately began to have doubts about making this call.

"Hello?" Dr. Winston said when Sheryl remained silent.

"Did I call at a bad time?" Sheryl asked quickly.

"No." She laughed, sounding sincerely friendly. "It's always hectic around here. Is this...Dr. Eldanis?"

Caller ID or a great memory for voices? It didn't matter. "Sheryl."

"Sheryl, hang on one minute, please."

She listened to the distant sounds of a quick conversation, where Dr. Winston handed the care of what sounded like a dozen children over to her husband. She must've moved into another room, because the commotion faded and when she spoke again her voice was clear and without interference.

"Have you found something I might be interested in?" Dr. Winston asked.

"I lied to you when you called last week," Sheryl said.

There was a moment of telling silence. "I suspected as much."

Sheryl's heart skipped a beat. The woman sounded so cool, so completely undisturbed by the confession. "The files that were stored in the basement of my clinic when I bought the building are worthless, for the most part."

"You can't be sure," Dr. Winston began.

Sheryl didn't slow down. "But last week I think we found what you were looking for."

There was a very short pause before Winston said, "We?"

For herself, she'd be better off to let this all die. The danger was over; the man who'd wanted the file on Deanna Payne had what he wanted. She could repair her clinic and get back to her life. The life she had built for herself before Hawk had come storming in. The life where she didn't have to worry about things like broken hearts. Hers and others.

But this was very much not over for Hawk. The pain in his eyes, the pain she felt when she laid a hand on him and he tensed… No, for him, it wasn't over.

Sheryl took a deep breath and steeled her resolve. "I have a friend…."

Wednesday morning Hawk threw his clothes into his suitcase and carried the bag out to his truck. Time to go home. Baby was healing, though she absolutely hated the protective collar Sheryl insisted she wear. It was more of a nuisance to her than the healing bullet wound. Once they were down the road he would let her take it off, as long as she promised not to lick her bandage.

Sheryl was waiting for him when he walked back into the house. "Where are you going?" she asked sharply.

"Texas."

"Not yet!" She looked at him as if he'd told her he was going to the moon.

"Baby's not ready to make the trip."

"Yes, she is."

"I'm her doctor, and I'm telling you she's not ready." Sheryl crossed her arms over her chest, trying for a forceful pose.

He knew her too well to be taken in by a sharp word and a straightened spine. She was trying to keep him here. "Sheryl, it's time—"

"One more day," she said. A blush rose to her cheeks. "Maybe two."

This wasn't simply a reluctance to see him go. Sheryl was trying to stall him. She was obviously waiting for something to happen in one more day. Maybe two. "What have you done?" he asked softly.

She wrinkled her nose, ruining her fearsome pose. "Someone's coming to Wyatt to see you."

"Who?" he asked sharply.

"An FBI agent named Liam Brooks."

"Why?" His question reverberated through the house.

"I'm not really sure," Sheryl said. "Dr. Winston—Faith—she said it was too complicated to go into over the phone. But Agent Brooks is very anxious to speak with you."

"Winston's the one who called asking about the files, right?"

"Yes," Sheryl answered softly.

"She called again?"

"Actually…" Sheryl looked decidedly sheepish. "I called her."

For a moment there was dead silence in this house that was never completely still. The truth hit Hawk like a boulder landing in his stomach. "You told her about me."

"Yes." Sheryl looked so innocent, so pretty and warm. And it was all a lie. "She understands completely, Hawk, and—"

"What's next? A phone call to the tabloids?" He had never trusted anyone but Cassie with his secret, and now he remembered why. He'd actually told Sheryl who and what he was, and what had she done? She'd betrayed his trust and called in the freakin' FBI.

"I'm only trying to help."

"If this is your idea of help, please don't."

He could tell by the expression on Sheryl's face that her feelings were hurt, but at least her eyes didn't tear up. Instead, she seemed to grow a bit tougher. "Just stick around for another day or two and meet with this guy. Faith said he had a lot to talk to you about."

"You talk to him," Hawk snapped. "I'm going home."

"This is home, you jackass," Sheryl snapped right back.

He didn't argue with her. Maybe because in a way he had never expected, this place did feel like home. It was Sheryl, he knew. She was home to him, in an undeniable way that absolutely terrified him. He had to get out of here before he was in so deep he could never walk away.

He would never live a normal life. He couldn't have a wife, a family, friends who knew and accepted him. And if he ever did have kids, would they be freaks like their daddy? Was that a chance he dared to take?

At least Sheryl wasn't pregnant. He couldn't fathom how he knew, but he did. At night when she was sleeping, he touched her hair and smelled her skin, and he knew.

"I have to go."

"So this is it, huh?" Now she sounded angry, "You're just going to walk away? That's your answer to every problem, isn't it? You run."

"That was always the plan. I didn't come here to settle down. To be honest, I've already been here too long."

She shook her head slowly, as if she couldn't believe

what she was hearing. "Do you think ignoring everything that's happened between us will make it go away?"

He didn't know how to answer that one. "I'll mail you a check." He lifted Baby and carried her out the front door, half expecting Sheryl to follow.

She didn't.

From the bushes across the street Ricky watched as the big fellow carried his dog to the truck. He wasn't supposed to let him leave, but how could he stop the man? Especially in this condition.

Ricky glanced down at his trembling hands. He didn't feel good; he didn't feel strong. He felt as if he was falling apart, his mind and his body, one molecule at a time. Something was wrong. Dr. Sheridan had said no more than one shot a day, but that wasn't enough. And sometimes the injections had no effect at all.

Dr. Sheridan had ruined him with that damned drug of hers. He'd always liked her. Always, from the first. She was smart, and while she wasn't dishy like the veterinarian, she was certainly striking. He had always been able to tell, even when she wore those lab coats, that she had a killer body. He'd always imagined that one day she'd get tired of that stick-in-the-mud Titan and turn to a younger, more handsome, more attentive man. Someone like Ricky Driggs.

She'd left town before they'd had dinner. How rude of her. How inconsiderate.

Yes, he'd once liked Dr. Sheridan quite well, and what had she done? She had ruined him. She had killed him.

What had Titan said before he left? *Don't hurt the man, but the girl is expendable.*

The truck pulled away from the curb, and Ricky turned

his attention to the little yellow house where the veterinarian lived. A curtain fluttered, but that was the only sign of life.

She hadn't walked her friend to the truck, but she was home.

Since the boss had obviously used and betrayed him, Ricky didn't feel any obligation to follow the orders he'd been given. As if he could stop the man in the truck now. It was too late. In fact, he rather hoped that the big fellow showed up where he was least expected to give Titan and Janet a nasty surprise.

No…what was he thinking? Ricky pressed shaking fingers to his temple. Of course he would do what Titan had asked of him. The boss would reward him when the job was done. He'd make sure Ricky was never without the drug he needed.

The woman he'd been watching for days finally was alone. There would be no muscle-bound lug to get past.

Maybe she had something in there that would make him feel better. Something to take away the pain. Gathering what little courage he had left, Ricky left the bushes where he'd been hiding and walked toward the little yellow house.

Chapter 15

When the doorbell rang, Sheryl's heart skipped a beat. Had Hawk forgotten something? Or had he just come back to torment her a little bit more?

She had almost reached the door when she realized that something was wrong. Laverne was not pacing anxiously in the entryway, but standing well back and watching the door warily. Neither of the dogs or the other cats had even bothered to rush to the door to greet Hawk.

Which meant it wasn't Hawk ringing her bell.

She could very well imagine who was out there. Debbie had seen Hawk leaving and wanted all the details. Problem was, Sheryl wasn't ready to share those details with anyone. She'd started out by having a purely sexual affair with a studly guy, and ended up falling in love with a man who had more problems than she could even imagine.

What kind of idiot was she?

Since she wasn't in any mood to talk to anyone, she didn't answer the door. Debbie would understand. Not now, maybe, but later, when Sheryl could talk about Hawk Donovan without making a fool of herself by sniveling like a pathetic girl.

The ringing of the doorbell was replaced by furious knocking, and then a shout. "Let me in, luv! I know you're in there!"

Could Agent Brooks be here so soon? She guessed it was possible, but the man at her door certainly didn't sound like an FBI agent. He had a British accent, and a fury in his voice that kept her well away from the door. No way would she open the door for this obviously frantic man. Whoever he was, he had the wrong house, and he would realize it soon enough.

But he didn't. The knocking was replaced by a kick that splintered the door. Sheryl turned and ran for the kitchen and the phone, but she hadn't gone far before a second kick all but took the door off its hinges. The door flew in, Laverne hissed and fled, and the man who'd been shouting burst into the house. He gave chase and caught Sheryl from behind two steps before she reached the phone.

He was breathing too fast and his heart beat too hard. She actually felt that pounding of his heart as he clasped her to him tightly. The hand that clamped over her mouth when she tried to scream was clammy. But that hand was also strong.

"Not running away from me, are you, luv?" he asked breathlessly.

Gradually the hand over her mouth relaxed. Sheryl knew if she screamed or spoke too loudly, he'd just clamp the hand down again. "What do you want?" she asked.

The intruder dragged her back to the front door, and

while he held her in place with one hand tangled in her ponytail, he shut the broken door so it might look normal to anyone passing by.

The man looked like a vagrant. His blond hair was oily and mussed, his clothes were dirty and there was a smudge of dirt on his face near his long, pointed nose.

Had anyone seen or heard him break in? Sheryl wondered. Or was she on her own?

Bogie and Howie came running into the room, barking frantically and dancing back and forth on their short little legs. They moved in as if to bite the man and then scurried away.

"Make them shut up," the intruder ordered, no less frantic than the dogs.

"I can't," Sheryl said. "They're frightened."

Laverne burst from the corner, where the other cats cowered, and latched herself to the man's leg with her claws. She hissed while the blond man tried to shake her loose. She had some skin under her claws, but had latched on mostly to denim. The protective cat was more of a nuisance than a pain to the man who held Sheryl tightly.

It was the noise that seemed to hurt him most of all. Howie and Bogie barked; Laverne hissed. And the man who held Sheryl flinched as he tried to fight off the noise.

The intruder pulled a gun and aimed it at Bogie. "You make these nasty pets be quiet, or I'll shoot them all."

"I can lock them in the bedroom," Sheryl suggested quickly. She couldn't bear to see another animal wounded, not if she could prevent it from happening. "Besides, the gun will make a lot of noise if you fire, and all the neighbors will come running over to see what's going on. You don't want that, do you?" Would he listen to her, or was he beyond reason?

The hand that held the gun shook slightly. "No," he said

gruffly. "I don't want to alarm the neighbors. I can't deal with that complication at the moment."

The intruder held on to Sheryl by the hair, jerking her this way and that as she removed Laverne from his leg, shepherded all the animals into her bedroom and closed the door. The barking didn't stop, but the sounds were dulled by the closed door.

The man with the gun hauled her down the hallway and into the living room, obviously trying to get away from the sounds that disturbed him. "What about that thing?" He wagged his gun toward the parrot in her living room.

"He's in a cage," Sheryl said calmly. "He can't hurt you. And you don't have to worry about Bruce making any noise. He's a very quiet parrot."

The man laughed, short and hoarse. "Bruce. What kind of a name is that for a bird?"

For once, Bruce was wisely silent.

"I don't know," Sheryl said. "He already had the name when I got him." The gunman's pupils were dilated, and judging by his jerky movements and his obvious distress, the clammy hands and the sweat, she assumed he was a junkie looking for money or drugs. She hadn't even known there was a drug problem in Wyatt until it had burst through her front door. Somehow she had to calm him down so no one got hurt.

"What's your name?" she asked gently.

"Why?" He latched pale-blue eyes on to hers. There was no life in those eyes, just a dull chill.

"I have to call you something, don't I?" She tried to keep her voice serene, completely nonthreatening. "My name's Sheryl."

"I know," he said gruffly.

Sheryl swallowed hard. She had been so hoping it was

chance that had brought this man to her door, but if he knew her name, apparently trouble hadn't left town on Hawk's heels.

"Ricky." Those odd pale eyes swept over her from head to toe. "Ricky Driggs. My mum used to call me Richard, but she was the only one. I haven't seen my mum in a long time," he added almost dreamily. "These days some people call me Rick and some call me Driggs, but most call me Ricky. You can call me Ricky."

He didn't mind at all telling her his name, which either meant it was false, or he didn't expect she'd ever have an opportunity to speak to the police about this incident. "Okay, Ricky. Why are you here? What do you want?"

He leaned in close, placing his face much too near hers. He still had a gun in his hand, which kept her from fighting back. Yet. She had a feeling she was not going to be able to talk him down. She was going to have to fight, as soon as the opportunity arose.

"Before we get started, I need a little bit of something to take the edge off," Ricky said. "Something to make me feel better for a while. I don't feel strong. I don't feel good. Every now and then my thoughts get all jumbled and twisted about. I think my insides are turning to mush, and the organs are all switched around. My innards are topsy-turvy."

"I'm sorry," she answered. "I don't have what you need."

"Nobody does," he said hoarsely. "That's the problem, you see. There's only one man in the world who can cure my ills, and he left me here with a handful of syringes and a sorry-ass job to do. The medicine isn't working anymore, and the boss hasn't called like he said he would, so I can't ask him for something stronger. But you're a doctor, and you must have *something*."

Ricky wasn't nearly as big as Hawk, but he was much bigger than Sheryl. He was obviously suffering from withdrawal symptoms, which might weaken him but had also made him desperate. But she could fight him, if it came to that. And it would.

And then there was the gun...

"I can make you a cup of coffee, Ricky," she said, trying to keep her voice calm. "A whole pot. That'll make you feel better."

He laughed. "Coffee?"

"It might help."

Ricky shook his head. "No. Coffee is not going to help."

"What do you want, then?" she asked.

He gave her an odd smile, crooked and weak. "There was a time when I wanted you, luv. I had great plans for us. You're quite dishy. I imagine you'd put up quite a fight. I like a bit of fight in a woman. At least, I used to. The good doctor has unmanned me with her blasted drug. Now I can only think about one thing. I need more, and more. The relief doesn't last, the way it used to. I hurt. I think my blood is boiling. Is that possible, do you think? Could the blood be boiling in my veins?"

Sheryl tried to dismiss what he said about wanting her. The possibilities were too frightening, and she didn't need to be so scared she couldn't function. She'd break down later, if she got the chance. "There's a doctor in town. I'm sure he'll have something that will help you. All of my drugs are for dogs and cats. None of them would be strong enough to help you, and besides, everything is at the clinic. I can call the doctor for you. Is that what you want?"

"No. No more doctors for me. I want to die," Ricky answered softly. He laughed hoarsely. "That's the truth of it, luv. I hurt so bad I just want to die. Nothing but death will take away this agony, but I'm afraid to go alone." He dipped his head toward hers, and his hand gentled and wandered toward her breast. "I'm going to take you with me, Doc."

Sheryl twisted out of his arms, surprising Ricky with the sudden move. She spun and wrenched, slipping out of his grasp and scurrying away. She didn't get far before he grabbed her shirt, yanked her back and tossed her to the floor. Without hesitating, she kicked out and caught his knee solidly with her heel. He yelled and the leg buckled, but he recovered quickly. Too quickly. As Sheryl tried to roll away, Ricky stopped her cold with his foot on the center of her back. He pinned her there, pressing so hard he took her breath away.

The self-defense classes, the punching bag, the free weights she'd worked out with for so long… They didn't do her any good at all when she had her face in the carpet and a foot pushing into her back.

Ricky dropped down and reached inside his jacket to snag a half roll of duct tape. "Sorry, luv," he said as he pinned her to the floor with his knee and tore off a strip of duct tape. "But if you insist on doing this the hard way, we'll do it the hard way."

Hawk was more than uneasy as he drove through Wyatt, headed for the interstate and Texas and the life he'd left behind. A nasty knot had settled into the pit of his stomach.

In the past few days there hadn't been any talk about visits to Texas or Tennessee, about how a long-distance relationship might work. Sheryl deserved to have a normal man in her life, a husband who would love her without restraint, babies who wouldn't have to be hidden from the world to protect them from men like the one who had killed Deanna Payne.

He couldn't give her that, and he loved Sheryl enough to want the best for her.

What a kick in the pants that was, to finally fall head over heels for a woman after all this time. And he was.

Head over heels in love.

For all the good it would do him. He had definitely been better off before he'd met Sheryl. He didn't need this indecision, this nagging doubt that he shouldn't be leaving her behind.

Hawk slammed on the brakes and swerved in the street before pulling the truck onto the shoulder of the road and coming to a jerking stop.

Something was wrong.

His heart started beating too fast; his lungs constricted; his hands shook. He'd never sensed anything so strongly over a distance; he usually had to concentrate in order to get any sensation at all without touching an animal.

As he sat behind the steering wheel, shaking and breathless, Hawk realized what was happening to him. He wasn't sensing fear and danger from an animal, but from Sheryl. It was like she was inside him...calling him...reaching for him.... In the back seat, a resting Baby lifted up slowly and growled.

"Yeah, I know," Hawk said as he made a U-turn in the street and hit the gas.

Even as he drove, he saw more than the street before him. He saw a man's face, a gun....

And then he smelled the smoke as if a fire had started in the cab of his truck. Smoke dimmed his view of the road; it filled his nose and his lungs and all but blinded him. The smoke was here...and it was suffocating him. He drove fast, even though smoke stung his eyes and clouded his vision. He steered the truck down the middle of the street, taking corners sharply, squealing the tires as he made his way to Sheryl's house on instinct and fear.

He didn't pull his truck to the curb but drove into Sheryl's front yard, stopping with a jerk near the porch. "Stay!" he ordered when Baby made a move toward the door.

Hawk leaped onto the porch. The front door was in place but was almost off its hinges. Someone had kicked the door in, probably right after Hawk had driven away.

Someone had been watching, waiting for him to leave.

He pushed the door open and stepped inside, and the smell of smoke hit him. The same smoke he had smelled in the truck.

The farther into the house he moved, the denser the smoke became. The yapping and meowing of Sheryl's pets came to him from down the hall, and Bruce was cussing up a blue streak, but Hawk didn't hear Sheryl at all.

He felt her, though. He felt her to his bones. She was alive and afraid.

Hawk didn't know who had Sheryl, but he did know none of this was her fault. He was the one who had brought danger to her, and he was the only one who could take it away.

"Let her go!" he shouted as he moved into the smoky hallway. Thick smoke drifted from the spare bedroom.

"No!" a strange voice answered. "What are you doing here?" The man spoke with a decided British accent. "It's much too soon for you to come back. You're not supposed to come back until she's dead. Go away. You don't have long to wait, I promise."

"Sheryl!" Hawk shouted as he inched toward the open door.

"Get out of here. He has a gun!"

Hawk leaned against the wall and closed his eyes. He'd seen Baby shot and it had damn near killed him. What if Sheryl got hurt? What if she was murdered, all because of him? He couldn't live with that. He couldn't bear it.

He didn't want to lose her.

"I'm not going anywhere," he said softly. Then in a louder voice, "I'm coming in!"

The sight that greeted him as he burst into the spare room was enough to stop his heart on the spot, no bullet required. A slender, pale man sat on the narrow bed, a gun in one hand, a can of lighter fluid in the other. Sheryl reclined at an odd angle beside him. Duct tape not only bound her ankles and wrists, but lashed her to the bed itself. The files from the fertility clinic, the ones from the box Hawk had left here, were spread around them, on the floor and on the bed. The files Hawk and Sheryl had arranged so carefully had been negligently tossed about and many were on fire, small flames licking here and there, growing in intensity, giving off smoke and heat. There was a growing fire on the floor, in the center of the room, fed by old documents and lighter fluid and matches. The fire was inching closer to the curtains on one side, the bookcase on the other. There wasn't a lot of time before the flames spread out of control.

The man pointed his gun at Sheryl, as if he knew that would stop Hawk much more effectively than a bullet headed his way. "Come in and join us, if you'd like. There's plenty of room." He didn't move the gun away from Sheryl, but he did lift a sheet of paper and read a section. "Such a lot of fuss for such a lot of nothing."

Hawk stepped into the room as the fire spread, catching the curtains at the back of the room and spreading upward. Flames licked at the bookcase, caught an old book and climbed upward.

"Hawk, get out of here!" Sheryl ordered.

"Not without you."

Her eyes were wide and frantic, unlike those of her captor. He was calm amongst the flames.

"I figured you'd come back when you heard about the tragedy," the blond man said as he dropped a fiery sheet of paper onto the floor. "But I certainly didn't expect you so soon. You can go now." He shooed Hawk away with his hand. "Titan doesn't want you dead. Not yet, at least."

"Why not?" Hawk said as he took another step closer.

"I don't know. I don't particularly care, either. To be honest, I don't care about much of anything anymore."

"We can all walk out of here, Ricky," Sheryl said, her voice calm but her eyes frantic. "All of us."

Ricky shook his head. "No, I'm afraid it's too late for that. He can go," he nodded his head to Hawk. "If he hurries. But you're mine. You were promised to me. I will admit, this isn't the fun I had intended, but it's all I can offer. I had such plans for us...but Titan and Janet have turned me into a worthless pile of shuddering flesh. I'm no good to any woman." He laughed harshly. "I'm not good for much of anything anymore."

Hawk looked Sheryl in the eye while the man on the bed continued to ramble. He couldn't possibly leave her here.

Go. She mouthed the word. The fire moved closer to the bed, licking and growing slowly. Heading unerringly toward Sheryl.

Hawk moved fast; he had to, in order to get the gun before the Englishman fired. His hand manacled Ricky's wrist, and he forced the weapon away from Sheryl and out of the intruder's hand. Ricky was weak. Surprisingly so. Or else he didn't care to win this struggle. Hawk maintained his grip on the man's wrist and stuck the weapon in his waistband, then he reached into his pocket and drew out a knife. Ricky didn't kick; he didn't fight. He seemed, in fact, resigned to his fate.

Hawk opened his knife with one flick of his thumb and began to cut the tape that bound Sheryl to the bed, then the tape at her ankles and wrists. A few quick swipes of the sharp knife and she was free.

Sheryl leaped from the bed, escaping the heat and the flames and her captor to stand with Hawk. Her hands rested on his shoulder and his back, as if she needed that connection to chase away the fear that continued to course through her.

And she was afraid. Deeply, completely afraid.

"Go," Hawk said.

"You'd better be right behind me." She dropped her arms slowly, and then she ran, heading not to the front door but down the hallway to collect her frantic pets.

Still, the man on the bed didn't struggle. "Who is Titan?" Hawk asked.

"As if you don't know," the Englishman replied with disdain.

"I don't."

The man stared up at Hawk with the oddest, palest eyes he'd ever seen. And still he didn't fight. "Everyone knows Titan. He knows you, so you must know him, as well."

Hawk heard Sheryl and the pets leaving by the front door, and that was when he hauled Ricky to his feet. "Dammit, you will tell me everything!" Flames licked toward the ceiling, climbing the curtains and the books in the bookcase. The smoke was getting thick.

He pulled Ricky toward the hallway. "But not here." Breathing in too much smoke, he coughed once, and that was when his prisoner pulled away with a burst of strength. Hawk turned around to see that the man held another gun, a smaller and yet equally deadly weapon, much like the one that had already been confiscated.

"Backup weapon," the Englishman explained as Hawk stared into the barrel. "You should have expected that." The comment sounded very much like a reprimand.

"So, are you going to shoot me now?"

Sheryl and her kiddies were all safe. Either she or a neighbor had called the fire department and police by now, of that he was certain. The intruder with the gun wasn't walking out of this house a free man, and surely he knew that. There would be no escape. The flames that were fed by the fertility clinic files grew and flickered and moved into the hallway following a trail of lighter fluid that had been poured into the carpet.

Time was running out.

Hawk drew the pistol from his waistband and took steady aim at the man who had tried to kill Sheryl, threatening the intruder with his own weapon.

"Titan really doesn't want you dead," the man said softly.

"Then maybe we should talk. Who is this Titan? Why is he so interested in me?"

The blond man grinned. "The boss doesn't tell me anything of importance. I do know that he shot your dog. I was a bit stunned when he told me; for some reason it seemed very cold and unnaturally cruel. But it was a stroke of brilliance, really. He decided that if something so simple as a bleeding pup would bring you to your knees, killing the woman you were shagging would really stop you in your tracks."

In the distance, he heard sirens. So did the Englishman.

"Let's get out of here," Hawk said. "You're sick. I'll get you some medicine and then you can tell me all about Titan."

The Englishman aimed his weapon at Hawk's chest, and while his hand shook, his aim remained certain. "I don't think so."

"You said this Titan wants me alive."

The man with the gun shrugged. "Titan has screwed me over in the worst possible way. I'm a dead man, don't you see that? I'm dead! Why should I give a damn what the boss wants now?"

They moved, sharply and simultaneously, and one shot rang out.

Chapter 16

Sheryl stood in the center of the hotel room, still unable to believe what had happened this afternoon: that awful man breaking into her home; hearing the gunshot; watching her house burn.

Her house wasn't a complete loss, but it was too badly damaged for her to live in for quite some time. Only the spare bedroom and a part of the hallway had been completely destroyed by the fire, but there was water and smoke damage throughout the house. She didn't like to think that everything she owned had been ruined in one afternoon, but it appeared that was the case.

She should be more upset, and maybe later she would be.

The door to the hotel room opened and Hawk walked in, his stride easy, his face as dispassionate and hard as it had been the first time she'd seen it.

"How are the kiddies?" she asked, doing her best to put on a happy face. It wasn't easy, since she continued to tremble so deeply her teeth practically chattered.

"Fine," he said. "They're perfectly happy with Cory."

"Even Baby and Laverne?"

"Baby's fine. So is Laverne." She could read no emotion in his voice or on his face. It was as if he'd locked everything down so deep no one could ever reach it. Not even her.

When they'd checked into the hotel, Hawk had tried to get adjoining rooms. One for them, another for the animals. But the hotel manager—who had allowed Baby to stay in Hawk's room earlier in the week—had balked at the idea of three cats, three dogs and a parrot. By the time they'd finished dealing with the fire department and the police, there hadn't been time to make other arrangements for the night. So Cory, Sheryl's part-time employee, had taken all the animals into his own home. His mother was less than thrilled, since they already had a collection of their own, but in light of the circumstances she had agreed.

In a way Sheryl was glad they had this one night alone. She wanted Hawk all to herself for a while. No animals who could see a part of him she could not. No distractions.

He didn't move toward her, but stood near the door. Away from her. Always away. "I understand how you feel," she said softly.

"You have no idea—"

"I do now," she said. "When I heard that gunshot, my blood ran cold. Literally cold. I ran toward the house, but Debbie stopped me. She wouldn't let me go in and make sure you hadn't been—" The words stuck in her throat. "I was so scared that you might be hurt," she said softly. "I was terrified that you might be dead.

"And then I looked around and realized that all the animals, *all* of them, were calmly watching the front door, waiting for you to come out. They knew you were all right," she said, still amazed. "I didn't know. I didn't see what they saw, I didn't feel whatever it is they feel. And I was jealous. I envied them that extraordinary connection you've hidden from the world all these years. At that moment I wanted it for myself."

Hawk had soon come out of the house on his own, coughing but unhurt. Ricky had turned his gun on himself and had fired one bullet into his own brain and ended his life.

Hawk crossed the room with that graceful, sleek step that had captivated her from the beginning. Had he looked her in the eye once since he'd cut her loose and set her free? Had he uttered one kind word? No.

He was looking her in the eye now. She wondered if he would kiss her when he reached her, but he didn't. Instead he dropped to his knees and wrapped his arms around her waist. He was so tall, and she was so short, that in this position his head almost reached her shoulder. He closed his eyes and rested his head there.

Sheryl threaded her fingers through his hair. No, she wasn't terribly upset about the damage to her things. She and Hawk were both unhurt, as were all the animals. Everything else could be replaced.

"I saw his face," Hawk said gruffly. "I smelled the smoke. Through your senses, I knew you were in trouble."

She stroked his hair. "And that's why you came back?"

"Yeah." He stayed in place, holding on, pressing his large hands against her back.

In a way it broke her heart all over again. Hawk hadn't turned around because he realized he loved her. He'd come back because he felt responsible for her safety.

"I have money," he said.

Her eyebrows raised. She wasn't sure what was coming, but she was pretty sure she was about to be insulted. And still, she didn't release her hold on Hawk. "So?"

"I can fix your house, take care of anything the insurance doesn't cover. I can build you a better one if you'd like."

"Hawk—"

"I can rebuild your clinic, I can pay Cory and you while you're both out of work."

"Hawk!"

"I don't want you to be hurt because I came here," he said, his voice gruff and deep.

"I told you before, I don't want your money."

"I'm not finished," he grumbled.

"Fine." As if she wanted to hear him try to buy her off! "Finish."

"I can take care of everything here," he said. "Your business, your house, everything. Or you can come home with me."

She blinked twice. "What?"

"Texas needs veterinarians, too. And Baby likes you. She doesn't like the vet at home."

"So I should uproot myself because Baby likes me."

His hands worked up and down her back, barely touching her. "I like you, too," he said softly. "I'm not ready for this to end. I won't ever be ready for this to end."

She'd wanted more, she'd ached for more...and now here he was offering more and she was terrified.

"Why should I move to Texas?" she asked, more than a little defensive. "Why don't you move here?"

He didn't hesitate for more than a split second. "Okay."

It was not the response she'd expected. "Okay? What

are you thinking, Hawk? You have a business. You have a horse ranch and a home and a pregnant sister and—"

"And I love you," he said. "That changes everything."

She stroked Hawk's head and pulled him closer. She let go of every fear. Not fear of fire and bullets; that had already faded. But her fear of giving all of herself to a man, heart and soul; that had been hard to let go of.

"Love does change things, doesn't it?" she whispered.

Hawk began to unbutton her blouse without haste, his lips brushing against the skin he revealed as he folded the fabric back. He didn't wait for her to declare her love, as he had. But then, he knew, didn't he? He'd known all along.

Sheryl closed her eyes, unable to think about the future at the moment. They were both alive and unharmed, and they were together. Nothing else mattered.

There had been frenzy in their lovemaking in the past, but not tonight. They undressed each other slowly, kissing and touching as they shed their clothes, stopping now and then for long, deep kisses that made her head swim and her knees weak. When they were naked, Hawk picked her up and carried her to the bed.

"Can you…" Heaven above, she didn't know how to ask this question! "Now?"

Even though her question was awkward and incomplete, he knew what she meant. "No. The other times might've been aberrations. In the farmhouse, maybe I was so wound up over everything else I just imagined what I felt. And this afternoon, it's possible that I was seeing the intruder's face and smelling the fire through the animals, and I just misinterpreted. That's probably what happened."

Under the covers, with the lights burning all around them, they held on to each other. "Works for me," Sheryl said as she skimmed her hand along Hawk's side. "I don't know if I want to live with a man who can read my mind. A woman has to have her secrets, you know."

"Maybe I just imagined it," he said again. "If it was real, maybe it will only happen when emotions are cranked up or when I'm inside you. There's only one way to find out."

"How's that?" she asked as he rolled atop her and spread her thighs gently.

"Years of experimentation."

"So now I'm a lab rat," she teased.

He took a nipple into his mouth and drew it deep, while he stroked her intimately.

"A very happy lab rat," she whispered as she tangled her fingers in his hair.

The FBI agent Sheryl had been expecting arrived on Thursday morning. Finding Sheryl's house in ruins, he'd gone directly to the police station. Chief Nichols had directed Agent Brooks to the hotel. Considering the nature of their conversation, they decided to meet in the room Hawk and Sheryl had shared last night.

Hawk paced while Agent Liam Brooks told him a tale he didn't want to believe.

But his gut instincts told him every word was the truth.

Benedict Payne, Hawk's legal father and the man who had murdered his wife—Hawk's mother—had fled from the scene of his crime and disappeared. In recent years he had been connected with an international criminal, a ruthless man who was into drugs and smuggling.

Hawk and Cassie's other triplet was a man named Darian, and he had gifts of his own. Their older siblings, another set of triplets, were accounted for, alive and well. If he'd had the time to read the entire file he'd found at the farmhouse before it had been stolen, maybe he would have discovered some of these secrets on his own.

Liam Brooks was actually, if this tale were true, Hawk's brother-in-law, having married one of the older triplets, Danielle.

Hawk told Brooks what he'd found during his time in Wyatt, and of course the FBI agent was very interested in the contents of the file. Until Hawk told him that it had been stolen.

He and Sheryl had never actually compared detailed notes. Hawk had assumed the man who shot Baby was the same one who'd pretended to be a building inspector. But apparently that was not the case. The man who'd shot Baby had silver hair and had looked to be in his fifties, at the very least. Sheryl described the so-called building inspector as a man around thirty. When she mentioned the long black hair and earring, Brooks had actually smiled.

The ponytailed man who had pretended to be Tony Carpenter was actually one of the older triplets, Anthony Caldwell.

Overnight, Hawk had gone to being one of two children to being one of six.

Hawk told the FBI agent about the encounter with Ricky Driggs, trying to remember every word the man had said. At the mention of the name Titan, Brooks had gone very still. His anger was deep, his dedication was fierce. Hawk could almost feel sorry for Titan. Almost. The man who'd shot Baby would get his comeuppance, once Brooks caught up with him. If Hawk didn't find him first.

Brooks showed Hawk an old photograph, and though the hair color was different and the man was thinner and younger, Hawk recognized him.

"That's Titan."

"No," Brooks said. "This man is Benedict Payne."

Hawk returned the photo to the FBI agent. "Sorry, but you're wrong. Ricky Driggs said Titan shot my dog. This is the man who pulled the trigger. I saw him. Trust me, this isn't a face I'm going to forget."

For a moment Brooks was still and quiet as he digested the information. "They're the same man," he said softly. And then he said a few words not fit for Sheryl's ears. Bruce would be impressed.

Hawk held off telling Brooks about Cassie's episodes as long as he could, but since Brooks had told Hawk about the gifts the others had, it seemed like the thing to do. When the FBI agent heard about Cassie's flashes of precognition, he got very excited. And concerned.

"You have to call Cassie and warn her that she's in danger," Brooks said. "Is there a safe place she can hide out until we get there?"

The warning made the back of Hawk's neck prickle. "What makes you think Payne or Titan or whoever he is can find her so quickly?"

"Trust me," the man said sourly. "He'll find her."

Hawk tried to call Cassie on his cell phone, but she didn't answer. He ended the connection when the answering machine switched on. This wasn't answering-machine news. "No answer." His heart thudded hard.

Brooks snagged his own cell phone and started to dial. "I'll get my people out there ASAP."

Hawk gave Brooks the address, and then he laid his eyes on Sheryl. She'd been listening closely, but she hadn't said a word. Not to him, anyway. She'd answered Brooks's questions, and that was all. Now that she knew the truth about him, what would she do? He and Cassie weren't the only freaks in this mess. He came from a family of freaks apparently.

Of course, Brooks didn't use the word *freaks*. Instead he used words like *gifted* and *special*.

It was a nice idea, but inside Hawk was still fighting with the word *freak*. If Sheryl refused his offers, he wouldn't argue with her. If she wanted a quiet, normal life with a normal man, she wouldn't find that with him, and he wouldn't take that perfectly acceptable dream from her.

She loved him. He'd felt the love and he'd wallowed in it. But she would get over that if she had to. One day.

He wasn't sure he would.

"You're going home," Sheryl said as a moment of silence fell over the hotel room.

"I don't have any choice. After I'm sure Cassie is safe and this thing with Payne is over, I'll come back and…we'll see." He didn't want to say more, not with the FBI agent, his brother-in-law—and wouldn't that take some getting used to—listening in.

Brooks was charged, revved up about the coming encounter. He said a quick goodbye to Sheryl, shook Hawk's hand and said, "We're on a plane out of Raleigh airport in two and a half hours. I've got a rental car downstairs."

Hawk shook his head. "I'll meet you there. Maybe I can get Cassie on my cell phone before we get in the air."

As soon as the door was closed behind Brooks, Sheryl's arms went around Hawk's neck and she held on as if for dear life.

Sheryl watched as Hawk threw his suitcase into the rear seat of his pickup. Again. This time they were standing in the hotel parking lot. He'd swing by Cory's and pick up Baby, and then he'd be gone.

When he turned to kiss her goodbye once more, she slipped out of his arms and rounded the truck to climb into the passenger seat. He looked surprised, but didn't say a word.

"I need to make other arrangements for the animals," she explained as he pulled out of the parking lot. Besides, she wasn't ready to say goodbye. Not yet. "I did tell Cory's mother that I'd only leave the kiddies there for one night."

The short drive to Cory's house was silent. Awkward. Sheryl's mind was busy. Everything Hawk had told her, about his abilities and Cassie's, was true. She'd learned that for herself. Now she had to face the fact that his entire family was...special.

And somewhere in the back of her mind she wondered if all those sisters and brothers would like her when they met. Would they think she was good enough for a man like Hawk?

At the present time they had more pressing problems. This Titan or Benedict Payne. Whatever name he used, he was a very bad man, and until he was caught there would be nothing resembling a normal life for Hawk or any of his siblings. Could she handle that? Was she ready?

When Hawk pulled his truck to the curb and shut off the engine, he turned to her, pulled her gently toward him and kissed her goodbye.

Heaven help her, she wasn't ready for goodbye.

When he took his mouth from hers, he said, "I'm gonna miss you."

Without waiting for a response, he left the truck. She exited, too, and side by side they headed for Cory's front door.

"You're gonna miss me, huh?" she asked.

"Yeah. What a kick in the pants."

She wondered if Hawk Donovan had ever admitted that

much to any woman before. She thought not. He didn't
wear his heart on his sleeve; he didn't share his feelings.
Maybe he didn't even want anyone to know he had feelings.

He did, though.

"This has happened awfully fast," she said, trying to
sound strong and confident even though inside she didn't
feel either of those things. "It'll probably be good for us
to take things slow for a while." She even smiled shakily.
"That'll be a change for us. Slow."

"Yeah." Hawk's voice was low, distant, as if he'd already left her. "I'll call you, and when this mess with Titan
or whoever the hell he is is over, we'll…see where we are."

He sounded about as confident as she felt, deep down.

Hawk collected Baby, thanked Cory and his mother
and then looked at Sheryl with those gypsy eyes that had
a way of cutting right through her.

That was when she decided.

Hawk headed for the front door.

"Don't leave yet," Sheryl called softly. "I need a word
with Cory and then I'll be right out."

He glanced over his shoulder, then left the house without a word.

Less than five minutes later, with Laverne clutched in
her arms, Sheryl ran down the sidewalk to the truck, where
Hawk sat anxiously in the driver's seat and Baby lounged
in the back. She opened the passenger door and stepped
into the pickup. Laverne leaped out of her arms and joined
Baby in the back seat.

"Let's go," she said.

He hesitated for a moment, so Sheryl looked him
squarely in the eye. "I love you, Hawk Donovan, and I'm
not going to let you do this alone."

He smiled, started the truck and pulled away from the curb.

Cory was going to take care of finding homes for all the animals. Temporary ones or permanent, since she didn't know how long she'd be gone. Laverne had been with her too long to leave behind, and besides, the ornery cat didn't like anyone else. Except Hawk, of course. And Baby.

Cory and Bruce had bonded overnight, and he'd be keeping the bird himself. His mother was not amused, but since Cory had promised to continue the work of cleaning up the parrot's language, she'd relented.

The house, the clinic, insurance, repairs…she could handle most of that by telephone. Debbie had promised to help when she could. Anything to allow Sheryl to get closer to a man, to get a step closer to what she considered perfection.

A husband.

Babies.

The Home and Garden Channel.

As they left Wyatt, Hawk reached across the space between them and threaded his fingers through hers.

She'd never thought she'd be willing to leave everything behind for a man. Her experience with Michael had taught her to embrace her independence. She realized now that it had also taught her to close off her heart.

It wasn't closed anymore. She loved Hawk; she wanted to be with him. Now and always. Even if he could, on occasion, read her mind a little.

He hadn't mentioned marriage, but then they'd known each other for less than two weeks. Still, she reminded herself, it hadn't taken her long to fall in love with him. Her mother was going to have a fit! Sheryl laughed lightly. The way her mother had been talking about wanting more grandbabies lately, maybe she wouldn't mind that everything had happened so fast.

Hawk lifted their joined hands and kissed her knuckles. "Slow is for sissies," he said. "I think we should get married right away. As soon as possible."

She watched his profile, one eye narrowing as she wondered. Had he just read her mind?

"Your mother is going to be a very happy woman," he added. "I want kids. Soon, if it suits you. As soon as we get Titan out of our lives, I want to start a family."

Sheryl gazed at his profile, so strong and beautiful in the sunlight that shone through the side window. Yes, she wanted his babies to grow inside her. She wanted little Hawks and little Sheryls, and if they had talents the rest of the world didn't understand, she'd help them deal with that, the same way she planned to help their father.

"You've been reading my mind again," she said accusingly.

"Can't help it." At least he didn't try to deny it. No, Hawk had always been brutally honest with her. She didn't expect that would change.

"So, can you read everyone's mind now? Did what you can do…change somehow?"

He shook his head. "No. It's just you, Sheryl. Just you."

But why? How?

"Because you're the one," he said, even though she had not asked her question aloud. "We're linked. Physically, spiritually. Even mentally. Don't ask me to explain it. I can't. I just know that's the way it is."

Linked. It was a scary thought, but it was also comforting. She had never known something could be both frightening and a blessing at the same time.

"Can you teach me?" she asked softly. "Can you teach me how to do what you do? Not with the animals," she added quickly. "I know now that's a gift no one else can ever learn. But with you... Do you think one day I could read your mind?"

"I don't know," he said. "Let's see." He squeezed her hand, and after a long moment of silence he asked, "What am I thinking?"

Sheryl began to smile as a mental picture formed in her mind. It was jumbled, sure, but in an odd way it was also very clear.

She saw Baby and Laverne, curled up together before a stone fireplace. Her hand and Hawk's were intertwined, much as they were now, but with two simple gold rings in the picture. Wedding bands.

She saw those babies—a little girl, a little boy.

She saw horses, galloping across a pasture with green grass and gently rolling hills, and in her heart she knew those hills were home.

She saw and felt Hawk holding her at night. Every night. Forever.

"Yeah," she said, not knowing or caring at the moment if the pictures in her mind were hers, his or theirs. "I want that, too."

* * * * *

Look for the story of Cassie Donovan when
IN SIGHT OF THE ENEMY
by Kylie Brant hits the stands.

Don't miss the fifth part of the exciting continuity
FAMILY SECRETS: THE NEXT GENERATION
Coming in October 2004.
Available wherever Silhouette Books are sold.

On sale now

girls' night in

21 of today's hottest
female authors
1 fabulous short-story collection
And all for a good cause.

Featuring *New York Times* bestselling authors

Jennifer Weiner (author of *Good in Bed*),
Sophie Kinsella (author of *Confessions of a Shopaholic*),
Meg Cabot (author of *The Princess Diaries*)

Net proceeds to benefit War Child, a network of organizations
dedicated to helping children affected by war.

Also featuring bestselling authors...

Carole Matthews, Sarah Mlynowski, Isabel Wolff, Lynda Curnyn,
Chris Manby, Alisa Valdes-Rodriguez, Jill A. Davis, Megan McCafferty,
Emily Barr, Jessica Adams, Lisa Jewell, Lauren Henderson,
Stella Duffy, Jenny Colgan, Anna Maxted, Adèle Lang,
Marian Keyes and Louise Bagshawe

www.RedDressInk.com   www.WarChildusa.org

Available wherever trade paperbacks are sold.

™ is a trademark of the publisher.
The War Child logo is the registered trademark of War Child.

RDIGNIMMR

If you enjoyed what you just read,
then we've got an offer you can't resist!

Take 2 bestselling love stories FREE!

Plus get a FREE surprise gift!

Clip this page and mail it to Silhouette Reader Service™

IN U.S.A.	IN CANADA
3010 Walden Ave.	P.O. Box 609
P.O. Box 1867	Fort Erie, Ontario
Buffalo, N.Y. 14240-1867	L2A 5X3

YES! Please send me 2 free Silhouette Intimate Moments® novels and my free surprise gift. After receiving them, if I don't wish to receive anymore, I can return the shipping statement marked cancel. If I don't cancel, I will receive 6 brand-new novels every month, before they're available in stores! In the U.S.A., bill me at the bargain price of $4.24 plus 25¢ shipping and handling per book and applicable sales tax, if any*. In Canada, bill me at the bargain price of $4.99 plus 25¢ shipping and handling per book and applicable taxes**. That's the complete price and a savings of at least 10% off the cover prices—what a great deal! I understand that accepting the 2 free books and gift places me under no obligation ever to buy any books. I can always return a shipment and cancel at any time. Even if I never buy another book from Silhouette, the 2 free books and gift are mine to keep forever.

245 SDN DZ9A
345 SDN DZ9C

Name	(PLEASE PRINT)	
Address	Apt.#	
City	State/Prov.	Zip/Postal Code

Not valid to current Silhouette Intimate Moments® subscribers.

**Want to try two free books from another series?
Call 1-800-873-8635 or visit www.morefreebooks.com.**

* Terms and prices subject to change without notice. Sales tax applicable in N.Y.
** Canadian residents will be charged applicable provincial taxes and GST.
All orders subject to approval. Offer limited to one per household].
® are registered trademarks owned and used by the trademark owner and or its licensee.

INMOM04R
©2004 Harlequin Enterprises Limited

e**HARLEQUIN**.com

The Ultimate Destination for Women's Fiction

For **FREE online reading**, visit
www.eHarlequin.com now and enjoy:

Online Reads
Read **Daily** and **Weekly** chapters from
our Internet-exclusive stories by your
favorite authors.

Interactive Novels
Cast your vote to help decide how these
stories unfold...then stay tuned!

Quick Reads
For shorter romantic reads, try our
collection of Poems, Toasts, & More!

Online Read Library
Miss one of our online reads?
Come here to catch up!

Reading Groups
Discuss, share and rave with other
community members!

For great reading online,
visit www.eHarlequin.com today!

INTONL04R

Silhouette®

COMING NEXT MONTH

INTIMATE MOMENTS®

#1321 NOTHING TO LOSE—RaeAnne Thayne
The Searchers

Taylor Bradshaw was determined to save her brother from death row. Bestselling author Wyatt McKinnon intended only to write about the case, but ended up joining Taylor's fight for justice. As time ticked down their mutual attraction rose, and with everything already on the line, they had nothing to lose....

#1322 LIVE TO TELL—Valerie Parv
Code of the Outback

Blake Stirton recognized a city girl when he saw one, but leaving Jo Francis stranded in the bush wasn't an option. She had information he needed to find his family's diamond mine before a greedy neighbor foreclosed on their ranch. When his feelings for her distract him, it puts them both in danger. And the explosive secrets they uncover as they work together up the stakes—for their relationship...and his family's fortune—exponentially.

#1323 IN SIGHT OF THE ENEMY—Kylie Brant
Family Secrets: The Next Generation

Cassie Donovan's ability to forecast the future had driven a wedge into her relationship with Shane Farhold, until, finally, his skepticism had torn them apart. But when a madman saw her ability as a gift worth killing for, Shane took her and their unborn child on the run. And not even Cassie could predict when the danger would end....

#1324 HER MAN TO REMEMBER—Suzanne McMinn

Roman Bradshaw thought his wife was dead—until he found her again eighteen months later. But Leah didn't remember him—or the divorce papers she'd been carrying the night of her accident. Now Roman has a chance to seduce her all over again. But could he win her love a second time before the past caught up with them?

#1325 RACING AGAINST THE CLOCK—Lori Wilde

Scientist Hannah Zachary was on the brink of a breakthrough that dangerous men would kill to possess. After an escape from certain death sent her to the hospital, she felt an instant connection to her sexy surgeon, Dr. Tyler Fresno. But with a madman stalking her, how could she ask Tyler to risk his life—and heart—for her?

#1326 SAFE PASSAGE—Loreth Anne White

Agent Scott Armstrong was used to hunting enemies of the state, not warding off imaginary threats to beautiful, enigmatic scientists like Dr. Skye Van Rijn. Then a terrorist turned his safe mission into a deadly battle to keep her out of the wrong hands. Would Skye's secrets jeopardize not only their feelings for each other but their lives, as well?